# THE LORD'S RIGHT IN LANGUEDOC

# THE LORD'S RIGHT IN LANGUEDOC

## An Historical Novel

by

## S. FOWLER WRIGHT

## THE BORGO PRESS

*An Imprint of Wildside Press LLC*

MMX

# CHAPTER ONE

"I CALL it not an ill world," Lucette said, "though there be perils for those who walk not with a sure foot and a seeing eye. And these are days when a comely face and a quick wit may buy the best that the market holds, though there be little skill with viol of harp, or at the reading of scrolls. Look you, if you care little for Guilbert now, yet it may come. For how know you the sort of man he will be until you put him to proof? You know naught, being a maid; and, beyond that, being one who will look aside from a pleasant sight, or be deaf to a knowing tale. Yet, if you be wed, and you like him not, you may look about with a better eye than you do now. You may have pleasure enough. He may be brother to me, yet I would not blame you for that if it be done in a quiet way. Think you he would be faithful to you? And what men do, women may, as I hold, they being much alike at the end. For the priests may say as they will, but the sins both of women and men, they must be of the same count. For if a man sin, must there not be a woman there? And as to you, you may do your choice, and never a guess, if it be not seen; for you would go to a lover's bed as a Madonna goes to her prayers."

Yvonne said nothing to this. She liked her cousin better than she liked her words when she spoke in this way. And what use was there in words? She knew Lucette well, but Lucette knew not her. How indeed could that be, when she did not know her own mind?

She cared for Guilbert little enough, yet of itself she was not loth to be wed. More than most things, she wished to get away from this house where she had lived for so many years—they seemed many to her—and her uncle's eyes, which she feared.

Besides, it is the way of life that we fret least against that which we know we cannot turn. Be there a hope—a chance—it is enough, though it be no more than a wafer's weight. But Yvonne's cage was secure.

She was not alone in that she dreaded her uncle's eyes; there were few in the town—nay, there were few in Provence or in Languedoc—but would have owned to the same fear. Yet he was an old man, frail enough, and with a cough which gave him little peace in the winter days. He wore no sword, and his servants were only two. But he was an alchemist whose name was a word of dread, even to Flanders and to the Empire beyond. It was he who held the famous charm which was sold to Charles of Orléans at a later date, but which did not save him from death in Paris streets:

Aring that in a corpse's mouth hath lain,
Dipped in a he-goat's blood at Easter slain.

So the rhyme ran.

Yvonne knew that her uncle could have made her to love his son, had it been worth his pains, or had he doubted that she would fall to his will. He had charms enough at his hands. There was that one of which all knew, though it was of such price that it could be seldom sold. It was of powdered cherry wood, made into a paste with the blood of a red cock, which had had no white feather at all (being a bird less easy to find than those might think who have not sought), and the blood of an untrodden pullet, of which every feather was speckless white (being another search which may take more time than would be said at a quick guess); and who had this paste could bring any woman to his touch, as close as are two cherries on a twisted stalk. Everyone knew of that charm. It was the whole world's talk. Yet it was a simple thing to some of those that the old man sold. Yes, she would go from that house with a glad step.

Thinking of a freedom so soon to be, and of no will to give heed to her cousin's words, Yvonne broke into song:

"Two lances rode from fair Toulouse
At sun-dawn on the Virgin's day;
They had the jocund world to choose,
And jocund as the merle were they."

But then she thought of Guilbert, and the song died. She did not hate him at all. He was not one whom it would be over-easy to hate. But she had little will to wed him, as they both knew. It would be done (if it were done at all, which it were idle to doubt) at the old man's will.

For she was in his hands, even apart from the bond of fear. It was not a time when a woman could walk in her own way, except it were that of shame. So he had said, on a day which was not long past.

He had counted all she had cost since, he said, he had taken her, being penniless and his sister's child, she being dead of the plague, and from that hour she had been reared at his cost. He summed it all in good Burgundy crowns. Surely, it seemed, she must be his while the debt stood. And how could she pay such a debt, having no gold? There was one way, as he had not scrupled to say. He could have got a large price had he sold her at Arles, that she might be a woman of the public baths. It might be thought that he would not so, she being called of his blood. Yet such things were at that time. Nor had they always, as it was said, a poor end. There was one such at Artois who sat at a Count's right hand, being Countess now.

But Livron did no shame to his niece. She should wed his son. That Guilbert was willing for that need be no wonder, for he was young and had eyes. And for her, a maid need not be too willing before the day. There will be time to learn and to know.

Yvonne's song ceased, and she said no more, looking out on the town—for the window was not low—and on to the high white towers of the castle of Faucon-haut, which was on the steep hillside overhanging the town, it might be three miles away. Why, she thought, were women thus, that they must bend to the strength of a man's hand? And what this traitorous weakness in their own bodies which drew them ever to that which they would not do? She knew it was in herself, though now it brought her no joy. She knew more than that. She knew that love might wake to a different tune. She had felt the beating of Lucette's heart as they lay shiftless in the same bed—as the way was at that time, when there came the sound of Henri's measured taps, that were no louder than ivy-leaves on the pane, when she would take up her cloak and go for a time to the inner room, that Lucette might do as she would with none to witness her play.

## CHAPTER TWO

MASTER LIVRON entered the room, and his voice broke the course of Yvonne's thoughts. It was a voice she had learned to dread, as he knew. Yet it was dread which she would not show. She faced the world with serene eyes, hiding her fears. So he knew, and he loved her less, if that might be, for the knowledge he had.

That he gave her no love she was sure. Yet he had done her no ill. Nay, he had done her much good. All men would have owned that, though he was not one they would care to praise. As a child, she had been tended well. She had been brought up with Lucette.

She knew nothing of blows. And Lucette had been beaten at times, even to a recent day. She had no cause for fear, except for the look in his eyes, and that he was a magician, and therefore one whom it was nature to dread.

He had done her no ill, and now she was to be wed to his son. There was no evil in that, on which he had shewn that he had a set mind. But now he said with a cold sneer in his speech:

"Mope you thus, Yvonne, with a bridal near? You would to bed with a sour face? You have shewn Guilbert that to his grief, who should have thanked the saints for a fouler fate.

"Well you may turn your eyes from that dread. There is one will have you bedded another way. The Count claims his right as of old."

He watched her closely as he said this, for it was a matter on which he had his own will, and it might be of moment to him to know her thoughts; but he learnt nothing, for, in fact, she did not know the meaning of what he said.

"The Count?" she asked vaguely, in a puzzled doubt. "What has he—? I know not—"

Lucette broke in with a wonder which was better informed "But that custom is dead! I thought it no more than an old tale. Is it not cursed of the Church? Oh, Yvonne, if you should bear the Count's child, and the Lady Isabeau let it live! I should build not on that overmuch. It is a thing which she is like to stop with a quick word."

Her father answered to that, "Peace, Lucette. You prate ever from a void mind. It is more like that it is the Lady Isabeau's wile to outwit the town. She would have us quarrel without the law. It is a thing, Yvonne, that you will not do, though they drag you forth. You must say that with a firm voice, or with tears if you will. But if you falter now, I will see that you get not that, but a worse fate. For you are pawn in a game that you do not see."

Yvonne looked at him with quiet inscrutable eyes "Yet I might see, being told." She was on her guard now, as he knew, and her thoughts would not be easy to read. His chance had been to learn what she felt at the first moment the news was told, and that was spoiled by her own ignorance, and Lucette's words. Yet he saw that she must be told in a plain way.

"It is a right," he said, "of the overlord of this vale, a right so old that there is none knoweth from whence it came, that he may claim a bride on her first night. He hath her for that once, and after that she goes to her husband's rule, and the Seigneur may not touch her again. There was an old time (so it is said) when it was counted shame to a bride that she was not claimed under this law, so that the

Seigneur must have those who were ill-favoured, or for whom he had little lust, lest his vassals were wroth. But that was in a far day, and it is a custom that is long dead."

"Can it be law yet," Yvonne asked, "being against the will of the Church, and so long dead?"

"The Church doth not forbid the law in this land. It is not of that strength. And it hath allowed this in older days, and maketh boast that it doth not change. There will be no help from the Church. Think you the priest sat with a shut mouth when this thing was planned? And for the law, there is our charter in proof. It is set out in the rights reserved, with a score of others which no one heeds at this day."

"Yet it is a thing easy to foil," Yvonne answered, as one who speaks of that in which she has but a small stake. "If there be no bridal, it sounds to me that the Count's claim does not come to its birth. We have but to say that, as for this time I will not wed, and he can make claim to another maid if he will."

M. Livron heard, but put this solution aside: "It is not to be answered thus. We must choose firmer ground. You need do naught at this time but to say that to Count Gismond's bed you will never go. You nay say that with a good oath, or with talk of a poniard in your own heart. You may say aught which will rouse the town."

Yvonne listened, and said nothing at all.

Her uncle, observing her in a cold doubt, was moved to add: "It may be that we shall do well to bring the bridal to a near day that we may talk of a thing done."

She said nothing to that either, though she did not look more pleased than before.

M. Livron went without further words. He went to confer with the maire and the chief citizens of the town. He had reasons, good to himself, why Yvonne should wed with his son on a near day, as will appear in its place, and it did not suit him at all that she should bear a son whose parentage might be less than sure. It was true that the law of Languedoc, and indeed of all France, was clear on that point. Let such a child have what parent it might, it was born in wedlock, and of its father's name. But there were lands beyond France which might read their laws in another way. It was a thing not to be risked.

He was not one who could count on the goodwill of the town, being much feared but little loved, yet fear may be of avail where love were a weaker urge; and this thing was too great for such feelings to weigh overmuch, either for evil or good.

Yet he went with a fear that he could not speak, for he knew that the Count (or the Lady Isabeau, which might be a better guess) had not set up this claim from any will that such a custom should prevail in the land. The Count was not of that kind. It was to turn aside the wrangle over the market tolls, on which the Count was unsure either of the law or his neighbour's aid.

He had chosen, it seemed, to make quarrel on a ground on which those of his own order might give more support if a strife came, for if the terms of service on which there had been charter granted in the old days, or a fief held, could be broken at will, or with the plea of new age, where might it stop, if at all? The nobles at this time were a caste apart, and it was not yet in Languedoc or Provence that their order shook. They stood strong and secure. In Italy, the cities were of great strength. They must be cajoled to a lord's rule, or be stirred to strife one with another, that the nobles might hold their place in a land they had ceased to rule. But in France there was yet a nobility of unchallenged strength which few would make front to defy, and between noble and common the cleavage was clear and deep, and but seldom crossed. A custom might be fallen from use, but what of that? Such things must be as the Seigneurs willed. Who should give aught but thanks if a lord would deign to a peasant's bride?

The town provost, a man of less courage than law, shook a timid head. "I say it not in the street, but among ourselves it is well to know. It is old law, but it is not dead. The Count is in the right as to that."

The maire asked: "Will you say that a law cannot die of disuse, be its age ever so great? Do not men change with the years? It was the use of a ruder age, and unmeet for a Christian land."

"I say less than that," the provost answered. "Yet it is well to look to a journey's end ere you take horse for the road. This is in the charter by which the rights of our township stand. If we call it too old, may not the Count say that the charter itself is in the same case?"

"We could make answer to that. We could say that there are bonds which have been kept every year, whether on his side or on ours. They are alive, and this dead."

M. Livron listened to this talk and was ill-content. He said: "Sirs, may I speak?" He asked thus, for he was not of the Council, being there of grace, and he knew that he was little loved. Also, he made habit of a posture of lowliness, which was not of the mind.

"You may speak of right," the maire answered, "for you are nearly concerned."

"Then I would say this. The Count seeks not that which he asks. It is the market tolls that he will have in a fuller hand, as we all know. But he will test us thus that he may judge of what courage we be; if we should yield now, he would look that we yield again in another way."

"That may be so," the provost answered, "yet that is not all. He seeks quarrel where he is sure that the law is not on our side."

"You may be right in that," the maire said; "but there is more to be thought. We cannot strive with the Count except we have the common men of the town in a fighting mood. If we think not to yield in all, we must choose cause which will rouse them to a quick heat. And I think this hath the better sound."

The provost was less sure of that, but he was sure that it was an issue to avoid, if any way could be found. He sought delay, as a lawyer will.

So he would have said, but M. Sault spoke for the first time, and he was one to be heard, being of most wealth in the town. He had been a chapman in younger days who had travelled far, buying and bartering in strange lands, and he had come home with a heavy purse. We may judge from that that he had been both cautious and bold, the times being as they were. He had been skilled in the use of both sword and tongue, but he had ever trusted the tongue more, and the pen better than that.

Now he dwelt at home, sending his sons forth, for he was near the twilight of life, and his paunch grew. He asked:

"What sayeth the maid herself? There is much in that."

So they all saw. You could not rouse the town on the part of one who would go to the castle on willing feet.

M. Livron make quick reply: "She hath heard but an hour since. She is between anger and woe. She saith that she would liefer die than be handled thus."

Could he say that as yet she had said nothing at all?

M. Sault nodded. He thought it a likely thing. Had it been Livron's daughter, Lucette.... "If she takes it thus," he said, "it may be we could raise the town."

"You would deny the Count in plain words?" the maire asked. He became more fearful as the crisis threatened, as a man might well do at that time, holding the place that he did. The Count might not be of a great power, but there might be those who would join his part. He foresaw many deaths. More than that, he saw the town burn. He saw one who hung with a noosed neck, and it was like to himself.

M. Sault thought ere he replied:

"Nay," he said, "I would give answer in humble words. I would ask of grace, not of might, as seeking mercy from one stronger than we."

It was a counsel that suited all, and was quickly agreed. M. Sault might have said the same words had the town been ready for strife or siege, but in fact he saw gain in delay. He had thought of crossbows that were in warehouse at Arles, waiting payment from the Count of Angoumois. Well, they could come here now. But he gave no sign of his thoughts, having learned that silence has a high price. He would talk of that to his sons…and of other needs.

* * * * * * *

A week later there was a new talk. Konrad Wolvenstein, whose name had been heard from Prague to Paris in the wars of two decades, was camping, with three hundred of his condottieri, upon the river-bank a mile north of the town.

There was little doubt of the meaning of that. Soldiers of fortune do not come by chance to the place where a quarrel breeds. It was true that this was a small matter, and Konrad had a great name. But in times of dearth men must be alert for the landing of little fish. Besides, a great fire may be lit by a small spark.

It was said of Konrad that he was a man who looked far. The maire heard the news, and was glad. Condottieri were to be bought by the better purse, and there was no doubt where that would be found.

There was much wealth in the town, though it lay quiet, making no show. It hid in little houses, in narrow streets. It looked timidly forth, as a mouse peeps from its hole. But it would be brought out in willing hands if it could be used to free the town from the tax which the castle claimed. And it was known to all that the Count was a poor man, or, rather, one who spent to his purse's depth, which is to come to the same end.

## CHAPTER THREE

KONRAD diced at his ease with his two lieutenants, being one of the three who cared nothing whether he lost or won.

In the valley, the summer evening was warm. The tent was open, so that Halt Redwood, seated on Konrad's left, could see the fifty-tented camp which had been pitched to northward on the river-side.

Beyond the willowed bank, beyond his seeing, lay the beauty of the Rhone Valley, and further yet, blue in the advancing dusk, the mountains of Provence. Konrad was a small man, dark, quiet, neat. He carried no weapons. He might be able to use a sword, but it was a thing which no man had seen him do. He had a brain and a pen, and they had brought him repute, and a name feared from the Pyrenees to the Danube's mouths. Soldier of fortune he might be in a time which shines out of the past with a cruel light, yet there were many of whom men spoke in a worse way.

He had three hundred men in that place, and many more in a Florentine camp, over whom he had power even to life and death while the term of their service held; for in the breadth of Europe there was no power that would have the will (even had it the might) to dispute his rule. They were in his hands, and they had the hazards of the profession of arms, but, beyond that, they were safe as few were in the Europe of that day. Even a priest might be less surely immune from the civil arm of the law.

There had been a day when the Duke of Hesse had seized one of their number on a charge of wounding an ensign of his guard in a tavern brawl. Konrad had used no threats, he had shown no force. He had gone alone to the castle, he had seen the Duke, he had walked out with the man at his heels.

After that he had tried the case fairly himself, hearing all sides. He had acquitted the man, and the Duke and he had been better friends than before. He was a leader to trust.

Now there had been peace in Europe for nearly two years, except for bickerings of a local kind, such as were not likely to cease while the feudal order stood as it did; and there were ten thousand barons and counts who were kings of as much land as they could see from a height on a day of mist, or perhaps less.

There had been peace last summer, and again this, until the late August trees were losing their fresher green, and it would soon be too late for the stir of war till the next spring should come. It was a long, unnatural peace, causing grief and loss to craftsmen of many kinds, and filling the countryside with ragged disbanded wanderers, beggars to silk and steel, or bullies to those of a humbler guise, so that men of peace moved abroad in a greater fear than when the talk was of gathered armies and rumours of battles fought. Yet there was more labour for the harvest, and the smith and wright would mend gear more swiftly, and for smaller charge, than when the call was ever for horseshoes and halberd-heads, and wagon-wheels that the Jews would buy.

Peace everywhere, except in Italy, where there was always strife. Konrad had held his force together last summer, though the cost had been heavy. He did not wish to disband that which he had been building for twenty years. He did not believe that peace could last among the hundred jealous contentious powers who held precarious dominion in the world he knew.

When the last autumn came, he had reluctantly paid off half his men, and gone into winter quarters with the remainder. Then had come an offer from the junta at Florence. He would not go himself; he distrusted the Florentines. But when spring came, with no hope of more attractive enterprise, he had hired them two hundred lances, with his lieutenant, Bernardi; and then four hundred more, and recently another two hundred, always with instructions to Bernardi that he should be ready to strike camp if he should write him that the sum agreed to be paid monthly in advance was seven days late in reaching the hands of his agent at Amsterdam. He could trust Bernardi. But he would not put himself in the power of the Florentines. He could deal more safely from a distance. And Bernardi understood the methods of Italian warfare. It was very well as it was. So he had been lying on the borders of Burgundy, with a hundred lances that he had kept to his own control, idle as it seemed, but watching the tangled game; of diplomacy which it was his business to understand, and from which it was his business to stand aloof, when a tale had reached him of a petty quarrel a hundred miles to the south, and he had marched at the next dawn, counting, surely enough, that one or both antagonists would approach him for aid which should be decisive in such a strife.

The dice went badly for Halt. He lost quietly, giving no sign that his last three nobles were drawn forth to be staked on the board. His face, which, despite its tan, was rather that of a student than a soldier of fortune, maintained its pleasant impassivity. He looked boyish beside the lined face and short-cut grizzled hair of his leader, and the massive form of Raoul.

Konrad played as one whose thoughts were not in the game, and who cared nothing for the coins he staked. Raoul played as he fought. He was no strategist, but there were few better men in France or middle Europe to judge of tactics when the battle joined, or to lead the storm of a doubtful breach. Raoul had a quality that would flash in extremity to surprising ends. He might be dull at the council table, but was inspired by tumult, and coolest when crisis came. Men spoke of him as an indifferent swordsman. He had little skill with the foils; but it was different in the battlefield, where few would choose to meet the rush of the giant form, and the sweep of the heavy sword. He played now with the ease of long experience in a routine way, but with an occasional audacity which, being infrequent, was incalculable in its results.

Halt Redwood was the only one to whom the game was of any moment. He knew the limit of the gold he carried, and that he had no reserve or resource beyond it. He knew it to be near its end, and he lost steadily, as men will under such conditions. In any case, he was no match for his more practised opponents in a game in which skill had its place, though chance ruled.

Konrad may have guessed this, but he was not one to share his thoughts. He looked a moment at the young Englishman who had walked into his camp three months before, and whom he had enlisted with few questions, and trusted already as he trusted few. His glance told nothing. He had not made his reputation by losing, whether at dice or war. He called carefully and won again. Then Raoul called high, too high—and lost to both of them with doubled stakes. He reached for the dice-box to throw again, with a jest at his folly; but Konrad rose:

"I will walk," he said. "I would have you with me, Raoul."

Halt understood it was indicated that he should not accompany them. "Shall I set guard for the night?" he asked. This had been his duty on the march; having camped, his lack of experience caused him to ask for orders. Konrad paused for a moment, with a hesitation that was unusual to him. They were in a peaceful country. Certainly they had nothing to fear from town or castle. Either might hope for their help, but could gain nothing by molestation. Besides, their own troubles were sufficient. "There is no haste," he said at last, "till the roll be called. After that, you will place sentries as in the way of war, and with reliefs during the night. You will give orders that none leaves the camp till the roll is called again at the dawn."

Saying this, he laid a hand on Raoul's arm and they went out together. Halt sat watching them through the open side of the tent. The river was low in the dry August days, but still of a great breadth. The camp was stretched along a strip of sloping pasture beside it. To the left was a spreading copse, with undergrowth dense in places. Halt thought it a poor place for a camp. But there was no fear of attack from any quarter. He knew Konrad to be a practised soldier. He had chosen ground where water was near, and grass for horses, and wood for fires. He did not wear a cloak on a warm day. Yet he would have a full watch kept. Why was that?

He saw Konrad and Raoul pacing between the camp and the wood. Konrad was on the right. He looked slight beside the burly form of his lieutenant. He stooped a little as though wearied. He was a man who carried himself well, but it was the end of a day of toil, and he was not young. He appeared to be talking earnestly. Yet Halt had observed that he was a man who measured words with care.

They passed out of sight as the river bent. Halt remained seated in his leader's tent, thinking idly. His pay would be due in a week's time, and meanwhile that last throw had left him sufficient to carry on. He did not wish to show need, or to borrow. Konrad had asked him nothing when he had given him his position; at least, nothing that mattered. He had asked some things, keenly enough. But he judged men for himself. Free companions would enlist with such pasts as were often best forgotten.

Halt knew that he had been fortunate beyond reason. He believed Konrad to be one of the best soldiers in Europe. And he had seen nothing, in these months of peace, of the fouler side of the trade to which he had taken. There was an iron discipline in the camp to which all must bend: there was no license allowed. While they had loitered on the borders of Burgundy they had done wrong to none. A child of ten might have walked through their tents without fear; a merchant could have driven a mule unplundered, though its saddlebags had bulged with gold. He had not learnt that the condottiere was a beast that endured the chain, knowing the time would come when he would be loosed.

The tent where he sat showed some comfort without ostentation. There was a plain trestle table covered with a velvet cloth. The camp-stools were upholstered in leather. There was a camp-bed. There were two chests. One held Konrad's clothes, as Halt knew. The other, iron-bound and very heavy, his treasure, and his private records. It was unguarded.

Its keys hung at its owner's belt. Its weight would have made it difficult to steal. Its publicity was its protection. While Konrad lived, he would be a bold man who would enter that tent unbidden.

Stark ruthless discipline was the basis of the order which the camp maintained, though it was a discipline which dealt only with essential things. Halt knew already how ruthless it could be if the need came. He had seen a man hanged for an offence which would have meant no more than the stocks, or a public whipping, in the England from which he came. But there had been no protest, even from the sullen silence of the man condemned.

A sudden uproar broke his thought. It rose from beyond the river-bend. It was not too far off for him to hear Raoul's great voice roaring an order. It sounded as with a strange excitement or urgency. Men within his sight had leapt up, and were running toward it. He rose quickly, not knowing that there was anything to fear, yet he had a sense of disaster given by that distant voice, and he drew his sword as he ran.

Round the bend, he came on no scene of fighting. The men were scattering through the wood in pursuit of one who had already fled.

Konrad was supported on the ground by Raoul's arms. He had a crossbow shaft in the back.

## CHAPTER FOUR

KONRAD lay on the camp-bed which had been carried out from the tent. He knew well that he had not many hours to live. He would have been sooner dead had he allowed them to draw the barbed head from the wound. But the bolt had been cut with sharp shears, close to the flesh, so that he could be propped in comfort, and that the life might hold for a few hours, and here he lay with a grey face, giving no sign of pain, with his lieutenants beside, and three hundred men paraded before him.

He spoke very slowly and very low, as though he feared to breathe deeply; but the words came clearly in the silence:

"Comrades," he said, "you have sworn in all things to do my will; will you do that for the last time?" There was a murmur of assent. "Some of you," he said, "have been with me for many years. I have spared neither myself, nor any. I have been hard, but I have kept faith, and my hands are clean as to you. I have not wasted your lives, nor hired you to a foul cause. Now that I am near death, I have work undone, which I must pass on to other hands. For the times that you have sworn service to me, I will appoint you a new leader, and I will have you while I yet live to swear service to him. That is my right, and I will take denial from none."

He motioned Raoul to come closer. He pointed to the keys at his belt, and Raoul loosed and took them. He did not doubt that he was to be lord of that band. Even Bernardi was to be beneath him now. Men watched, but there was no murmur. Raoul was well liked. He would be good leader enough.

Then Konrad motioned also to Redwood, and as he came more closely to learn the will of the dying man, he saw him turn again to Raoul, and speak so low that, though he was near, he did not hear the words.

Raoul started. Then he flushed darkly, and a look of protest, almost of anger, came into his eyes.

Konrad spoke no more, but gazed at him in silence, and his glance fell. Then he stepped across to Halt and placed the keys in his hand.

Halt was slow to take them. He stood bewildered He did not understand, nor, for a moment, did any. Then there was a murmur of voices, and the note of dissatisfaction was not hard to hear.

Konrad took no notice of that. He turned to Raoul again. "Call them three by three, that they may swear in my sight."

Halt Redwood found words at last. Through the confusion of his mind, one thought was clear, that he had no right—that he was not fit—to take that which was so strangely offered.

He was ignorant and unpractised. He had already been advanced beyond any proved deserving. He made a motion to return the keys to Raoul. "My captain," he began, "I cannot—"

The low level voice of the dying man cut short his protest. "You are not asked."

Three by three, Raoul called the men forward. To each he repeated the oath which they had first made to Konrad. An oath of loyalty, obedience, and service, an oath absolute and unreserved; but it was now sworn to Halt for the remaining term of the service of each man only. That was just, as they saw.

There was no protest, nor any overt unwillingness, till more than half the number had sworn, when Raoul called the names of three, and but two came forward. He called again the name of Gustave Meyer, but the man, from where he stood, shook his head, and moved a step backward

As the swearing had proceeded, Konrad had lain with closed eyes. None could tell whether he heard. He looked very near his death. Now he raised his head once more. His voice came low, but very clear. It held no sound of anger. "Gustave, come here."

He came forward with a more confident look than he had shown before.

Halt saw a heavy, swarthy man, with very black eyes, having an expression that was at once insolent and furtive. His forehead was divided equally by a wide livid scar, almost straight down from hair to nose. It did not look like a sword-cut. It had, in fact, been given by a woman's hand from a hot spit in a kitchen brawl.

He looked at Halt with an open contempt. His youth, his inexperience, his slighter frame. Halt was conscious of all these as he looked back, though he gave no sign.

Konrad spoke again, even more gently than before. He was speaking now with a very visible effort, as though he found it hard to control either his voice or his consciousness. "Gustave," he said, "I do not order twice. You will swear."

Gustave looked at him in a sullen doubt. Plainly he was dying. His day was over. Raoul was the better man. If he stood out for Raoul, who knew that he might make him his lieutenant in a natural gratitude?

He looked down uneasily, but he shook his head.

He was beginning to speak his mind, when the slow voice startled him to a sudden fear:

"I do not order twice. You will hang."

The man looked at Raoul, but he got no answering glance. Raoul had already signalled to the two men whose hands were on him. "Nay," he said sullenly, "I will swear if I must."

"You will not swear. I do not order twice. You will hang at dawn. If I live, you will hang. If I am dead, it will be as your captain wills."

They led him away.

When the swearing was over, Konrad was carried back to his tent. The long summer twilight had given way to the light of a crescent moon. He called for lamps, and for writing materials. He wrote slowly, but with a firm hand. He wrote to the junta at Florence. He wrote to Bernardi. He wrote to a goldsmith at Amsterdam, to a Jew in London, to a merchant in Hamburg. They brought hot wax, and he drew the signet from his hand, and sealed them one by one with his wolf's-head crest. They were curt notes, for he wrote as he spoke, sparing words, but with a meaning direct and clear.

As he wrote, his lips were tightly pressed, and his face was greyer. When he had finished, he turned to Halt, and placed the signet-ring on his hand. Then he looked to Raoul again. His lips opened: "You will tell him—" he began. The words ended in a rush of blood. He did not speak again.

# CHAPTER FIVE

HALT REDWOOD sat by the side of the dead man. He did not think of rest. The letters lay on the table. Each was sealed at the foot, but had been left unclosed for his reading. They made mystery deeper.

To Bernardi, Konrad had written:

> I am dying at Faucon-haut, being a tower that looks at Provence from the right bank of the Rhône. An Englishman, Halt Redwood, is my successor. You will take his orders in all. Adieu.

> Konrad

To his agent at Amsterdam he wrote with an almost equal brevity:

> I am dying. You will account for all to Halt Redwood, an Englishman. He has my signet. Raoul is witness. Send him schedule of that which is now his by a very trusty hand. I recommend you to him as a proved friend, knowing you will not fail. Adieu.

> Konrad

To the London Jew he had written to like purpose, but at greater length. There were instructions for the settlement of debts in various parts of Europe; for the realization of certain properties, if possible before his death should be known; for dealing with certain Florentine bills of exchange; and in respect of financial claims against the Dukedom of Hesse. It was a letter only vaguely understood by him who must now take up the matters with which it dealt, for he had little knowledge of the international financial methods by which the Jews of that day had subjugated the Europe on which the nobles strove to their gain.

The Hamburg letter was merely a curt line over his signet, ordering certain stores, for which payment would be made by his London agent, as usual, against Bernardi's certificate. It showed something of the character of the man who, stricken so suddenly, could yet remember such a detail, and hold his death at bay while he provided for those who were dependent upon him.

The letter to the junta at Florence, though as curt in tone as were the others, contained a matter over which its reader paused for a time, as indicating that there was more than a random favouritism in the choice which had placed him in such an unexpected and unearned authority.

It ran thus:

> My Lords, I am dying, and time is short. I have appointed my lieutenant, Halt Redwood, my successor and heir. He will carry out my orders for eleven months from now, for to this he is sworn. For such purpose he may require the troops which are now with you, under my captain, Bernardi. I do not know. Should he thus, they are pledged to you for four months only. I give you such notice as I may. I had written tomorrow to the like purpose had I lived.

It seemed from this that Konrad had been at the threshold of some enterprise for which his full strength might—or might not—be needed, and that he was now passing it on to his heir, whether he would or no.

Even yet there might be a high price to pay for the authority and wealth which had been thrust upon him. And he had no choice! For though he was captain to the living, he was still the servant of the dead.

But how should he learn the purpose for which he had been so strangely chosen?

Something, as he had understood, Raoul could tell. More might be learned from the iron-bound chest which was now his, but which he made no haste to open. There, doubtless, was the record of the dead man's life, the intimate things of one who had been aloof and reticent beyond the habit of most. Six hours ago to have touched it would have been an outrage beyond pardon.

Halt had seen something of the revelations which might come from the chest of a Free Companion. He had been placed in charge of the opening of that of the man he had seen hanged a week ago. He remembered its shabby mean utilities, its sacred useless things, its surprising oddities, its shames. He could not imagine what might be in the chest before him, but he had little will to look while the dead man lay so near. That was absurd. His thoughts wandered to the other hanging, which was to take place at dawn—unless he forbade it. He started to consciousness that issues of life and death were his, not, as they had been, at his sword's point only.

Raoul came in. He saluted in the routine manner of a life's habitude, but with respect, and an under-aspect of geniality. Perhaps the place made it more natural for him to do so. He had never entered that tent without the formality of deference while Konrad lived.

To Halt it came strangely from one who had been his senior officer but a few hours before, and he repressed a start with difficulty. But he was inwardly pleased, and most so at the expression which underlay the action. He thought that he could trust Raoul, and on that much might depend in the enigmatic days which were before him.

"Did you find him?" he asked. Raoul said they had not; they had traced the man's flight from where he left the further side of the wood. There was a treeless meadow beyond, undulating at the further end.

Lest he should be seen as he crossed this open ground, he had continued along a ditch that flanked the wood for some distance. In the dry weather, what would otherwise have been a ditch of water was of mud only. It showed his footmarks—recent marks of a man who ran. Not large feet. The right always made the heavier impress. Possibly an old wound in the left leg. When the ground favoured him, he had left the ditch, and his track was lost until he had leapt a little dyke beyond it, that bounded the high road. It was scarcely more than a long stride, but he seemed to have leapt short, and slipped down on the further side. Clearly a somewhat lame man. The road shewed no marks, but he must have gone by it, for on the farther side was swampy ground, and a spreading pool.

It was a way no man would choose who fled from a near pursuit. There was more than this. By the angle at which he crossed the meadow he must have intended to take the road to the left—and that led to the town or round it, and to the castle beyond.

And—Raoul pointed out—the gates of the town would be already shut, for they had learned that they were closed early while the trouble with the castle continued. It seemed likely that he had gone on to the castle, or that the town gates had been opened to let him through. Even had they not been shut at the time, such a man must have been very noticeable as he passed inward, lame, breathless, soiled from the ditch, bearing a crossbow.

Well, it must be left till the dawn came.

Halt turned to the letters on the table. He would not hold Raoul at arm's length. He must lean on him too greatly. "You should read these," he said, "and you shall tell me what you may to explain."

But Raoul shook his head. He was no scholar. Halt closed them carefully, sealing them with Konrad's signet. They must be sent at dawn. But how?

He knew little of how letters were conveyed in safety through the troubled Europe of those days, or whether he should detail men of his own to carry them, or who to trust to that length; but he need not show his doubt.

"You shall send them at the dawn in the speediest manner, but by a sure hand," he said; "they are letters of weight." He handed them to Raoul, who dropped them into his pouch. "I will send Werther," he said, "on a lean mule."

Halt wondered a moment how one man should bear letters to places so far apart; but he was slow to expose his doubt, and Raoul added: "There is a Jew in Lyons who makes boast that he never fails with any missive placed in his hands, though it be for Tartary or the Afric Moors."

So it was done on the next day. Werther rode in a mean habit, and on a mule such as would tempt few to its theft. There was a clump of spears a furlong back on the road, bearing the arms of the grey wolf's head which most men knew. Should Werther be stayed by a thieves' band, there would be swift rescue enough; should there be trouble of higher kind, the escort might have blows to take or give, while the poor man's mule would ride on, for who but a way-side thief would take heed of him?

## CHAPTER SIX

HALT slept little that night, having many matters of which to think. When the morning came he must question Raoul; he must explore the records in the iron-bound chest; he must learn the power which was now his, and the burden which had been cast upon him.

He must take order also in many things. There was the dead man's funeral to arrange, his assassin to be sought. For the routine control of the camp he could trust Raoul, as Konrad had done before. Konrad had not been one to interfere in the smaller things, which made for the ease of one who must take his cloak before he had fitted it to his own wear.

Falling into a troubled sleep as the dawn neared, he was roused by Raoul, who asked: "Shall the man hang?"

Halt saw that there can be little peace for one who leads. He should have had that on his mind without Raoul's aid. Raoul might be unable to read, and for that, or other cause, he had not been placed in command. Yet, at this first test, he had shown himself the better fitted to rule.

Halt saw that the man would have hanged while his mind wandered on other things, or in the absence of sleep. Now the power of life and death was in his hands. How should it be used on his first day? He would be merciful if he might. He said: "I will have the man here. He should have learnt sense in the night."

Raoul looked at him while a second passed. It was no longer than that. His shoulders may have lifted an inch, but no more.

Halt knew, in that second's time, that he had been judged, if not for a fool, yet for one who walked in a foolish way. He saw also that Raoul would be one he could trust, as Konrad had found before. Indeed, there was no difference to Raoul. He had obeyed Konrad for many years; he obeyed him now. He brought in the man.

Gustave looked at Halt in a sullen way, though there was hope in his heart. He was of a shrewdness to see that he had not been brought there had it been determined that he should hang. A minute ago he had thought that the ropes which bound his arms would be there to his life's end.

Halt looked at him coldly enough: he was a man he disliked. The world would be no worse when he died. Halt saw that; but having brought him here…. That had been his mistake. He said only: "You have had time to learn sense in the night. Will you hang, or swear?"

Naturally, the man swore.

He went back to his tent with his hands free. He found his chest open, his possessions shared among those who were of his own troop. Some things were returned, others not. He saw a gold chain in a man's hands. It was not worth a life, being of light weight, yet it cost two. Daggers shone in the dawn. Gustave rolled on a bench, holding his side. There was a man whom Halt must hang when the tale came to his ears. There could be no doubt about that. There had been refusal to surrender a stolen thing, and a fatal blow. He gave judgment in a cold way, being wroth at himself. The men saw that he was one who would rule, and they gave him the fear which he might have lost had Gustave lived, and had that been the tale's end.

But he was condemned in his own heart. He had lost two men of those he led by a weakness he should not have shown, when it might have been no more than one.

But Halt had done and heard much beside this ere the noon came. He had sent out riders to search for word of a lame archer who fled in haste. He had sent complaint to the castle and to the town. He knew enough of how matters stood to guess that there would be little will to quarrel with him from either side, and he wrote in a bold way. He let it he seen that to find the assassin might be to win a friend, but that to shield him would be to have a most certain foe.

He had request made also that Konrad should be buried in the town, in the great church of Ste. Sarah.

That brought a priest to his tent. He had questions to ask. Konrad had been excommunicated ten years ago; once, if not more. Had the Church lifted the ban? There was a doubt about that. Had Konrad sought the aid of Holy Church when he died? It could not be said that he had. Halt could have thrown some light upon that. He had learned from Raoul at an earlier hour that Konrad had held aloof from the Church for many years.

He had made vow that he would not ask absolution till he had revenged a wrong, which was still undone when he died.

Halt might know this, but he felt that it would be the wrong thing to say. He replied that a man who stops a crossbow bolt with his back has little time to think of such things before his life goes. There had been no priest in the camp.

As to the question of an excommunication of earlier years, Halt knew enough of the politics of Southern Europe to make little of that. Had not the papal power mixed in all the confused quarrels of the last fifty years? Had it not taken active part in the wars? Had it not become a routine to excommunicate those against whom it fought?

The priest said it was beyond his power to decide. He must ask the Cardinal's will. Halt was impressed, though he gave no sign, by the mention of so high a dignitary of the Church. He showed simplicity in that. They were but a day's ride from Avignon, where the Pope dwelt at that time, and around which he was then building the wall which still stands, massive and high. His palace rose in the midst. Cardinals in Languedoc and Provence were as thick as fleas in a bed.

But though he did not know that, he knew that it was a point on which he could not take denial. Konrad must be buried with honour in blessed ground. He was an Englishman, and in that country the priests had less power. They were taught to walk in a meeker way. He said something of this. The priest answered that he would put the case to the Cardinal in the best light, using such arguments as he could.

"There are a hundred here, on which you should dwell ere it be too late." The priest understood that. He knew that a hundred spears was the total of Konrad's force. (Three men counted as one spear in the jargon of that day.) He came to the point then, talking of gold. There was a price agreed, which was high. Konrad should have a noble grave, in the chancel itself.

Halt felt that he had done well. The boldest fiend, seeking the soul of the dead (as he knew that fiends are alert to do) might turn in terror from the chancel of a church of such ancient fame.

The next day there came maire and provost in deputation from the town, but he told Raoul to send them away. There was the same dish for a deputation from the castle, though it was a bishop who came. Halt said he would do business with none till he had buried Konrad, unless they could bring the man by whose hand he had died. The town protested that it knew nothing of this man; the castle's tale was the same. Raoul said he believed the castle's word; of the town he was less sure.

Konrad was to be buried on the third day, and meanwhile Halt held his camp as though he were in a hostile land, suffering none to enter or go forth, except for certain bartering, which he allowed, having no will that his men should starve.

For himself, he had matters of which to think, for the tale which Raoul had told him was this:

For some years he had been in Konrad's confidence to this degree, that he had known that he had one purpose that ruled his life. He sought ever for one who had seduced his wife from his side, and had deserted her in such strait that she died, and who had taken his child. The man had been a soldier at that time, having a reputation in the Italian wars. Konrad had found him with the dead woman and the living child, which he had refused to surrender. Konrad had challenged him to a duel which would have decided the child's fate. It was to have been fought on the following day. But on that day the man had gone, and the child also.

From that time he had disappeared. He was heard of no more in the wars. Konrad supposed that he had changed his name. He sought him ever, reckoning that he must find him at last. He searched among the prisoners that fell into the hands of himself or his allies, looking at every face. He reviewed the inhabitants of every taken town. For eighteen years he had learned nothing at all.

But a month ago—or it might be less—he had had news, at a time when search had become a routine of life, rather than the urgent impulse which it had been at the first. His London agent, whom he could trust and who could learn of all that moved in the world of European finance—which was at root much as it is now—wrote that there was question made of a secret kind as to the wealth he had, and of where it lay. Konrad was vexed and angry at that, pondering who it should be, though he thought he would gain but little, his agents being the men they were, both in London and other parts.

He could see none whom it would serve to make such a quest, for which crowns must be paid from a full purse. Then he thought: "There is one. There is he in whose hands my daughter lies. He would use her again to have my wealth when I die;"

When the idea had once entered his mind, he saw that it was no less than a likely thing. He had been active in Europe's wars for a score of years, and he had been fortunate in himself or in the sides he chose. It was easy to guess that he would have wealth in a safe hole; and, for such as he, England was ever the surest hoarding-place, being oversea, and of the settled order which comes to a land which is not ravaged by foreign foes, though there might be strife between baron and baron, or prince and prince, from which no land can be free for more than a short space. The man who had taken his child might well be of a will to take his wealth too, either for himself or for her. He might have grown fond of her, making her as his own. Or he might have fallen to poverty in these days. Or he might be near his end, and think that, if he would ever assert her claim, it must be swiftly done.

He might think also that Konrad could not have much longer to live. It was true that he had no feeling of age, but his years were as many as were gained by most in those days, and especially by such as were spent in the wars. They might not be slain, as few were, but their lives would be weakened by fevers and many ills before they could come to the fifty years which he had passed at that time.

As he thought thus, he became sure. And with the surety that the man he had sought in vain had now doubled upon his own tracks, all the old hatred revived, and the lust of chase wakened anew. He wrote that no coin should be spared to find from whence that enquiry came.

In a few weeks he had word. It had come from Paris, from a goldsmith there, of whom Konrad knew well by repute. He had had it from Faucon-bas, which was a town in Languedoc on the border of Provence, which the castle of Faucon-haut overhung. The enquiry had been of a very secret kind, and supported by a large fee. It had been in the name of Livron, or Louvaine, or one like to that, which might mean little. He might be no more than a scrivener who had been given the charge, and paid to keep a still tongue.

More might have been learned, but the goldsmith's clerk who sold this tale was discharged suddenly on the next day and could tell no more than his memory held, which went no further than this. But Konrad thought it enough.

He could not tell whether that which he sought would be found in castle or town, and he thought the castle the more likely place; but he would search them both to their cellars' depths, though it should mean storm and siege in a private war, such as was often waged at that time.

He moved south from Dijon where he then was, and as he marched, not swiftly, nor by a direct route—for he would seem to come there by a wandering chance rather than as one who sought a prey of which he had scent—he heard tale that there was strife of words between castle and town, such as might soon turn to a strife of steel. That would give him all the pretext he would. As a circling vulture swoops to the spot where the carcass falls, he marched straight and hard down the Rhone Valley till he saw the high ramparts of Faucon-haut dark against their background of hills and a sunset sky.

Konrad had told Raoul of this, of which he had known something before, though not much, as he had walked with him outside the camp, on the night when the bolt came from the wood.

He was told as much then as might be needed to make him of better help.

At a later hour, when Konrad knew that his life was done, he had had to think whom he should trust, that his vengeance did not fail in the end. Could he cast his cloak on the back of one who was unable to read? He chose the best he might at that pass. He judged Halt Redwood to be one who would keep his oath. Halt did not doubt that Konrad had done the best he might in his own cause, but that he himself had any cause to be well content he was less sure.

## CHAPTER SEVEN

SIR LANVAL DE VENCE rode down the Rhône Valley. He had tired of the Court of Burgundy, and would go further, seeing the world, not caring much where it might be.

He came in no state, having but one squire, who rode with a sumpter-mule on his right hand and a spare charger upon his left, and who carried also his master's spears, and his shield bearing his device of the flying swan.

He who could show that shield had no need to flaunt wealth, nor to ride in state that his rank be known. The harp that was slung over his back, where a two-handed sword had been a more likely sight, would win him an honoured seat at any Court in the lands of chivalry. He gave lustre to where he stayed. Had he not proved at a dozen Courts of Love and countless contests of song that he was the first trouvère of the day?

He wore a sword also, and of his valour there was no spoken doubt, but men differed as to his skill either in the art of war or in single strife. For he was one who would quarrel with few, and if he fought (which he would be slow to do, even in the mock-strife of the tilt), he would jape at his own skill, so that it seemed but a little thing. Men gave Fortune praise when he won rather than his own arm, at which he chafed naught, being one who cared more for the art of song. And he had moods when he would mock at that too.

Now he looked on a fertile valley of corn and wine, and the broad river shining blue in the cloudless air, and the great hills beyond. There had been no war in these parts for two summers and more than that. The scene was peaceful and fair. The sun shone warm overhead; there was a cool wind from the distant Alps. It was a gay world at its best.

As he rode, he hummed a half-made song, seeking its tune. It was a love-song, tender of words, but with a mocking lilt.

> Oh, mignonne mine, though parting be…

There was a line beyond that which he could not get to his will.

Well, let it wait. It would come. He had found that it was of little use to fret his mind in such quest. He would turn thought to another song, one that would win him fame at the Court of the French King at a later time, for it would sing of the ancient banner of France, which was then powdered with golden lilies on a field of blue. The white banner was of a later day, nor was it yet impaled with the red arms of Navarre.

> Gold lily on its dusk of blue,
> There is but one of lordlier hue:
> The Flower of God that lit the stem

Of David's line in Bethlehem.

The metaphor drew his thought to the high dream of the deliverance of the Holy Land, to which all knighthood turned at that day. Could he not frame the song to that end, so that it would be call to a new Crusade which must surely win? He knew how much may be done with a good song. It is true still, and it was more so at that day. He had vision of a great host that moved under many banners; but first and widest, from a thousand staves, fluttered the golden lilies on their ground of blue. Could not men be roused by song to the high effort that was needed now?

> Until the winds of Canaan kiss
> The tossing field of fleurs-de-lis,
> And Mahound's hordes shall yield to them
> The ramparts of Jerusalem.

He must give more time to that song. His mind went back to that which had held it before.

> Oh, mignonne mine, though parting be
> The end of every love, ma mie,
> Yet while...

He forgot the song again as he became aware of white tents ranged along the riverside, and a banner-staff in their midst from which drooped a lowered flag.

"Now what have we here?" he said, and as he spoke the flag spread to the wind.

"It showed like to the grey wolf-head of Konrad of Wolvenstein. But what doth it at that height? And there is little stir in the camp. Is the man dead? Lambert, you shall ask for me of this."

The squire went at his word. He got down from his horse, for he must climb a stile, and there was a field to cross, with a cherry orchard upon his left, and the north end of Konrad's camp at the far right corner. He was soon back with a tale we know. He added that Konrad Wolvenstein was being buried that day at the church of Ste. Sarah within the town.

Sir Lanval gave him a short epitaph: "Worse men live." He considered the tale. He added: "Lambert, we will lodge here a night, or it may be more. There should be things to see or to do."

He rode on to the town gate, at which he paused, and then turned aside. He said: "I see not why I should watch another put to earth, being neither sexton nor priest. A man may wait his own turn, which is too soon for most. He will be present at that."

Lambert said nothing. He heard much of his master's words without making reply. He did not always think they were wise. But his own wisdom told him that there are other things that are best unsaid.

They went on to the castle by a climbing path.

## CHAPTER EIGHT

IT was the banquet hour at the castle of Faucon-haut. The Count sat at the head of the higher board, with his sister, the Lady Isabeau, on his right. Sir Lanval sat at her other side, as an honoured guest. It was such a place as he often had, even at tables of kings; for he was not only of a high race, he was first of the trouvères of northern France. He was the only one of that band who could win honour against the troubadours of Provence. Kings, doing grace to him, might do the like to themselves also, for he could set them so in a song that they would be more great than they were before. He was also one whose songs came with himself, for he could both sing and play, which few could or would at that time, whether troubadour or trouvère. For some could make songs, but had no skill to the making of a good tune; and if they had skill in both, yet they might lack that of hand or voice, so they made songs that the jongleurs sang in their names.

But Lanval had the arts which would make both music and song, and could touch viol or harp in the right way, and he had the voice also to sing. Is it wonder that men were glad where he came?

So he sat now in the best robes that the castle held for a guest's use (for a knight did not ride at that day bearing his clothes with him, as though he thought that he might halt where there would be none to spare), and he looked round with eyes that were used to see, and though he spoke in a free way, he heard much more than he said.

He saw the Count to be much as he had thought to find, from the talk he had heard before. He was a man of a formal pride and few words. He had lost a part of his right hand, with three fingers, more or less, in a duel when he was young; so he had excuse that he was not one of a ready sword.

He had lost his wife three years before, she having gone her own way with the Count of Thale. He had made little of that, even on the day she went. He would have men think he was rather glad of that loss.

He could play well at the chess—or so it was said; but that was made less sure by the fact that he was slow to play, except against those he could always beat, lest his pride fall.

He was not savage of mood, nor would he take pleasure in cruel deeds, as many did of the nobles of that time; but he would be obeyed, even to a great price; and he was hard to move when a thing had been once said. Only Isabeau could change him from that. She was his sister—or, at least, there was but a whispered doubt, which was not spoken aloud, lest the castle gallows silence the tongue. She was of a pride that was like his own, and a fiercer will.

It was said that she, rather than he, had forced quarrel upon the town to a point when it came near to a strife of swords; but, indeed, there was little choice on the castle's side, they having been free of gold as they were in the better times.

The town read its charter in its own way, now that much merchandise passed up the Rhone Valley in a time of peace, and its tolls had risen to a large sum. The Count had men on his hands whom he must needs pay. Should he let them go, his power went. Before, they had been engaged in the wars, as had many from the town also. It was the strange length of the peace from which this quarrel was bred.

But whether it were the Lady Isabeau or the Count himself who had brought that quarrel to where it stood, it was common talk that it was her wit which had given it the new turn which it now had.

Isabeau told it in her own way. Sir Lanval heard her, giving little sign of his thoughts.

"Well," he said, "if it be good law, as is like enough, there may be no trouble in that. Doth the jade wince from her joy?"

"She may take that as she will," Isabeau answered, as one who turns from a little thing. "She can be whipped if the need come."

Sir Lanval looked at her with a glance which she could not read. "Doth the Church stand with this law?"

"The Church will tell you of that," she answered. Her eyes went to the Bishop of Nîmes, who had a near place on the Count's left. He was a priest, thin and tall, with a hollowed face, whose age would be hard to tell. He drank little wine, which he chose with care. He cut from the best joints with a sparing knife. His discreet and moderate amours were such that his dignity was not smirched.

He had confessed most who sat round that board (except at its lower end), and he knew them for what they were. He was suave of speech, with much Latin upon his tongue, which can be left to itself. Now he said:

"It is good law; there is no question of that. The Church doth not strive with the law, except at a great need."

Sir Lanval smiled with his lips. "Doth the Church bless?"

"She hath not been asked. There would be bull from the Pope if it were put in the right way. It is a small thing in itself, at which some maids would be pleased, and some fret. It had a good use in an older day."

Isabeau would have him speak more plainly than that. She said "Father, being the law of the land, it can be done without sin of the flesh, or the breaking of marriage vows?" She knew his answer to that, for she had had it before.

"Surely," he said, "it can be done by a bride without sin, for she doth it not of her choice, but by force of law, and to the intent that her first child—if a good fortune be hers—shall be of a better kind than she would have from one of her own rank, such as she must needs wed. It is a custom from which our race rose to its strength, as we know it at this day. Nor can it be sin to him who doth it of duty, and at a set time, rather than by the mastery of a lewder will. Nor is there wrong in its end, being within the cloak of the law."

"It hath a fair sound," Sir Lanval replied. "Yet for one who is loth—"

The Bishop answered as one who solves a point of logic which has caused dispute in the schools. "That were a thing hard to re-solve, for who knoweth a woman's heart at its most depth? Yet you may see that to give her choice would be a poor rule, for there would enter the feet of sin to her heart. Nor would it lead to her peace, for should she choose at her will, would she be lightly forgiven by him to whom she had vowed her faith and her love? There was much wisdom in those who contrived this law in the form which it still bears. And you must see beyond that, if a maid be loth, as some would, or if she be roughly used by one who would go beyond her own will at a single chance, yet it is a world in which there is little pleasure without prelude of pain, or its after-coming (which is a worse thing), nor, as the scripture saith, is such the purpose of God." He crossed himself as he said this, as did several of those who heard in an absent way. "Even to Paradise, is there not a Purgatory to be gone through? Shall she wince for a night of pain, if it lead at last to her lover's arms? It were to think little of love that we should hold it too hard a way."

Sir Lanval answered him in his own tone. "There is much reason in that, yet if a trouvère may speak when the Church's wisdom is said, doth not that somewhat impute the high feeling of gentle kind to those of a baser blood?"

It was a question that brought a murmur of assent from those who heard. What did the common kind know of the high mysteries of the Courts of Love? It was enough for them that they mated and bred, and that the fairest of their women might hope for the honour of an hour of a knight's regard.

Sir Lanval did not wait for an answer to the question he had raised, on which the Bishop paused in reply. He turned to his host to enquire courteously, "Would you bring this custom back as a live thing, Sir Count, or is it only to test the town if they be loyal and meek?"

It was a question to which Count Gismond had little will to reply. It had been discussed in his presence from various angles from which his dignity flinched. There had been those who had counted what it might mean. They had reckoned how many scores of marriages there might be in the town in the year's course. They had made jests at which he was wroth in ways which he shrank to show. He wished Isabeau had never noticed this bond in the old charter that the town held. And the Bishop had been less adroit than his habit was. Could it be purgatory for a common woman to come to a lord's bed? It was class-treason to make such a comparison even in jest.

It was an honour for which they should kiss his feet, as he had little doubt that many of them would be ready to do.

Yet he was not fool enough to suppose that their men would take it in quite the same way. With the town in the mood it was, they might well make it a cause of strife, such as would win them more sympathy among those of their estate throughout the land than would a question of market-tolls, on which an old charter was less than clear. It may seem that there was no gain to the Count in that, but he cared little, though they might have the succour of every town in the land, if he should have the like help of his own kind. Let the quarrel be for the privileges of his order, and though it might be about one that had fallen from use, there would be no difference over that; they would not let him go down beneath the feet of the common mob. He saw that Isabeau had been right in that. But he would have the talk cease.

He said, with a formal courtesy, as one who speaks from a height, which was more weakness than pride, rising from the need to assure himself of how great he was: "We do small courtesy to our guest, telling thus of our own jars. We would rather hear of the talk he brings from Burgundy and beyond, or a new song he hath made, if he would do us so large a grace when the meats are cleared. Sir Lanval," he added, addressing his guest directly, "our minstrels have a new viol which we think to be of a good tone. They would value it to a greater height had you once touched it to song."

It was a long speech for Sir Gismond, and the careful formality of its phrasing did not hide the fact that he spoke with a good will. His words worked also to the end he sought, for there was a murmur of assent as he ceased. There were those who had not heard Sir Lanval either sing or play, though they knew his songs as they were rendered by other minstrels. They forgot the talk on a matter of which they had heard enough in the last week in the pleasure that was to come.

It was a request to which there could be but one reply. "If you will honour my poor art so far, it must be pleasure to me," Sir Lanval answered, and as the hall was cleared he took the new viol which was brought, praising its tone, as a guest should, and touched its strings to such notes as were not often heard, even in that hall where music was the nightly use, as it was in the castles of most of the nobles of southern France at that day.

"I will sing a song," he said, "by your grace, which it is most like that you have not heard, for I made it for one in Picardie, whom I sought to honour when I was there in the summer days, and when it was made she would not have it joined to her name—she being as wise as she is fair—lest those who should see her, after it had been heard, should think her too small for the song."

"Yet," he added, "I meant it well; and it may be one that is too good for a dumb death." And having said this, he lifted the viol, and the hall grew very still to hear the words of the song.

> Hear a song a knight hath made
> Who beneath the hazel's shade
> Lay beside the loveliest maid,
> Elle, la belle du Picardie.
> Think it not a jongleur's song,
> Tale of plundered maiden's wrong,
> Garlands to her name belong,
> Elle, la belle du Picardie.

Sendal soft her chimisete,
Gleaming hose of golden net,
Cloak of ermine lordlier yet,
Elle, la belle du Picardie.
Braided shoes with flowers of May
On her feet as white as they;
Now she casts her clouds away,
Elle, la belle du Picardie.

Those were clouds that hide the sun,
These are beauty's tale begun,
Now she bares the loveliest one,
Elle, la belle du Picardie.
Loose she breaks her beauty's screen,
Plaited leaves her girdle green
Where the recent rains have been,
Elle, la belle du Picardie.

Ermine for her cloak she had,
Now in flowers her limbs are clad,
Naught has tender grace forbad,
Elle, la belle du Picardie.
Heaven would to itself prefer
All the yielding grace of her,
Love's surrendered almoner,
Elle, la belle du Picardie.

Cavaliers who greeted well,
As she left the lonely dell,
Asked, "Art mortal maid, pucelle?"
Elle, la belle du Picardie.
"Nay," she said, "La France's gage
Drew me from the elfin mage."
High she called her parentage,
Elle, la belle du Picardie.

Farthest branch in farthest vale,
Where the winds of winter fail,
Bears her sire, the nightingale,
Elle, la belle du Picardie.
Siren of remotest cave,

Sunk beneath the deepest wave,
Her, with birth, her beauty gave,
Elle, la belle du Picardie.

"There would be few ladies," Isabeau said, leaning somewhat toward him, as the song ceased, and he gave the viol to a waiting page, "who would not do love's pleasure for the guerdon of such a song."

"It may well be," Sir Lanval answered, "for of that you should know better than I. Yet there may be those of another mind."

"Nay," she said, "you should know, for men know best how a woman yields."

"Lady," he answered, "I doubt naught there be those who do; but we who would sing of love in a high strain are not of those who should give witness thereon, for if we drink of a common cup, then the song dies."

Isabeau looked at him at times after that, while the jongleurs played in a clear space of the lower hall; but she said no more. Once she licked her lips as she looked, in a way she had, and the Count, who watched and understood (as did some others who knew her ways), thought of her as of a tigress choosing her meal.

When the jongleurs had ceased their tricks, and some would rise for a dance, and there was bustle and talk, she leaned toward him, and said, in a low voice: "Lanval, have you found lady to love?"

"Nay," he said. "I have found none yet." He spoke as one who would have liked better to make other reply; but it was a thing known.

"Will you be knight to me?" Her eyes said more than her words.

"I am knight," he answered, "to all ladies of gentle blood. It is to that I am sworn."

She showed no sign of rebuff, nor did her eyes change. She had wooed men before now who had not come to the first call, though not often, for she was fair in the way of a mating beast, lithe like a lustful cat, and yet as sleek as an autumn doe. She said:

"You will make me a song?"

He could not say no to that.

## CHAPTER NINE

WHEN the evening ended, Sir Lanval was given a bower for the night for his separate use, as his rank required. The bowers were small rooms set round the great hall, in which others slept on the straw. Lambert lay across his door, as a squire should.

He waked early, while the castle slept. He would not go forth at first to make disturbance among those who lay in the hall, ere it was time for them to wake. But for that thought he would have climbed stairs, to walk on the high walls in the dawn, or gone out to the hills. Yet he was not too much concerned for their peace to lift his harp in an idle way, and to touch the notes of a song. As he did this, he recalled that he had promised the lady Isabeau that she have one for herself. His fingers mocked on the strings.

> The toils you ask I would not dure,
> The knight you choose I would not be,
> For all Provence's dancing lure,
> And all the wines of Burgundy.

It would be simple work to make a song on that note, but he saw that it would not do. He had no will to make any song to her name. Yet it must be done. He made songs of love and of war. He could make her no song of love, and, if he could, he saw her to be one who would read it in the wrong way. He might have made her a poor song, but he would not do that, for he valued his own repute. He would have his songs known as far as men could speak in his tongue.

Well, he must make her a song of war. He found that to be an easier thing. That night he gave her the song. It made her name the battle-cry of a winning fight, as it well might be. "Swords for Isabeau" was its name. It was good for a time when lords threatened and vassals stirred into strife. He was asked to sing it again, which he did. Other voices caught at the tune. It ended in a shout of song.

> The shout their shaken ranks shall know,
> "Swords, swords again, for Isabeau!"

Isabeau purred. She liked the song well.

Doette, sitting at Lanval's side, lifted fawnlike eyes. "Lord," she asked, "would you make song for me?"

"I would with a good will. But it should be song of love, not of war; and it is of your own knight you should ask that, rather than me."

"Lord," she said, "I have no knight that is mine."

He turned his glance fully upon her as she said that.

He had eyes that had learned to see. She added: "Of a truth, no. I have none."

"Lady," he answered, "you walk in a wise way."

So she would have had him think, though she was less sure. She had lived more than twenty years, and her virginity was still hers, which was the jest of her friends. There were few of her time and rank of which that could be said, whether in jest or truth. She had been wooed of all of good birth that the castle held, and by many guests, and had she met one to whom she could do the service of love with a glad heart, she might have yielded more lightly to others in later days. But she had drawn back on the brink, being afraid.

Lanval looked at her again, but not at the fawn-brown eyes, over which the lids fell. "Lady," he said, "I will make you a song. But it is a song that should be made in the spring days."

She made no answer to that, being afraid in a new way.

Doette was one of Isabeau's maids, of whom there were three. She sat where she did, being of noble blood, as such ladies most often were. Isabeau was, in fact, of the lower rank, Doette being half-sister to the Count of Poitou.

Now she kept her eyes down, looking serene enough among those who had more heed to themselves than to her, but with a heart that beat in a sudden way that she could not still, so that she feared that it must be heard by the stranger who sat on her other hand.

That was Halt Redwood, the new captain of the condottieri, who sat in that high place with assurance enough, though he did not speak much, unless it were to reply to that which might be said directly to him; and then he would answer, but in a foreign way, so that it might not be easy to understand unless you should listen with care.

It was plain that he was not a boor, for he spoke with courtesy and address, and he had a knowledge of tongues, or he would not have been able to talk at that board, he being the Islander that he plainly was. And when the Bishop of Nîmes had tried him with Latin words (whether of courtesy or not it were hard to say), he had answered readily in the same tongue, which all would not have been able to do. And yet he was a man of no certain rank, for even knighthood he disclaimed in a quiet way.

It was a difficulty which leaders of condottieri would cause often enough in the minds of seneschals who had a lifetime's practice in the ranging of ranks, at a time when, in France at least, such barriers were not easy to break.

There was a tale of Konrad that he had once been placed low at a duke's board, and the Duke, fearing his displeasure, had tried to show courtesy by addressing him over the heads of the intervening guests. Konrad would talk of nothing but the price of the aid which the Duke sought at his hands, and of that only in a voice that the Duke could not hear, so that he must send the seneschal to enquire what had been said.

"Your Grace," was the report, "Captain Wolvenstein saith that he hath an infirmity of the ear. He cannot hear aught unless it be the talk of a very high price, the distance being too great."

It was an error which cost the Duke some thousands of Paris crowns, and the seneschal such a whipping as one of his dignity would not think to feel; but the Duke was not one who forgave a fault.

The condottieri were hard to place in another way. They did not fight with the lance, after the tilt-yard fashion, as the nobles did, having few knights in their ranks. Neither could they be compared with the common levies of footmen, with pikes and bows, that a king would lead to war, being gathered from the vulgar herd, and fit only to fight with their own kind, or for knighthood to slay.

The condottieri bore heavy spears such as it must take two men to wield, they being on foot, but it was on foot only that these weapons were used. They were all mounted men; but if they fought on horseback at all, it was with axes and swords; and there were many that would bear bows at their backs. They were mounted infantry, rather than cavalry, and, above all, professional soldiers, whom both knight and common had learned to fear.

It might be thought that the existence of many bands of this kind would add to the ferocity and the bloodshed of war, but it had a different issue from that. If they had no enmities among themselves, why should they kill and be killed by those who might be their comrades tomorrow, though they were paid for striving today? They were paid well enough, but life itself has a higher price. They moved as a chess-player will move who aims less to take than to mate. If there were needless clashing of men, and blood spilt to no final end, the captains who led them thus would find they had few to lead when they would enlist service anew.

There might be marching here and there, gathering or division of troops, seizing of height or bridge, or cutting off of supplies, and at the end of such tactics as these, with no fighting at all, the two captains would meet, and agree that the one had gained and the other had lost, or that the issue had been no more than should mean some yielding of ground, and they would march off by their bargained ways, and manœuvre for a new bout in the coming month. There was much work of this kind on the Italian plains, where the cities quarrelled ever, and, having more money than fighting men, they would hire these soldiers of fortune to make their wars. And these men would come back, asking their pay and saying: "We did not fight, finding ourselves equally matched, and on even ground. It would have been foolish, seeing that we stood thus. We agreed that this war is a draw." Or they might say: "When we came face to face, we found we were four to one, so we made peace on terms which we thought fair in your name. Why should we have died to no better end?"

Those who hired them took such words well enough, for what else could they do? Besides, the condottiere asked a high wage as it was. How much more would it be if he were expected to get killed every year?

It was from this cause that they were valued little by the English for aid in the Scottish wars, though they hired them at times; nor did the condottiere welcome such service, though his quarters might be good and his pay sure. He said that these battles were more near to those of beasts than of men. For they would go on, the one slaying and the other holding their ground, after the issue of the fight had become clear to those who were skilled in the art of war. And if they would not stay on a lost field, but marched off, who should blame them for that?

Yet when they saw cause to fight they could fight well, which they would do—though not only then—when they were offered town or castle to storm. For they fought then, not for a wage alone, or their captain's will, but for plunder, and for the women that could be bent to their lust in a taken town. For the condottiere, living a wandering life, with no more than a crowded tent for his home in the summer days, had, as it most often happened, no wife, nor any love of a good kind. He took what he could when the chance came. For the rest, he had dice and wine, and the watching of jongleurs' shows, and the tricks they played, and there were talk and tales to be heard in the tents as the daylight fell. Also, there would be new places to see. It was not a high manner of life, but it suited some, who had been less willing either to toil or to starve.

Halt Redwood, having three hundred of such men sworn to his will, and more in a further place, and much wealth at his call, though he had little practice in ordering either wealth or men, found that they had brought him already to this high seat, with the Lady Doette on his left hand, and another lady upon his right of a more forward mood, who whispered light words at times which we need not pause to regard, though they were not without wit of a lewd sort, which had been better welcomed by one of a liker mind. Captain Redwood, as he was now called, had more thought for Doette.

But before we listen more to the talk of this board (to which we may come again), we must turn back to see how he came to be there when it was no more than one day from when he had buried him to whom he owed all, whether for thank or dole, in a vault of Ste. Sarah's Church.

## CHAPTER TEN

IT was yet in the morning hours of the day following that of the burial of Konrad Wolvenstein, when Halt had the trestle-table within the tent which was now his spread with parchments which he had drawn from the iron-bound chest, from which he would learn all that he could. As he read, Raoul entered to say that there was a messenger come from the castle of Faucon-haut, asking if he would receive the Bishop of Nîmes, and at what hour it might be.

Raoul added: "There are others upon the road. They would be first here from the town."

"Well," Halt answered to that, "we can hear both. Let the Bishop know he may be seen at the third hour after noon."

It was not long before Raoul came again. "Captain, there are here three rats from the town. They would see you now if they may."

His tone said as much as his words. If they were to hire themselves to this quarrel, he would have it be on the Count's side. Halt knew that he had one reason for that in the fact that he had formed an obstinate conviction that Konrad's assassin had found refuge within the town, which had no more reason than lay in the failure to find any who could speak to having seen a lame bowman who fled over the countryside. But Raoul might have separate reasons for preferring that they should bargain with castle rather than town. Halt knew that he had a hundred times more experience than himself of the conditions of such service as it was their business to sell, and he was one whom Konrad had trusted far. Yet there had been a limit to that trust, or Halt would not then have sat where he did. And the reasons of that limit were easy to see; the mere fact that Raoul could not read rendered him unfit to be the leader of such a band.

Halt understood this better when he had studied the documents which the chest held. For he saw that it was not enough that a captain of condottieri should be one who could lead men well in the field, which it might seldom be needful to do. But he must be expert at accounts, one who knew much of language, custom, and law, and one who could bargain well.

He had found agreements in that chest in half a dozen languages, and of great length and elaboration. He had selected that which was now current with the junta at Florence, because it was the one the provisions of which it was most needful for him to know. He found that Konrad had contracted to supply good lances for the service of Florence, at a monthly charge of 13,250 gold florins; and he found careful calculation in Konrad's writing, that this would leave 4,640 florins as clear profit to himself. That was while peace held. In time of war it would be a more elaborate estimate of a less certain, though it might be a larger, gain.

But the agreement was not as simple as that might sound. There were conditions as to the quality and conduct of the men supplied; as to their arms and horses; even as to the responsibility for the loss of a horse, which might fall variously upon either of the contracting parties, or upon the man himself, according to the circumstances of the case; as to the time allowed for its replacement; as to prisoners of war of various ranks, the division of their ransoms, the right to settle these amounts, the ownership of their arms; the allocations of booty under a numerous variety of hypothetical conditions. The agreement went on to a great length, giving material for endless deductions from that 13,250 florins, endless questions which could be raised to delay payment, if pretext were sought, endless rights of inspection, the result of which there would be no impartial arbiter to resolve.

When he came to the final clauses, it was easy to see why a sum of three months' payments was to be deposited in advance by the Florentine junta with a goldsmith in Amsterdam, and why Konrad was to deposit security for his own good faith in the same hands. Even so, how could there be effectual security, with no independent authority—unless it were the Amsterdam banker—with the power to settle any dispute which might arise?

Yet, in practice, the system worked well enough to establish itself in Europe during the disorders of nearly two hundred years. There were fierce quarrels, instances of bad faith and duplicity. States made bad bargains, and captains-general made bad debts.

But reputation counted, as it always must, and it was not to be lightly lost. An unscrupulous city might find itself bare of defence in a coming year; a captain-general, having broken his faith too far, might find himself unable to make a further bargain, and obliged to hire himself and his men to serve under another condottiere of a better name.

It worked well enough; and with such as Konrad, whose ways were known, there would be many clauses in such a bond of which no one thought after the wax which sealed it was dry.

But Halt saw that the making of such bargains was less simple than he might have thought it to be. And there would be limits to the help that Raoul could give. He could keep order in the camp, he could marshal men for the field, he could do his part if a fight joined. But there were other things in which he might be little able to render counsel or aid.

Halt put back the parchments which were strewn around him. He closed the chest. He put on a cloak of Konrad's, which was dull enough, being of damson-blue, but of richer cloth than his own, and having silver buttons and loops. He had stools placed. He ordered service of wine. He told Raoul to take a seat at his side. He said that he would see these three who came from the town.

## CHAPTER ELEVEN

THE maire introduced himself. He was of a pompous manner, but not entirely at ease. He introduced the provost. The man of law had his mind still full of a dispute they had had on the way from the town, on which he had much to say, which there had been no time to conclude when they reached the camp. The maire introduced M. Sault, who was more the master of himself than were the other two, and might have been the better man to transact the business on which they came. But the maire held the official right. It was a matter for him.

And if he had not been at his ease at the first, he became more adequate to his office when he commenced to speak, for he was a man of affairs. He knew what he would have. When he asked, he was brief and clear.

"We are threatened," he said, "by the seigneur of Faucon-haut, and in such ways as none could endure, being of honest blood. He will have strife for his own ends.

"We are not weak on our side. We might bear him out with our own swords. But we would end this in a short way. With your help, it were soon done. We will pay well for a month's aid, giving a good price for every lance you can bring at a call. We will pay you half in Paris crowns when the bond is signed, and the balance shall be secured."

Halt looked at Raoul, but his face gave no sign. He asked: "What would you have us to do? Shall we hold your walls for a month from your lord's assault?"

Raoul still gave no sign, yet Halt, glancing at him again, felt that he had asked the right thing. He felt it the more as the maire paused on his reply, though it was but for a second's space.

"Nay," he said, "we would make short work. We would storm his walls. With your aid, it were lightly done."

"What force hath he in Faucon-haut?"

"He hath but threescore men, or it may be four, and there be those of them who would slip away."

"But he may have strong friends."

"He hath friends, but they are unsure. We would end this too soon for any to come to the seigneur's aid."

"Count," said Raoul.

"To the Count's aid," said the maire, as though there were no difference between the two words.

But Halt took the hint as it was meant. The nobles of Languedoc might bicker among themselves, but would be likely to join their strength to chastise rebellion of the common herd, whom they despised, if they did not hate, and whom they had yet scarcely begun to fear.

"Faucon-haut hath strong walls?"

"Thirty feet," Raoul said, as one stating a fact.

"They were soon mounted by such men as you lead," the maire answered, without challenging Raoul's figure, "and being held by so few."

He spoke in a confident tone, which was not assumed. The condottieri were trained in the storming of walls. They carried lengths of ladder, strong and light, which could be hooked together with speed, while their crossbows threatened death to any who should show basnet above the wall. But it was deadly work to swarm up those slender ladders, and to be first to leap the parapet.

"How many men have you armed in the town?"

"We have thirteen hundred who bear arms, but they are not trained for that work. There are those who would do their part."

"And the spoils, if the castle fall?" Halt had learnt enough to know that that was a vital point. It was not merely his own profit or loss that would be at issue. His men would expect reward of pillage if they took such a risk. It was so expressed in the terms in which they were hired.

But the maire was cautious in his reply. "We would make good terms. There is much wealth that the castle holds. Monsieur the Provost is here that he may draw a bond to your fair content."

Halt felt little satisfaction in that. He doubted that he would be fairly matched with M. the Provost in the drawing of bonds. He had a fear lest he might pledge his men to a desperate adventure, with no adequate reward. He feared also lest there should be disaster at the threshold of his command. Konrad had made a name for success, for caution as well as courage. He did not wish that he should fail at the first fence. In fact, he was unsure of himself.

He turned the subject to ask:

"What is the cause of this strife? Is it bitter beyond hope of accord?"

"Captain," the maire began.

"Captain-General," interjected Raoul.

"Captain-General," the maire corrected himself, "the seigneur is of a great greed. He would tax us beyond that which the town can bear, or our charter yields."

M. Sault interposed. He had been watching with the observation of one who had travelled in many lands, and was skilled in the judging of men. He said:

"It is more than that. He would have our maids for his lust."

M. Sault had a clear conviction that the maire was not winning his case, though less clear as to the cause. He felt that they were held off by this young, impassive man of the foreign accent, and the slow, reticent words. He was equally sure that the burly soldier who was seated at Halt's right hand was of an unfriendly mind. Yet, with both of them, it might be no more than the spirit of bargaining, which will be slow to close till the price be named.

The maire, who was a good enough businessman, though of narrower experience and inferior intellect to his colleague, felt the same. He might have done better with one of his own race, or one who was freer of speech. Now he was quick to take the point of M. Sault's interruption. He explained the demand which had been made upon them, putting it with such indignation as he could voice, for, in truth, he cared little for the nuptial experiences of M. Livron's niece, nor did he think that the Count would give fifty crowns for that of which he had made his demand.

It was the market tolls he would have, and it was those tolls which the maire was concerned to hold. Still, he put the case well enough.

It sounded strange to English ears. For the first time sympathy and interest were aroused. Halt saw that it might be difficult for him to maintain that aloofness to the causes of quarrel on which such as he must live, which the condottiere was expected to show. But for the thought of the crossbow shaft that had found its way into Konrad's back, and the belief that it had come from the hand of one who dwelt in the town.... Yet even so. He asked:

"By what right can he make such claim?"

The provost spoke in reply. He admitted that there had been a right in an old day. But it was a dead thing. He would have instanced other laws which had fallen to disuse in the same way, beyond the patience of those who heard.

Raoul interrupted this talk: "Is the maid loth?"

The maire was emphatic on that point. She would liefer die.

"Well," Raoul answered, "she may do that if she will. There is none could stay her therefrom. Or she could remain unwed, and the Count foiled of his law."

Halt was aware that his lieutenant's sympathies were unmoved. To himself also this issue had a sound of unreality. He asked shrewdly:

"Yet should you make accord on this matter of tolls, your lord might withhold to vex you in other way?"

"It may be, or no," M. Sault interposed again; "but they are tolls that we will not pay. We will give good price for such aid as should tilt the scale, if it be used in a speedy way."

This talk of causes and rights went beyond the etiquette of the bargain they came to make. So he felt, as would most in his place. The condottieri might be blessing or curse, but they would have introduced a different, perhaps a greater, complication to the troubled politics of the time had they asserted the right to judge the causes of those who had the wealth that could hire their swords. It was as though a shopkeeper were to ask the character of a man before he would sell him a cloak that would warm his back. Questions of quarters, and rates of pay, of risks to be taken, or hardships to be endured, of the qualities of horses and arms, of the soundness and ages of the men that were lined up in the ranks—all these were of the routine of such a bargain as they would make. But this talk turned into other paths. Well, the man was foreign and young—young also to his command, as was known. M. Sault felt it time to bring the talk to its point.

Halt felt the same from another cause. He had resolved that he would decide nothing till he had heard what the castle offered and asked, and till he had talked to Raoul. But he must discuss the terms of the bargain that they would make, or he would have nothing to compare. The provost was ready enough. They went into figures and facts, into which it would be tiresome to follow at the same length.

Halt was able to show that he knew much. He had made good use of the last hours. He used silence well, concealing ignorance where he must. He gained Raoul's respect to a degree that he would have been glad to know. It had not been Konrad's custom to have his lieutenant present when such bargains were made. Even Bernardi had never sat as Raoul sat now, though he was trusted in many ways. It was not for those who were hired to know what bargains or profits their leader made.

Raoul had not understood so well, in the twelve years that he had been selling his sword, how complicated such bargains were.

In a generous mind he admitted that Konrad had chosen well, and that he would have been no good at the lawyer's work. It is against any man's advance in the world that he cannot read, even though he live by the sword.

The provost felt also that he had met one who understood how such hirings were made somewhat better than he did himself, though he would not have said it aloud to a living man. He was of much learning in the law, in which he had a repute which went beyond his own land. But in this matter of the hiring of condottieri he had no experience on which to draw. He had been glad to pick the brains of a scrivener he employed who had worked for some years for a lawyer in Mantua, where such business had been of a frequent kind. When Halt, being secretly unsure of himself, had said, "There will be the usual clause as to that," he had been glad to assent.

When they had agreed the main terms on which his aid might be hired, Halt rose, as though the business were closed. He said:

"I must give some thought to the offer you make. I will send answer by tomorrow's prime, or it may be sooner than that." The maire showed his sense of rebuff. "We had thought—," he began.

The provost interposed. The delay seemed more natural to his legal mind. It was better tactics to assume that all would go smoothly to its natural end. He felt that the terms of the treaty had been liberally made. Five crowns extra to each lance, if the castle were stormed and no booty taken; ransom of prisoners to be equally shared. There were friends of the Count in the castle now who would pay well. He said: "When we hear from you, I will draft the deed; it should be sealed in a few hours."

M. Sault was as much concerned as the maire. He had an instinct that their cause would fail should they leave it thus. He made a last effort to weight the scale to the side he would. He said frankly:

"Captain-General, this is much to us. We would not stint gold, could we be sure of your aid. You may be approached by the Count. We were babes not to see that. If he makes written offer which you can show we will go five hundred crowns beyond that." He saw the consternation on the maire's face, and added: "Yea, though it be from my own purse, though I am poorer than some may think."

They argued over that on the way back. The provost said it was of no matter. The Count would not make written offer. He would make it by word of mouth, writing naught till there were a bond to seal. M. Sault explained again that he was a poorer man than many thought. He did not want those five hundred crowns to be remembered against him in other days.

## CHAPTER TWELVE

AT the hour appointed the Bishop came. He came with some retinue, riding a white mule. He was an experienced diplomat, who knew that it is better to stoop and win than to remain erect while the stalk snaps. He was of an importance which came from intellectual ability and many powerful connections, rather than personal wealth or following. He had a care for his own dignity, and his eventful life had not previously included any transactions with captains of condottieri. He saw clearly that such men should call upon him. Yet it was not as though he were so demeaning himself with any of a defined social inferiority.

It was not, for instance, as though he had mounted his mule to wait upon the maire of the town. The condottieri were outside the social order into which they intruded with naked swords. In their own unconscious way they were commencing the disintegration of the feudal order for which they fought. The Bishop stooped in a quarrel which was not his, but he was to have his own price.

Isabeau had favours for sale. They had been favours that he would have bought at any time in the last ten years, as he had let her know with few words; but he had not bid to her price. Now she had taken that in hand which she must bring to a good end, be the price what it might.

"Get me these lances," she had said, "that they come not against our own walls. Get me them that we may chasten the town." She had lifted slow eyes of allure, and they had understood one another as well as though they had talked for an hour…

If we judge the Bishop of Nîmes without thought, we may go down a wrong road. He was a man of intellect and of ordered days, He was one who faced the issues of conduct and of life and death with a clear mind, and he had a conscience at peace. He believed in God. He had helped those who sought his counsel to the firm anchor of faith. He had comforted penitence many times. He believed that a celibate priesthood was necessary to the temporal prosperity of the Church, and he accepted that condition of life. But he believed an absolute chastity to be beyond what man could expect, or God require. There were fanatic priests who were more austere in practice than he, but they were few, and he thought they did harm rather than good. He had argued with such at times. He thought their spiritual pride to be of the devil, who can work in most subtle ways to the loss of the souls upon whom he may lay siege. He would not fall in that trap.

Yet he was of a careful life, bringing no scandal upon the Church.

He was one, also, who withstood the heresies which were rising at that time in the land, and that cried aloud at the gates, even in Avignon, where the popes dwelt. He had preached with power against those who denied God, asserting, as many did, that men were not a creation apart, but had been carnated in other forms before they came to a human womb, as they would be again. He had shown that such would fry in a sure hell.

Now he did that from which he saw no wrong that could come, but a clear gain upon either hand. He knew that the chief officers of the town had been to the condottieri camp in the earlier day, about which he was well content. He had made his appointment before the hour when they had been there, and he judged that no final bargain would be made with them till he also had been heard. Besides, there would be little time for the drawing of such a bond as he knew to be the custom, if not the necessity, of such a hiring. Under such circumstances he thought that he who went second would have the first chance. M. Sault had felt much the same, which was why he had made his offer in the form that he did, so that the castle should not outbid the town, let them bid as high as they might, thinking that they bid last.

The Bishop felt some confidence in the power of his own tongue. He did not expect to fail. And he had no doubt that he was doing a good thing.

It was the will of God that there should be noble and common, rich and poor, for so He had made the world, and it was of the nature of men that the poor should envy the rich, and do them service with dragging feet. Yet it was easy to see that all could not be rich, though to make all poor were a simpler thing. Nor could all be of learning or gentle ways. There must be many boors, that noble living might come to its perfect flower. There had been enough darkness over the world after the power of Rome sank to its knees, and such shadow might fall again, which would be dreadful to think, except that the noble held down with a firm heel the rough boors of the land. And what said the Scripture on that? The poor have ye always with you. It was the settled order of God.

And this order was easy to keep with men who toiled on the land; but when they gathered in towns they might become of a very insolent strength, though being neither of gentle blood nor being learned in gentle ways, holding back the wealth of which their lords had need, and which they could spend with more skill, that the strength of the state might grow, and to foster beauty and grace of life. That was how the men of Faucon-bas would now act, and to chasten the town must be to the will and pleasure of God.

If he used his skill of words to that end, was it not well that he should have his reward in a way which the weakness of the flesh must crave—and that all the more that he was a man of controlled life, having never fallen to evil ways? And now he would bring evil to none, for Isabeau was a woman of wanton moods (had he not confessed her at sundry times?). There must be several in the last ten years that she had had to her bed, or with whom she had lain in the little garth that was private to her own use.

There might be a dozen if those were added whom she had met when she would go to Dijon, to the Duke's court, or further yet to Poitou. And he could absolve her for what she did, serving the Church, as the Cardinal would absolve him. So he would have thought, had he given thought to these things, but in fact he gave them no thought at all. His conscience slept at its ease. Had he been asked, he might have said that he did well, for she, being the kind she was, might have asked a worse price of a worse man, who would have had more than his due.

Before he came to the camp, Halt had had some talk with Raoul, and though he had not said overmuch, for it was his part to take orders, and he would fight for castle or town with an equal will as his new captain might decide, yet his own choice was easy to see. The castle walls might be stormed, though they were of thirty feet? Yes. He did not deny that, the garrison being no more than it was. But he remarked that the town walls were of no more than half the height. There were many men in the town? Yes, but the town walls were of the greater girth. They would need many to man them at every part; and the townsmen were less trained and practised in war. There might be rich ransom to share if the castle fell? Yes, but the spoil of a town may be rich too. A town may give ransom also, to save plunder and rape and fire, and its ransom is quickly paid. It would be found in a few hours. You wait ransom of prince or count, and you may keep them for months ere the gold come, and there will be their charges to pay for that time, for you must keep them in such state as their rank can claim. It was clear that if Raoul had his way he would turn his sword on the town

Halt found also that to make terms with the Bishop of Nîmes would be much easier than with provost and maire. The Bishop had no thought of a bond, nor did he talk of the counting of men, or of soundness of horses and arms to be inspected or pledged, nor of division of spoils, or of ransom to be split up. Halt was to bring the force he had to aid in storming the town if it would not submit in a quiet way, and for that he was to have a sum down in silver florins, which might not be as much as the town would pay (it would have been less had not Isabeau gone her own way to a loan from the Bishop's purse); but beyond that it was hard to compare, for the offer was that he could hold the town to such ransom as it could pay, or, if it would not give him content, his men could sack it for two days, taking all the spoil they could find, so that it were not burnt. Halt saw that there was, at the least, as much to be got in that way as any sum that the town would pay for his hire.

"And I would put it to you," the Bishop said, "as one more practised than I in such bargains as we would now make, that if there be no bond—in the drawing of which I should have but a poor skill—we do trust you far more than we ask trust of you, for if you be once in the town you may do much as you will, even to put it to flame, and we ask but your word that you will hold your men back from that which were loss to us, for you must see that it is from the town that our wealth comes. At the last it is the Count's town which we give you to spoil."

Halt saw that there was reason in that. He saw also that the offer was of a simpler kind. If he did all that the town asked, there might be long haggling before he closed account to his own content. Yet the Bishop was shrewd enough. The town might pay much, yet it could not pay more than the coins it held. It would remain, and so would the tolls it took from the merchants who must come by that way. Or, if it were spoiled, there is a limit to what can be found in two days, when all of worth will be hidden away. It was they of the town who would go short in the future days, and the Count would be lord of a place that had been chastised to his will.

"You should know," Halt said at last, "that I have here but three hundred men. Think you that they are enough to storm a walled town of this size in which there are many more who can bear arms? I would know what aid you can bring."

"We can give but few," the Bishop said, with a frankness which was wise enough. "We may not leave the castle bare of defence. We will find twoscore men, but they will be well furnished and trained in the arts of war. You do not need me to say that it is not numbers that most avail."

"First or last, is that all you can do? Could you muster more at a later day?"

The Bishop paused somewhat in his reply. He had not yet had the pledge that he sought, and all he said might be used to his own loss, if Halt should decide at last to take part with the town. Yet he judged it best to say how the truth stood, which was less than a secret thing.

"We can have aid at a sharp need from the Count's cousin at Péray; it might be to three hundred knights at the most, and it is aid we must ask, whether we will or no, for reasons it is needless to tell.

"A messenger should have gone even now—though it may be delayed for a day or more—asking such aid. But it is aid that we do not wish to have. We would have this thing ended ere the Count Raymont could come. Which is a reason why we think to bring it thus to a sharp end."

The fact was that Count Gismond walked on a narrow plank. He owed large sums to Count Raymont, which was one reason why he could not give ground on this matter of market tolls. There were sums of money overdue on the debt, which should be paid with speed.

If the Count knew of this broil, he would be quick to come. He might make it cause of quarrel that he had not been told, if things should go ill. Yet if he came, who could say how soon he would go? Or that he would go at all? He was of another temper than Gismond, as well as of a much greater strength.

Halt felt that he would do better to take the Bishop's terms than to make a bond with the town; yet he was slow to close, being yet unsure of himself. Ever he had the fear that he would bring to a swift disaster those whom he had come so strangely to lead, and who had been led in a better way.

It was but a year since he had trod the cloisters of Oxford having no thought of such life. We must allow something for that.

The Bishop did not think him a fool, though he saw that he was cautious to pledge his word. He judged it a word which the man who gave it would be likely to keep.

"I see not," Halt said, "how you can bring this thing to a swift end if the town should seek to delay. You have asked that they yield a bride, as is required by an old law. That, you say, is no more than a feint, knowing they will refuse so to do. Yet if they say that as yet the maid will not wed, then is your point foiled."

"That is so," the Bishop agreed. "And then should we ask that they yield on this matter of tolls in a plain way. We will bring it, whether by black or white, to a swift end.

"And if they accord with the Count when they see that they have no succour from this camp, how do I stand then?"

"It was that which I was about to make clear. If you come to the castle tonight, the Count will give you what entertainment he may, and the florins shall be paid down. If the town accord thereon (which it will not do), you have earned the fee with not a sword drawn, and we shall be content on our side."

Halt considered this, and it had a fair sound. "Yes," he said at last, "I will do that. But that they will not accord, I am less sure."

In the next hour he sent letter to the maire to let him know that he could not give aid to the town. It was easy to read the meaning of that. Yet it did not bring the town to a will for the making of peace. It stirred them to different mood. For they heard also that one had ridden north to St. Péray from Faucon-haut and they could guess the meaning of that. Also, M. Sault had spoken of the crossbows which he was having brought to the town. He had spoken of more than that. There were about forty men trained to use of those bows whom his agents at Arles had hired, and who would be coming up the valley on a near day. There was the same thought now in the minds of all. The Count thought to crush them to earth. Not content with the aid of the condottieri, he had sent for Count Raymont and all his knights. It must be their part to force the quarrel to a quick head if they could. Let him be stirred to attack before Count Raymont should come. So it came about the castle and town were both seeking the same end. The town thought it best that the wedding of Guilbert and Yvonne should be fixed for a near day, and be loudly talked. It was fixed for as soon as the bowmen would be due to enter the town. Let Count Gismond interfere if he would.

# CHAPTER THIRTEEN

So it came that Halt Redwood sat that night at the high board in the banquet-hall of the castle of Faucon-haut, with the Lady Doette on his left hand, with whom he would have had pleasure to talk, but who had eyes rather for Sir Lanval than for him, and with the lady Louise upon his left, to whom he was less drawn, but who would talk to him as much as she might, either with a bold jest, to which he was not quick to reply, or with such words as sought to know more of himself, which he would turn with a quiet skill.

She thought him slow and cold, but one whom it would be a fair sport to bring to another mood, as she had hoped that she should be able to do. He thought her fine in a foreign way, save for a broken tooth, which would show when she laughed, as she often did; but she was not of his kind.

Yet he must show her the regard that a guest should. She had hair, glossy and black, in which she had a just pride, and a white skin which she did not paint, thinking it looked best as it was. Her face was rather broad and low, the eyes bold and gay, the full lips very red. She had on a gown of silk, which was as red as her lips, to which Halt would not have given its right name, he being little skilled in questions of women's gear. He saw that it was figured in black in a quaint way. It was cut loose and low, which was not the English style at that time, so that her breasts showed to one sitting beside, as she leaned forward to take her food.

The English ladies of that time wore gowns that came high to the neck, fitting like a close glove, so that they showed as slim as they were. They were gleaming sheaths of silk, showing the body's shape in a true way, which they were glad to do, being more finely formed at that time than were the women of France, as they have been since. Yet there were fair women in France, as Halt could see at that board.

While Sir Lanval talked with the Lady Doette, as we have heard, there was a space cleared at the lower end of the hall where the jongleurs might play their part. There was a troupe at the castle at this time, being there for a week at the Count's charge, which had the name of being one of the best in the French lands. They wandered thus from castle to castle, and from town to town, through the whole year, either in time of peace or of war, except only that they might not perform during Lent, for this was a law through the breadth of the Christian lands which there would be none of so great a folly as to defy. Yet they did not rest even then, for they had schools of their art, to which they would then go, where they would change knowledge of trick and song, and teach novices at a fee which might seem high but it was a good trade for those of skill to excel, though its honour might be a draggled rag. For the most, the jongleurs were of common sort, whether women or men, and of a low repute, even among those who would pay their japes; and there were towns of a strict rule which would drive them out, or give them a time in the stocks, thinking that their shows would corrupt the young.

But the gentlefolk of the land welcomed them without scruple, and would give them gold with a free hand if they were pleased with their shows.

The songs of troubadours and trouvères at this time had become fantastic rather than passionate. They were more free from verbal coarseness than they had been at the first, and had a formal quaintness which removed them from the world of reality. They might be lascivious or of a very innocent beauty, according to the interpretation of the mind that received them. But the jongleurs used a lower art to a lower end. It had the grossness, if not the banality, of the comedians of a day that we know better than theirs.

There were those of all ranks, of religious or sober minds, who would turn from them with aversion or mere contempt; there were many others who would join in the moment's mirth, but who yet regarded it as something apart from their continent and ordered lives. They laughed at the ridicule of marriage or chastity, which were the stock subjects on which the jongleurs played, but they did not therefore think to deceive their husbands, or suspect their wives. Yet there were others, as there must always be, to whom these ribald shows were no less than portrayal of life at its normal mean, or even at its desired height.

Tonight there was a show, at the first, of acrobatics and juggling, in which men were of much the skill that they are now, with dances that were derived in part from the traditions of Italy and France, and in part from the Moors of Spain; but they would blend these arts, the troupe working as one, rather than making a separate turn of each, and the pace and changes were such that none had time to tire, even of that for which he had little love.

And then, at the last, they gave a balérie, which was a dramatic dialogue, acted in character and costume, with an accompaniment of quick-beating music, and a commenting chorus of song.

This one was new, having been first rehearsed in the Lent season, and now being spread through France by a dozen troupes who must each keep to the road that would be left only to them for the first year, after which each might use it where they would. It turned aside from the theme of the lover and faithless wife making jest of a husband's trust, which was the routine subject of these plays, to show the seduction of a maiden who was wooed to give up the cold folly of her virginity, which at the last she would do with a light mind, as the knight argued, and the chorus urged.

> Maiden, you must stay awhile,
> Learn—learn—to play awhile,
> Doing what you may awhile,
> As—your—youth—can.
>
> Do not seek to fly away,
> Maid—maid—why away?
> Turn about to try a way
> That—your—youth—can.

There was intoxication in the quick steps of the dance and the quick movement of the melody, which would alternate with a slow, drum-like insistent beat. As the final surrender came, the chorus closed round the protagonists, as though to hide the consummation of the event.

"Now if they should break apart," the Lady Louise proposed, with the laugh that showed her strong white teeth with their broken gap, "I wonder what we should see. I thought at times that there was more warmth than art in the wooing that endeth thus."

Doette watched the show, and her fawn-brown eyes were not hidden, nor did she blush, as she knew that she was too prone to do, though there was much lewdness in the dialogue both of gesture and word, into which some new jests had been brought, as the way was, glancing at the issue which now divided castle and town. She was, in fact, rather bored, having seen many of such shows since she had crouched, a barelegged child, in the rushes at the side of her mother's chair in the glittering court of Poitou. Nor had the balérie power to hold either her eyes or her mind, for her heart was stirred to unrest by the knight-trouvère at her side, who was to make her a song, and she had thoughts also, though there were less of these, for the English captain who sat on her other hand. She noticed, being one who would always see more than she spoke, that the Lady Louise would talk to him in a freer way than he would answer to her. That might have meant no more than that he had less ease in a foreign tongue; but she noticed once, when the eyes of Louise were held to the show, that he looked at her with a doubtful eye, as a man might look on a strange beast of whose uses he was not sure, but from whom he expected little of any good.

She knew the English to be a strange, half-savage race of whom it was told that they were very fierce on the field if they were well fed. They were not civilized enough excepting the Anglo-Norman knights—to have the distinctions between the nobles and common folk as widely and clearly marked as they were here, or in her own land of Poitou, nor were their codes of conduct the same.

She knew also that the condottieri had a dreaded repute, but she felt that Captain Redwood was one whom it would be easier to trust than to fear. She was not much stirred by this talk of strife with the town, for the castle stood high and strong. It was matter to vex the maire rather than those who sat at that board. And she had heard talk of war since she had learnt the meaning of words.

So she went from the hall at last to her own dream, and to wonder what the song would be which would be made to her name in the spring days. And Captain Redwood received the silver florins that the Bishop of Nîmes had pledged he should have, and took them back to his tent under a strong guard.

Having got back, he found that Raoul had news that would not wait for the dawn. When he had heard it, and heard also the plan which Raoul proposed, he gave ready assent. After that, there was much stir in the camp, and while it was yet dark Raoul rode out at the head of a hundred men, who went westward among the hills.

Raoul came back three days later with less than three-score in his train, and some of them having bandaged wounds; but he did not look displeased at that which had chanced; nor did Halt, when he heard his tale.

It was that afternoon that M. Sault's crossbowmen entered the town by the south gate, bringing with them many wagons loaded with such stores as would be of use to the town at so strait a pass. They could be seen from the castle wall, but there was no motion to cross their way, for the town yet parleyed as to what it would do. It was known that Yvonne was to be wedded in Ste. Sarah's Church on the next day, but as to what would be after that, it had pleaded and urged, choosing humble words, as of those too weak to defy. But when the wagons were through, it closed its gates, and the talk ceased.

# CHAPTER FOURTEEN

"I KNOW not why you gloom as you do," Lucette said; "you should have pride in this, that it is for you that the town stirs, and that there is such sharpening of swords. Were it for me, I should have pride and a great joy."

Yvonne gave little answer to that. She had no will that men should fight in her name. She would have freedom and peace, that she might walk in her own way. Yet that way was not sure even to her own heart. She knew that the gates were closed, and that steel shone on the walls so that she might be wedded to Guilbert on the next day, and that there should be interference from none. Yet she had no joy in the strength of that secured from the castle's rape. Did she then desire in her secret heart that she might find herself in the softness of the Count's bed? There was no such thought in her mind. The fear—though it had not the face of a near dread—stirred her to anger and shame. She did not know how she would act if she should come to that pass. She tried to make her resolve, and was as one who looks into a crystal in which the scenes move in a dim way, so that their end is not clear. The event would tell her how she would act, if it should come, but before that she would not know.

She had a nearer trouble than that. She was more near to the blacksmith's bed than the count's, and there was no girdle of stone and steel to withhold from that. Rather, all hands pushed or drew her in that way. She did not think of Guilbert as of the Count, for she liked him well, but she had no will to be mated to him for a life's space. If he were better liked than the Count, yet he was to be given more than the Count asked, and it was the nearer dread. Would she have refused this wedding at the last, let the price be what it might, if the question of the castle's claim had not come up to confuse her mind? It was hard to say. She knew that as the hour approached, she was of a mind to refuse it now. Yet what escape could there be? What escape except death, for which she had no lust? The grave is cold, and it is a place where you lie long. There was one other resort, if its gates would open for her (of which she had a doubt), and she knew that she would have no pleasure in that which she would find therein. Yet now her mind turned to that way.

She did not say much of this to Lucette, though they were good friends. She had always had many thoughts that she would not speak to Lucette, for she knew that it would have been as though she spoke in a foreign tongue. Lucette would misunderstand, or she would understand nothing at all. Yet Lucette was loyal to her in her own way. You may be good friends with a dog, though you have dreams which he does not share. And Lucette was much more than a dog, though in some ways she may have been less. Besides, Guilbert was Lucette's brother, of whom she was proud and fond; and that one should grudge to wed him, being a maid, was not a thought which would enter her mind by an easy door. She did not look on marriage as closing the experience of a woman's life. Rather, it was the gate through which she must pass to a freedom that could not otherwise be gained without fear of shame. We have heard her views about that, which were such as were taught in the jongleurs' plays, and in the tales that were told in the castle sala, when the ladies sat by themselves in the afternoons, listening and talking together, while their fingers were busy with silk and wool.

Yet Yvonne must have shown enough to Lucette for her to see that she had no pleasure in what she did. For Lucette said, as the night came: "If you would flee, of a truth, having such dread of the Count, or I know not what, nor any cause that you should, I have talked to Henri, and he will show you a way over the tiles. It is one, so he says, that a child could take in the dark, except it be for the drop from the town wall, and you should manage that with a rope's help and the aid he would give."

"It was good of you, and of Henri," Yvonne answered, "to think of that." She was quiet for a time, leaving Lucette in doubt of what she would do.

It was not such a wild plan as it might sound at the first. The houses huddled close within the walls of the towns of those days. The towns grew, and the walls did not expand. Even space for the streets was grudged, so that the houses would be built with projections that almost met overhead. There were places where it was easy to step across on a night when the moon shone. The fluted tiles were easy to tread.

And it was a way by which Henri should be a good guide, for it was that by which he came to Lucette. There would be little peril till they should come to the outer wall; but that would be guarded now. There must be risk, at the least. And if she should be caught at that point, with what tale should she face the town? It would be said that she had a mind to go to the Count, whether they would or no. At the least, it could be turned in that way. And if she were caught after she were free of the walls, which was as likely a thing? That would be to have put herself in the Count's power, beyond rescue or hope, and by her own act, so that men would laugh at her for a fool, if they did not judge her in a worse way,

It was true that she would be unwedded then, and the Count's claim would be void under the law which he had invoked, but that might be little gain to herself. Having no home, and neither friends nor gold at her call, she would be in an evil pass, the customs of those days being what they were, and she being a maid who was fairer than most (which she knew well enough), and having no claim to gentle birth, which would have been her shield with many knights of that day, though with less than all.

She was of a half-mind to say she would go, but it was not a strength of will which would give birth to the needed word. She was of those who are more brave to endure than to move. It was her likelier mood to wait the event, and to face it as best she could. Yet she showed courage of her kind, being alone as she was. For, except Lucette, she had no friend in the world. There was none to whom she could speak her mind. So she was quiet for a time, till she saw that she would never make that resolve. She could not see what road she would take; but it would not be that of the tiles. There was one she would try, though it looked but sombre to her, whose youth was a strong flower.

So at last she said: "You must thank Henri from me, for it is the offer of a good friend, be it made for your sake or mine. But I cannot go by that way." And then, after a pause, "I am going out now. If my uncle asks, it is to the church."

Lucette asked, should she come. But she was told that there was no need. Yvonne would be alone with her thoughts. It was not strange that she should go to the Church to cleanse her soul before the mass of the coming day.

She did not go to the church of Ste. Sarah, but to that of Notre Dame de Bon Espoir, which was of less size, but of a great age, even in that day.

When she entered she sat for a time while the dusk gathered, hiding the holy scenes which were painted upon the walls, and causing the altar-candles to shine with a clearer light. She was alone in the church, which was a place of quietness and peace, though the devil walked in a world without, where men lusted and slew. The faith of those days had a confident strength, which it has told us in stone, so that it may be read still. Men looked up to a near heaven, and were aware of a waiting hell. Yvonne came to ask help of the one power that might outface both castle and town, and to pay its price, which would be bitter to do. Yet as she knelt there for a time, it seemed less hard than it had done in the earlier day. So at last she went to the priest, both to confess and to ask counsel and aid, which she supposed that he would not refuse to give.

## CHAPTER FIFTEEN

FATHER AMBROSE was a man who strove with the flesh, at times using a scourge that reddened his own back. At other times he would fast till his legs failed, so that he must steady himself with a groping hand as he moved from pallet to stool. He would fast till his sight wavered, and the voices of men would sound distant and very faint in his ears.

Yet, fast as he might, he must eat at last, and when he did this, and the voices of men resumed in a natural way, there would be the devil's whisper again, which he would hear as plainly as theirs.

We may call him fool that he fought thus, and we may think that he could have done his work in a better way had he had peace in his own loins, yet men would heed his words who took little count of the priests of Ste. Sarah's church, who were sleek and suave, and whom they would not trust with their wives in a place apart; and there were times when he had the eyes of one who had seen God.

Now he heard Yvonne confess her sins, or what she thought to be such, and he gave her the peace of absolution more readily than he would to most, for he had learnt much of the hearts of women, as well as men, since he had been priest of that church, and he heard Yvonne's voice, and he saw that she had grave and very innocent eyes. He was always moved by the beauty of women, either to revere, as though he saw that God bared His own thought for the marvel of men, or to a fierce and evil desire. And to the women who moved him in the latter way, when they confessed their shames (of which they thought not overmuch themselves, for did not all their neighbours the like?), he would give such penance that they would not come to him again, while they could find a priest of a milder mood, for which they would not have to walk far. For he saw that Satan had such power in their hearts that he could enter with them even into the Church of God.

He looked at Yvonne, and there was peace in his own soul. Yet when she asked his counsel and aid, opening her heart, as she had not done to any before, she did not get the answer that she had thought to hear. For she asked the sanctuary of the Church, and that she might be given to the charge of the abbess who ruled the convent at Beauregard, which was but few miles down the Rhone, on its further bank.

The Convent of Beauregard had an austere repute, and was said to be strictly ruled, as were not all the convents of southern France at that day. Its nuns had done much for the folk of their town at the time of the last plague, and had had the comfort of God, so that few fell sick, and but three died. Its Abbess would not ask one who would seek to enter its peace with what wealth she came, or what name was hers, though it was true that she seldom took in those who were not of a gentle blood, or that such would seek entrance, knowing that it was not for them.

Yvonne said she was being forced toward a marriage in which she had little joy, and was threatened with a worse fate, of which she had a great fear, as to which, as all knew, the town was to fight on her part on the next day, if the Count should seek to enforce his will, as he was certain to do.

The priest heard her tale, and was slow to speak. He asked at last:

"Would you seek to take the vows of those who are brides of Christ if this marriage were put aside?"

"Nay," she said, "for then were my dread gone."

"Then," he said, "would you lose your soul with a false vow? Would you blaspheme God? Do you say that you will be bride to Him rather than earthly spouse, for which you have little will, but had you more freedom and time that you might choose among men, you would put Him by, thinking that there may be men who are better than He?"

"Father," she said, "there are many who would be brides of men rather than take such vows. God doth not blame us for that, as I have heard you say before now."

"I said truth in that," he replied; "but their case is not as that which you would have me allow. They are content with the lesser thing, as God hath willed that most men should be. They go their way, being blind, and He doth not blame them therefore. There are heights which they do not climb, thinking them too hard and too high. They do not climb and contemn, as you would do in your secret heart, even though your lips might be closed, which is less than sure.

"You would take the vows not as one who seeks God, but that you would avoid the handling of men whom you do not choose.

Having done thus, do you think you would have any joy in your life, or peace in your soul's depth?

"I tell you no, for either you would sell your soul at the devil's price, breaking the most holy vows by which you were joined to God, or you would chafe ever at a chain which you had locked with your own hands. Do you think it too hard to join in an earthly bridal which is not to your utmost wish, and that a heavenly one may be taken in the like mood, as a lighter bond? You know not that you would do.

"For it is plain to see that you do not ask me this being chaste either of body or mind. For were you that, it could be but a small matter of choice as to which man it should be, whether smith or count, who should deal with you after the flesh. You would think of it as no more than the holy Judith, who entered the tyrant's bed that she might slay him the while he slept. It is naught in the eyes of God who it may be who deals with your body in carnal use, be they many or few, so that you have no joy in their arms, holding your soul pure and apart."

So he said, and with that she must be content. He may have counselled well, if the high mysteries of God were as he thought them to be, which it is not our part to decide here; and Yvonne knew that he spoke from an honest mind, as the priests of Ste. Sarah's church would have been less likely to do.

He did not weigh whether she would bring wealth to the Church, or the ill will of the nobles of Languedoc, if it should take her within its gates. He did not shape his words to the policies of the time, nor think of what might be said at Avignon, when the cardinals met in the great Council Hall that the Pope had built in his palace there, and the talk would be less of the things of God than of the exigencies of his temporal power. (For the things of God could wait very well for a quieter time, He having more patience than men.)

Yet, if his mind were free from such thoughts as these, he knew, after Yvonne had left, and he considered what he had said, that the devil had whispered behind his ear. For had he not envied her in his heart, as well as he who was to have her on the next night? Had not the starvation of his own flesh caused him to look on her as one who complained having little reason for woe? What did he know of the hearts of women, who might look in the eyes of none save those of the Holy Mother of God, which were sad with a great joy? He scourged his own back that night with a willing hand.

Yvonne went home through the narrow streets which were still lit by a setting day, though it had been dark in the church. She went thinking that she had had little comfort from the priest's words, in which she was wrong in part. For she had felt before as one who stands in doubt at a door which he may open at will, but of the further side of which he has a cold fear, and now she knew that that door was closed. Beyond that, the priest's word had convinced her mind (which was shaken with doubt before) that the way she had thought to take would be sin in itself, and would give her no joy. She saw now that there was no escape either to right or left, and with this knowledge she felt that she could walk ahead with a better heart.

As to Count Gismond—of whom she had the most fear—she resolved to put him out of her mind. The walls of the town were strong. It held more men than the Count could bring to assault, even with those of Captain Redwood's that he had hired. It would not be taken for many days, if at all. All the town was sure about that. Meantime, she would be Guilbert's wife, and the Count's claim would be lost, for she would be virgin no more.

She turned her thoughts to her uncle's son, and she knew him to be one that most would be glad to wed. She did not hate him at all, nor did she hold him in any fear. They had been good friends when they had been children of a like age. Only, as she grew she had drawn apart. He had been shyer of her, and she more distant to him. She knew that they were wedding now by her uncle's will. Yet she knew that Guilbert was glad that it should come to that end, or would have been glad had she not shown him that she would wed with a poor will. Well, she must do better than that.

If it were her fate to wed thus, she must make of it the best that could be. She had no thought but to keep her vows, for she was not of Lucette's kind. She had always been one who would eat from a clean plate, and would wash her hands both before and after a meal, as was the custom in palace and tower, but less certain among those of a common kind, even though there should be many plunged in the same dish.

She paused at a street's end, for there were two ways by which she might have gone home that were about equally near, and one led past the door of Guilbert's forge. It was this which it had been her first impulse to avoid, as she had done when she came, but now she put the thought aside with a steady will. For she was resolved that if she should wed him at all—which it was but a half-hour ago that she had decided that she must do—she would not fail on her part. So she went on to the armourer's booth, and the gleam of the smithy fire. Guilbert smote at the forge. It might be his wedding on the next day, but that was no cause that he should idle now. It would indeed have been to treat the town ill, and his own pouch at the same time. For there was clamour for the mending of arms, which were to be used in his cause, and for which they paid him with silver groats.

Yvonne stood at the smithy door. She called "Guilbert" in a low voice, and he was beside her in two strides, leaving a halberd-head in the fire.

"Guilbert." she asked, "would you wed me indeed, at the cost of this strife which will surely be?"

Guilbert was puzzled by this question, so that his reply was slow to come. He was always of more use with his hands than his head. It is a fact that he had not doubted that she would wed him till that moment, be she as cold as she would. That was, in the main, because he knew that it was his father's fixed will, and his father was ill to thwart. He was not likely to be defied by a maid under his own roof, and who was fed at his charge.

"Yes," he said at last. "I know not well what you mean. We have a right to do as we will." And then he added, with more wit, "It would not stay this strife, though I should not wed you at all. We are but the dice of their sport. It is the market dues which have brought us to where we stand."

There came a wagon of hay down the narrow street as they stood thus, so that they must withdraw into the smithy to let it pass. It was for the wall, where it would be ready for the discomfort of those who should lead the assault of the next day. Preparations for that strife were now urgent on either side. To delay the wedding now would have done no good to the town. Rather, it would have done evil, seeming a sign of fear, and men would have lost heart.

As it was, they were in good courage, having much faith in the strength of their walls, and making boast of the forty crossbowmen whom M. Sault had brought into the town. Even with Captain Redwood's band, it seemed that the besiegers would be too few for the town to fear.

Guilbert was closer to her now, as they drew inward for the hay to pass. She looked up at him with grave eyes in which there was neither shyness nor love. Rather there might be pity for both. He was a fine man in his own way, as she knew. He was comely and strong, and of an honest kind.

But he did not stir her at all. They had kissed in childhood, but not in these later days, when she had kept always as far apart as she might.

"Guilbert," she asked, "were it much grief if we did not wed? Do you love me much?"

He paused at that, as one lacking words, or the courage to use those that he would. He was far shyer than she. "Yes," he said. "I were a fool else. You are the best maid in the town."

He did not speak as in fondness of lover's praise, which may mean little enough, but as one points to a thing known. He did not say she was the fairest maid in the town, though that might have been true. He did not call her the fairest maid in the world, as some would have done with an easy tongue, being words that a maid may be glad to hear from a lover's lips, though it may be farther from truth than it had been then.

Yvonne was pleased by these words. She saw that he might have said more and meant less. She fixed her will that if she should wed him—as she saw that she surely must—she would give him such joy as she could. The marriage should not fail by her fault. Yet she knew that she had no love for him in her heart, and she was less than sure of his love for her. There might be many who would say she was the best maid in the town, but who would not fret for her love.

## CHAPTER SIXTEEN

THE town of Faucon-bas was not built four-square, its girth being controlled by the Rhone bank, and by the curve of the lesser river which came down from the western hills. This stream was a torrent in winter days, but now ran low in its rocky bed, which was hollowed narrow and deep. Its course was a wide valley at times, and at others a mere gorge through the hills. The Counts of Faucon-haut had ruled this valley for two hundred years, and something before that. The castle stood on high ground on the right bank of the stream about three miles from the town. Beneath the castle there was a bridge over the stream. It was built at a place where the river-gorge was so deep that no flood could reach to its top, so that the bridge was in no danger that it might be swept away at such times.

From the further end of the bridge the road ran down to the town to the western gate. It followed that, had the castle been attacked from the town, this bridge must be taken first, and it was narrow enough to be held with a little force. There was no road on the southern side of the stream, the bank at places being steep and sheer to the water-side.

This stream did not run straight into the Rhône, but took a southern curve at its last mile, and it was within this curve that the town lay. It had one wall that was straight enough, facing the Rhone bank. At times the river rose till it ran deeply along this wall; at times there was a stretch of shallow water, or mud, which could be waded or walked, but none would seek to attack the town from that side unless it had been by some swift surprise.

The southern wall was embraced by the curve of the smaller stream, over which was a strong bridge, giving entrance to the gate by which the merchandise of the sea-ports came to the town. The gate was strongly built, and the bridge could be raised at need. It was not likely that the Count would attack from that side, which would have been to have gone far out of his own way; and it was there that the wall was strongest, for it was from the south that the most peril had lain in the earlier years both for castle and town, which had been as one in those times.

Following the curve of the stream, the wall bent northwest till it came to the place where the road which was on the right bank of the stream entered the town. Here was the western gate, to which few came. Only those from the castle, or such as would come down from the valley farms to barter within the town, had any use for this gate. It was less strongly barred than was the great gate on the southern side, and the wall was lowest at this point. From there it faced west for a short space and then curved backward, looking over the flat land to the north, till it came again to the Rhône. On the northern side it had neither river nor stream to hinder approach, and in its midst was a third gate, by which much traffic would leave the town, which the chapmen who entered by the southern side carried north and west that they might sell it through the breadth of France and beyond.

It was this northern side of the wall against which the condottieri would be the most likely to come, for it was on that side that their camp lay. Here, on the past day, there had been ruthless felling of trees, which had grown too near to the wall, or which would give shelter to those who would come close while dodging the crossbow bolts.

The morning came, cloudless and still, with a promise of great heat when the sun should come to its full height. There was a stir with the dawn in town and camp, and in castle-yard, and it was but the seventh hour of the day when a trumpet blew at the western gate, calling for entrance in the Count's name to the town he owned, to which there was no answer returned. It was an hour later when the

Count rode out of the castle gates at the head of such force as his banner led. They marched at no more than a walking pace, for there were footmen, and carted ladders and tools, which could do no more; but there was shine and flutter of silk and steel where the mounted knights rode at the head, and a trumpet sounded at times.

Faucon-haut was built on a craggy knoll, of which it covered the top, the walls following the bends of the cliffs. There were higher hills at its rear, but they were more than a bowshot off, so that there could be no danger from them. It was not shaped as is a castle that is founded on a flat land, and laid out to a builder's will, but it had space within its walls that was large enough for courts for tilting and tennis-play, and two gardens that were well enclosed, and made private from oversight of window or wall, as the way was at that time.

It had a high, square tower at its outmost angle, from the top of which one could see far, both up into the hills, and out over the town, and the Rhône Valley beyond. Isabeau said that she would climb this tower, that she might watch with her ladies there how the fighting fared. But for this she must give the key, for she kept that tower locked at its foot, and none might enter except she willed. She gave a reason for this of which there was a doubt that few would be bold to speak, but the thought was that she would not have any climb there lest they should look down on the garth which was hers at a wrong time. For there was a little garth which could be entered only from her own room, and which was private to her. It could be seen of none at its upper end (where she would enter at first), which a row of cypresses screened, except that one should stand on this tower that was higher than all.

It was the day before that the Bishop of Nîmes had confessed her in her own room, having been locked therein with her for an hour, or it might be more. What of that? It was the room where she would entertain her friends, and to which her ladies came. Was it strange that she would be alone when she confessed her sins? Or that it was a matter of time, her sins being what they were? Or if she took him into her own garth, which was a pleasant place, scented with roses, and shaded from summer heat, we may say, what of that too? But she would not be overseen at such times, and none could challenge her will.

Now she gave the key of the great door that was at the foot of the tower to a maid, and with orders that food and wine, and an awning and cushions of silk, should be carried up to the roof, which was toil enough, for the stone steps were narrow and very steep. The walls of that stair had neither rail nor rope, and one who slipped might fall far. For, being so steep, and the tower being built four-square, there were but three long, straight flights of these steps without any curve, or any turn except at the corners of the tower; but the fourth flight was short, being no more than eight steps, at the end of which there was a door half sunk in the flat roof of the tower.

From this height, Isabeau, and those who were beside her there, could see the whole circumference of the town. They looked down on its walls, and, though it was nearly three miles away, they saw many men in the clear air, moving upon them like ants. They saw the shining line of the cavalcade that descended the castle road. They saw, far off on the left, on the level land, the regiment of con-dottieri moving slowly forward to the assault. It showed little flaunt of colour, and if a trumpet blew, it was not to sound defiance against its foes, but to make order in its own ranks, for the regiments of condottieri were formed for use, not for show.

Sir Lanval rode with the castle knights. He went rather to see than to do, having little lust to be killed or maimed in that brawl. But he must do his part, as a guest should, and for the rank in which he was born. His first thought was to see how men would bear them-selves in the strife, and of the handling both of assault and defence; for he who makes songs should know of all that the world holds, and of some further things beyond that.

It might seem that those who moved to the assault of such walls could have little hope to find more than their own deaths, the town being alert as it was; but they came on with a bold front, the Count's force to the western gate which was approached by the castle road, and the condottieri against the northern wall. For it had been agreed that they should make separate assault, to which Raoul's counsel had led. For these soldiers of fortune were ever loth to fight except under their own leaders, and the castle knights would have been as loth to take orders from those they hired.

"Beside that," Raoul said, "we shall be three to one, if not four, and it will be our work if the town fall. But if there be but three knights of rank whose pennons show on our front, they will take the praise if we take the town; and if we fail to do that, they will give us the blame, as being men of a baser blood." He spoke of that which he had seen before.

He added: "But if they be held apart, they will fight their best, for then men will compare, and they will not have it said that they are not better than we."

Halt saw the wisdom of this, and he went further, making a plan to which the Count had agreed, that there should be one feint, and one attack which should be earnest to force the wall; but which part should be done by each they could not tell till they saw how the wall was held.

# CHAPTER SEVENTEEN

ISABEAU looked down the valley, where the stream ran with the road, till the road entered through the town gate, and the stream turned aside, as though the town wall barred its way, though the truth was of an opposite kind, the stream's course having set bounds to the town.

At that point, facing the western gate, and spreading somewhat to the north, where there was no stream to hinder close approach to the wall, she saw her brother's force, showing a glitter of steel in the light of a sun that was now high in the sky, and a gay shine of col-our—pennons and tabards and painted shields. Using ladders that had been lent from Captain Redwood's camp, they were assailing the walls.

She scarcely knew what she wished to see. She would have the town scourged. She was sure of that. She would have its plebeian bride brought to her brother's power, for she loved sport of whatever kind. She hoped the maid would not come in a willing way. It might be as good as the baiting of bear or bull. Or she might be one who would show no sport, but just be stupid and dull, or a giggling fool. It is a mistake to expect too much, as Isabeau knew.

But while she would have the town scourged, and its bride brought to her brother's bed, she would not that the event should be to his praise, for she did not love him at all. He had made a brave show as he rode forth, and he could hardly come to a coward's shame, his hand being maimed as it was.

Yet he might be hurt in his pride, as would surely be if his own force should be flung away, and the condottieri should take the town. That would please her well. But, above all, let the town bleed. Should it store insolent wealth while they lacked gold to pay the charges that Raymont claimed? Let them learn what they were, and abate their pride.

But it looked as though Captain Redwood was not quick to face the issue for which so many silver florins had been paid in advance. Far off, to the north, if her sight was true, the condottieri manœuvred among the vineyards that lay beyond the northern wall. Keeping a long bowshot away, they moved as though seeking a weak place in the wall, or the chance of a sudden rush. And while they did this, the smaller forces of the Count carried their ladders forward to the assault.

"It looks," said Louise, "that the dogs bay; but they will not bite."

"They will bite hard when they do, and with the worse grip that they first heed where they shall spring," Isabeau answered, speaking that which she wished. Louise looked at her, and said no more. She understood well enough.

"Mother of God!" said Doette. "They are on the wall!" So it seemed that they were. Far as it was, they could see that the ladders stood. On the edge of the wall there was struggle and flashing steel. Some were flung back, or leapt down. It was little more than twelve feet that the wall rose at that point.

The fact was that the town had feared the condottieri most, being the larger force, and being trained and practised in war. Besides, they brought the fear of a strange name. The men of the castle were neighbours known, whom it is not easy to fear. The best of the town's defenders had been placed on the northern side, as had the crossbowmen that had come from Arles, whose special duty it was to hold the gate on that side.

Now there must be men brought in haste to the western wall. These came more than enough. Those who watched from the high tower of Faucon-haut saw that the assault which had begun so fairly had come to ruin at last. Their friends leapt from the wall, from which the ladders were flung away.

It was Louise who was the first to turn her regard from that sight. "It seems," she said, "that the dogs spring."

Her words turned all eyes to the northern wall, where the greater part of the condottieri had disappeared, having advanced too close under the wall to be longer seen; but there was a force of fifty men that were held backward, opposite to the northern gate. At some distance, both to right and left of that gate, the bustle upon the wall showed where the attacks came. For a time it was hard for those who watched to tell how the strife went, till, on the far right, a sudden flame leapt up from beneath the wall, and rose high into the air. To those who were familiar with such warfare it was plain what had happened there.

"As for this day," Louise said, "it seems that we are not taking the town." Her hand covered a wide yawn as she spoke, for she had been up late on the last night, and such watching is tiring work, even though you are stretched in cushioned ease, gazing over a parapet that was no more than a foot high, on which you can lean as you will.

"I hope Captain Redwood was not there," Doette said. Then she added: "The Count is attacking again. I think Sir Lanval is leading them on." She had eyes for those she knew, where her thoughts were.

"You are wrong, Louise," Isabeau said; "they are not beaten at all. See, they come on at a run." She did not know what that movement meant. There were things which had not been told even to her, for such secrets of war should be known to the fewest that must be told; but she saw those that had been held back beyond bowshot of the northern gate were now running toward it as such speed as they might, being burdened with weapons and arms. Isabeau watched, and that which she saw caused her to forget the sweetmeats which were beside her on the low parapet against which she leaned, and which she had been eating with greed, for they were of a new kind, brought by sea from Byzantium, and having come to her hands but a week ago. "Doette," she said, "you have the best sight; doth the gate stand?"

## CHAPTER EIGHTEEN

HALT REDWOOD, Captain-General of a military force which, small as it might be now, had a reputation which was feared through the breadth of Europe, knew himself to be without military experience or more than a superficial acquaintance with the science of war. It was a likely thing that he should have broken sleep on the night before he must direct attack upon a walled town.

He knew that Konrad had made his name without flourish of sword, seldom being seen in the van of battle, and often giving orders while he remained in his own tent in a quiet rear. But what he had thought well to do might not be a choice as fortunate for one who had a reputation to make, and experience to be gained. Halt had talked long with Raoul on the previous day, leading him to tell what he had seen of such assaults, and of the issues to which they came. He had given orders that twenty men should be left as a guard for the camp, and the stores it held, and that the rest should be ready to march at seven hours after the dawn. When they were arrayed, he set himself in their midst, mounted on a good horse.

Except himself, they went forward on foot, not bearing their heavy lances, for they were assured that the townsmen would not come forth of the gate to engage in the open fields, and that they could deal with them, if they did, with the swords and axes they bore. They went lightly weaponed, wearing little armour, and that only in front. They carried trenching-tools, ladders, and ropes with grappling-irons, which, being well thrown, might pull men down from the walls, and those who could use them with skill were armed also with bows.

Halting at something more than a bowshot from the wall, they waited till Count Gismond's trumpet told them that he went forward to the attack, and then Raoul moved leftward with about a hundred men; and another party of equal strength moved to the right, led by a Captain Vitelli, he being a young officer of whom Raoul spoke well, and who sought fame, leaving Halt with fifty whom he kept under his own order, who remained still, facing the gate.

The wall would have been stronger had it been twice as high, but, as it was, it had been a long toil to the town when it was built, and it looked high enough to those who would scale its side against hands and swords that would thrust them down. Yet such assaults would succeed at times, and may sound more desperate than they were. A ladder that is well hooked to the wall is not easy to thrust away. The more men that will clamber up, the firmer the hooks will grip. There is little comfort for those who would throw stones, or worse things, on the climbers' heads, if there be good bowmen awatch, ready to loose arrow or bolt at the first head that shall show. And there is the trouble of the length of the wall to be held, which must have store of missiles at every part, or they may be too late to arrive.

Captain Vitelli's men advanced to a point where the wall looked to be high and strong. He thought that there was little difference in that, it being of no more height than it was, and that such a place might be weakly held. They had six ladders, of which they fixed four. There were those who mounted the parapet and got a footing on the flat top of the wall, of which Vitelli was one. He wielded a quick sword. The townsmen gave way, being less than equal, each for each, to these who were skilled in the use of arms. Numbers would not tell here as they would have done in a wider space. Every moment there were others who scrambled up the ladders behind those whose footing was gained. Yet if some of the townsmen gave ground, others came quickly to their support. The narrow top of the wall became a fury of swords that slashed and stabbed, and clanged on helmet and blade. It became a shambles of wounds and death, a swaying, struggling crowd, from which rose the wild crying of men.

Raoul attempted the wall at a weaker place, and led his men to a worse fate. There is no cause to blame him for that, though he blamed himself on the next day.

His men fixed their ladders firmly enough. Raoul placed one with his own hands. He did his part well, and his men were of good heart, having the example he gave.

But, in fact, there was no effort to stay them at all. The townsmen were content that they should fix the ladders as firmly as they would, and that they should come more than halfway up, for against the inner side of the wall there was backed that wagon of hay that had passed by Guilbert's forge on the night before. When the ladders were loaded with human fruit the hay was tossed over the wall. It fell in heavy swathes, covering their shoulders and heads, choking them with its dust, bearing them back to the ground. It was soaked in oil, and as it fell lighted torches were flung upon it. In an instant a great flame leapt from the ground far above the height of the wall, in which more than the ladders burnt.

There was one man who had gained the top of the wall when they commenced to throw over the hay. That was Raoul himself. As his head rose over the parapet he had seen what was to come. There might have been time for him to leap free, or there might not, but it was a thing that he did not try.

"Back, men, back!" he roared in his great voice, and as he did so he was on the top of the wall, and making play with his sword.

He had thrust through two of those who were flinging over the hay before he came to one who met him with an equal blade, and when he had made him give ground with a bleeding arm he saw that it was too late to do more. Even where he stood he was scorched by the leaping flame.

He stood alone on the wall, with his reddened sword in his hand. For an instant there was no man who would be more forward than others to strike him down, as they stood watching the flames, being well pleased with what they had done, as they had cause. When they looked at him they saw that he was of some rank, and they knew that such men are better captured than killed. There will be no ransom paid for a dead man, and the ransom of captured knights was one of the best profits of the warfare of those days. With a common voice, they called on him to yield.

Raoul gave no answer to that. He looked down a wall where already the flames sank. Such a fire could last but a minute's space; but it had done its work in that time. Only the ladders still crackled and flared with a growing flame. Beneath them, in the blackening heaps of the hay, there were blackened forms that writhed, or that were already still.

Raoul saw that the ladders were not for him. He thought to leap; but he was a heavy man. He might lie there with a broken leg, and he did not like the idea. He looked along the wall to where its line was pierced by the northern gate. It was there that the crossbowmen were stationed that M. Sault had brought into the town. He looked out over the vineyards, and he saw that Captain Redwood's company was moving toward the gate.

Suddenly he raised his sword in his two hands, circling it around his head. He commenced to run along the wall toward the gate. He shouted loud as he ran, "*À moi, à moi*, Raoul, Raoul!" Men gave way from that rush, and the great sweep of the circling blade. They were not trained to face such blind fury as that which did not turn to see where its wounds fell.

Raoul came through to the crossbowmen with no hurt that would vex him a week, and from them he had nothing to fear. Some of them were now scattering the townsmen who had been with them to guard the gate, others were flinging it wide. They had each a white scarf tied round the upper arm, showing the crest of a grey wolf's head.

Raoul had no cause for surprise at that, for he had waylaid M. Sault's men a few days before, and replaced them with two score of his own. M. Sault's men were in a cave in the hills. They had no reason to fret nor to risk their lives in an effort to break away, having been promised their full wage, and something beyond, when they should be set free.

The assaults which had been made upon the wall, both from west and north, might have seemed to fail, but they had drawn the strength of the defence away from the northern gate so that it had been easy for the crossbowmen to overpower those who had remained to guard it. Halt rode through the gate in the midst of fifty men who had not used weapon nor taken wound, and those who had attempted the wall, both to right and left, formed in a heavier rank at his rear. He left the crossbowmen to hold the gate, and took a straight course for the Hôtel de Ville, which flanked the central square of the town.

He met with no resistance at all. His entrance had been too sudden, his force was too strong, for any organized opposition to obstruct its way.

They who bore arms fled by side streets and alleys from the advance of those disciplined ranks. It was a little later that the Count's men-at-arms established themselves upon the western wall, against an opposition which had become weakened by cries of treason and that the town was taken. The Count drove the defenders from the western gate, throwing it open to those of his followers who had not mounted the wall. Guessing well what had happened elsewhere, they advanced boldly into the town. Less disciplined, though not less valiant than the condottieri, they scattered somewhat as they advanced, and were opposed with a better heart, so that there was confused fighting in street and square, even after the maire had yielded the town, as he had no choice but to do.

# CHAPTER NINETEEN

SIR LANVAL came by a narrow street to a square where men fought. He was not cumbered with heavy arms, which were for tilt-yard sport rather than for men who must mount a wall. He wore a helmet of steel, but such as left his face bare, save for a downward bar. He wore gorget and shirt of mail which had not been bought at an armourer's booth, but made in Spain to his own shape. It fitted light and close as a glove to a girl's hand, and every link was of tested steel.

Sir Lanval looked round, seeking rather to see than to do. What he saw would not wake into song at once, but when it had sunk into his mind it might give seed of song on a far day. He had a heavy sword in his right hand which must be swung of both if the need came; but he stood at ease for a minute's space, he not being one that all men of the town would be quick to cross. He looked round. "The rogues lose," he thought, "yet they fought stoutly enough."

He saw Michael Sault, M. Sault's elder son, and at the same time Michael saw him. Michael was bigger than he. He wore a quilted coat, making him seem bigger yet. He had a heavy sword in his hands, like to that of Sir Lanval, and there was a moment when the two men looked at one another, as men may look at such times.

"Turn aside," Sir Lanval said, "if you will, and it may be better for both. I would not kill a good man."

Michael paused, with his sword ready to swing. "Will you go back over the wall?"

"Nay, you call too high if you ask that."

Their swords met. Sir Lanval might not wish to kill a good man, but he would rather that than be killed, as most would, and he soon learnt that the issue was less than sure. Had it not been for the mail he wore, he had been a dead man while the fight was still short. Michael's sword circled round by a way for which his guard was too late. It smote his side under the left arm, with its full edge. The mail held, though it was a great stroke, and he was near to a fall which had been his end. But he would have a black bruise on his side, and sore ribs for many days after that.

That was the worst of this new fashion of linked mail, which was so light and easy to wear, and of such strength, if it were truly made. It did not break, but it bruised as padded plate would not— nor would Michael's quilted coat, which had stood that blow with less hurt.

Sir Lanval fought hard after that. The great blades circled and clashed. The sound was of a smithy when the anvil works.

Michael went to his knee with a hand on the ground. He had had the point through his ribs. That was the worst of the quilted coat. It would take the edge well enough, but the point would go through. Over his head a sword shone. His brother came to his aid.

Andrew Sault was a youth, not yet being of full growth. Michael looked up at Sir Lanval. "Kill him not," he said; "he is the last of our house."

Sir Lanval beat down the boy's sword, using the utmost strength that he had. His own point came to the ground.

"Get him home," he said. "He is sore hurt."

Andrew looked his surprise, for there were few knights of that time who would act so to those of the common blood, though they might at times to some of their own rank.

He went off with his brother's weight on his arm. Michael had strength to walk thus, though it might be a hard thing. But in the evening he died.

Sir Lanval looked round again on a square that emptied of men. The fight had moved on. He judged that it neared its end. He followed where the noise led, humming the song he had made, that he might shape it a better tune. "Swords, swords again for Isabeau!" It was a good song, which would do no harm to his name. Yet it gave him less joy than he had had from a worse tune. "Swords for Isabeau," he said. "Swords for a she-cat!"

He walked on, looking round as one who looks at a fair. It might be thought that he had done his part in that fight of which he had little joy. Yet he had done more good for the town, and more evil to Faucon-haut, than any who fought on the town's side. But he could not know that. For M. Sault became a wroth man, seeing his dead son, where before he had thought only of market dues, and to count the coins that he staked on a measured gain; but after that, his wealth was the town's purse, and the town must move at his pace, being driven by him.

Yet at this hour, M. Sault, not knowing of his son's hurt, and seeing a lost cause, was very active for peace, for he would save the sack of the town.

# CHAPTER TWENTY

THE maire sat in his place at the table's head, with the provost upon his right. Around him were such of the principal citizens as were at hand, M. Sault being one.

They had made space for Captain Redwood to be seated opposite to the maire, and it was to him that all eyes turned. They knew that his men were drawn up, a silent menace in the square without. At his word they would scatter, to put the town to plunder and fire.

He had walked in among them with no guard, which, if he had had more experience (especially in the Italian wars), he would have been less likely to do. Yet it did nothing to strengthen their nerves that he should hold them, as it seemed, in such careless contempt.

The maire moved uneasily in his chair. "You ask," he said, "a price which we could not pay, though it were at our lives' stake. We would do what we can, but there is not so much wealth in the town."

He looked down as he said this. It was a plain lie, as all knew who were seated there, unless it were Captain Redwood himself, whose ignorance might be used to their gain.

But Captain Redwood was unmoved. "It is the price," he said, "which was agreed with the Count, if we should take the town, that it should not be plundered or fired. If it be too high, you must show him that, and it may be he will make up that which is short. He should be here by this hour."

They looked at one another and showed no pleasure at this proposal. The provost said, "Captain, we would meet you the most we might, that the town stand. But it is a very great sum. There would be no help from the Count. But he should be lightly content, if you would meet us in the same mood, having that for which this strife was stirred up, which we can no longer withhold."

"Yes," said the maire, "he will have the maid." There was a murmur of assent. They were of one mind. With their wealth at stake, there was no thought for Yvonne. Perhaps we should not blame them beyond limit for that. They had their own wives and daughters of which to think, and the condottieri, like leashed wolves, were without.

M. Sault interposed. The maire's words reminded him that the castle's claim was for that which was of more weight than an alchemist's niece. "Captain Redwood," he said, "we would be plain. If we pay such ransom now as may be agreed to save the sack of the town, and if we yield you the demoiselle—Madame Livron, as I should now say—will you go thereupon, pledging us that you will do us no further wrong, and that we have back our own gates?"

"Livron?" Halt asked. He remembered that name. It brought his mind back to his own quest, and he misunderstood M. Sault's doubt in a natural way. Did he know that Konrad's assassin was in the town? Did he know even more than that? He added: "Why should you doubt that?"

The second question had first reply. M. Sault spoke in a plain way. He was too able a negotiator to make frequent use of evasion or guile. "We should doubt it for this reason, that there was dispute between us and the Count of another kind, before this matter arose. It was a question of the share he claims of the market dues which are levied on all stuff which enters the gates. We say that he has no claim upon aught save that which is here sold, but he would have it upon all the tolls we levy on that which must pass the bridge. What we ask is this. If we make accord on this ransom that you would claim, and if we yield the maid to the Count's will, do you withdraw in peace, or will it then be that another matter is to be brought on?"

Halt saw that this question was fairly asked, but his own position was clear. He would have done all that he undertook, and the question of market tolls was one that he had not been asked to settle, nor did he know on what basis it could be done to the Count's content. Yet he knew that it was the root of the strife that had brought them there.

"I can say nothing of that," he answered with an equal frankness. "If the maid be yielded, as you are willing to do, and the ransom paid, the town will have no more hurt from me, and I will give you the gate I hold. Yet I should say you will have no peace if this be not lesson enough. I should say you would do well to make accord with the Count on the best terms that you may."

"It may be," M. Sault answered, "that we shall be of the like mind. But we would know where we stand. We would not have it claimed at the sword's point."

The maire and provost had been whispering together while this conversation proceeded. Now the maire spoke. "Captain Redwood, could we raise half the sum which was first named—"

"It is waste of words," Halt interrupted, "to say more. I named that which I meant, and the last florin must be paid down if you would have the bars of your own gate. But I will offer this. There is one I seek who may be now in this town, and who, as I think, is known to him who caused Captain Konrad's death. If you will help me so that I find these two, I will pay a thousand crowns to the town's chest on the day when I have learnt this beyond doubt, and there are two hundred more to be earned by any who will give me good aid to this end."

M. Sault had the instinct that knows when there is no more to be gained by any spending of words. He spoke quickly, lest there should be less wisdom from those who had better right. "If we agree to this, you will give some space of time to assemble the gold? Such a sum is not to be paid in an hour's space."

"It shall be paid as to the first half in an hour's time, and the balance tomorrow noon. Until then I shall hold the north gate, and if it be not paid by that time, you must look that I shall make sack of the town."

It was not a bargain that Konrad would have made, having seen more of how such things went. He would have had the whole sum in an hour's time, or hostages that would make it sure. The maire should have spent the night in his own camp, or a castle vault.

The town was cowered for an hour; but its fighting men were four to one, if not five, though they might not be of equal sort, and they lacked leaders of skill. They would have time to think during the night. When Raoul heard, he wondered what the next day would bring. Yet it might be well enough. The town had been chastened well.

The provost was busy with inkhorn and parchment. He would have the terms clear, and that, if possible, before the Count should come on the scene. Halt said: "There is one more thing I would ask. Who is this M. Livron who is wedding the maid that the Count claims? Is he beyond his youth? It is a name I have heard."

"He is a young man of about twenty-two years. An armourer of the town." Halt saw that he could not be the man he sought. There might be many of that name in the town.

"It is an older man with whom I would meet, if there be such. A scrivener, as a likely guess."

The provost looked up at that. He knew the men of his trade for ten leagues round. "There is none of that name in these parts, nor hath there been in my time."

M. Sault said: "The young man's father is widely known. He is an alchemist, and a seller of charms."

"He is one," Halt suggested, "who may have been in the wars in his younger days?"

But M. Sault thought not. He spoke with decision. M. Livron was not of that kind. He appeared to be a man who had always been poor in health. Not a man of his hands, nor one who would endure the hardships of war.

"Has he children besides this son?"

"He has a younger daughter—Lucette."

"Is she surely his own child?"

They were old men who sat round that board—men who knew the town. They considered, consulted, agreed. They remembered M. Livron's wife. Not a woman of roving mind. And Lucette had something of her father's looks, in the way that a girl may. Yes, they said. They thought the Captain-General could be sure of that.

Halt saw that he could not learn more at that time, but he saw that he might be on a trail which would take him far. He did not think to make enquiry concerning the woman that M. Livron the younger married. She could be nothing to him. And it seemed that the father could not be he whom he must seek. Probably he was no more than an agent through whom enquiry had been made. Well, he would see him, and might learn more.

Meanwhile, he had the young woman to take in charge. Let him have her, that she might be handed to the Count's charge, and the ransom paid, and he would withdraw his men to the gate.

The provost passed him a scroll, neatly and fairly written, for he was a man skilled with the pen.

The maire said: "The wedding was for the noon hour, which is now past. If you will go to the church with sufficient guard, the maid may be put in your charge in a quiet way. I will go with you myself, to give order that there be no protest nor brawl." For he felt the relief of a timid man now that peace was come again, at whatever price, and he saw that a spark of strife might yet rise to such flame as would wreck the town.

## CHAPTER TWENTY-ONE

THE Church of Ste. Sarah was not in the centre of the town, but lay somewhat aside, among the meanest habitations and narrowest alleys, as was natural enough, for the growth of population which had impelled its erection had made it difficult to find space for its site. That was the frequent problem of the walled town. For such an edifice, other buildings must be pulled down, and the choice was made where those that already stood were of least value and greatest age. Any demolition would be undertaken with reluctance, for in that age men built with enduring materials. Whether they laboured on castle or cottage, they aimed to build that which would last.

It followed that those who crowded the church through the length of the wedding-mass were not quick to learn how the day went. There was a great crowd there, being women for the most part, and children, and men who did not bear arms. They heard tumult at times, but it had ever a distant sound. They had no active fear, for it had not been thought that the town could be taken on the first day. Indeed, there was little dread that it would be taken at all, with such force as was near its walls; and had not the crossbowmen been way-laid as they were it might have been a hard thing to do in a longer time. It was the common talk that they would make the Count to re-spect their strength, and would then come to accord in a fair way, rather than take strife to extreme, or risk that there would be those who would come to his aid, beyond their power to endure.

Guilbert came with no thought that his bride would be snatched from his arms. It was to deny that that the town had made fast its gates. But he knew that there might be fighting around the walls, in which he should do his part, wherefore he came to the church wear-ing a stout leather coat, and with weapons hung from his belt, which he left for a time, with a morion of steel, at the church door.

He did not think much of the Count's claim, yet he had not the joy of that bridal that a man should who had come there by the right path, for he was wedding one who had become distant from him since childhood days, and who might not have been his free choice, though he might call her the best maid in the town, had he not been pushed to that point by his father's will. Yet he did not feel loth. He was rather as one who walks by a poor light, not seeing well where he will end, though he have a will to go on. Such a bridal might come to a good end, which would rest most with the woman's will, and Yvonne was of a fixed mind that it should not fail on her side.

In this mood, she came in a willing way, looking serene and content, and, being clad as she now was, she was of a fairness for which most who beheld must envy him she would wed, even though he might not value that which he won at the true price. She had the look, so it was said as she came into the church, of a knight's wife, and there were few of those that would be as well favoured as she.

It was a time when each man would wear the garb of his own rank, or his own trade, and the women were held apart by the dress they wore in the same way.

That was the custom in every rank, and in most parts of the Christian world, whether in palace or hut, excepting only that there were breaches of these rules in the towns, as their wealth grew. A man might wear the garb of merchant or scribe, or of the trade that he owned, so that all might know him for what he was with no questions asked, but his wife would be less easy to rule.

Besides, there would arise many in the civic life who were not easy to range. Who could say how an alchemist's niece should be fitly clad? M. Livron had opened his purse for this day, and Yvonne had bought to her own will, which, be she troubled as much as she might, she had not been unready to do.

The marriage service was done, and the last blessing was being said, when there was a stir at the main entrance of the church, and two men advanced together up the central aisle. The chancel was barred and latticed from the common throng, as was the custom in those days, but the maire, who wore the garb of his office, such as he used when he walked abroad, entered without ceremony, with Captain Redwood upon his heels.

It was not of Halt's nature to turn from that to which he had set his hand, or to which his word had been pledged, but as he came close to the thing, he was not sure that it was to his mind. It was not such as he would have thought to do in an English town. But he had the sense to see that there must be other customs to meet for those who wander abroad. He thought that there could never have been such a law in his own land. He supposed that these people were not to be measured by the same yard. Yet he was ill-at-ease, wondering how the woman would take that which he came to do.

On his way to the church he had been met by a squire who had brought word from the Count that he had ridden back to the castle, relying upon him to have ruled the town as had been arranged, and that he would bring the bride to the castle gate.

Halt had been unsure how to take this. Would the Count throw upon him that which would soil his own hands? He was not clear that it lay within the bounds of that which he had undertaken to do.

In fact, it was the Count's dignity which had been alarmed in another way. As he rode through the town, he had heard how long Captain Redwood had been in the civic hall. He supposed that matters might be agreed by that time, and he feared that if he should enter he would appear to be shown to a second place. It was a doubt which would not have come to an abler or more confident man, nor to one less jealous of his own state. He thought it best to ride back as one whose work had been done by those who were under his rule.

Halt considered what he should do. He resolved that he would ride no errands for any count. He said: "You can tell Count Gismond that I have a pledge that the woman be given up. If this be done, she shall be sent to the castle gates in an hour's time."

The squire saw by his tone, and by the way in which he stressed his words, that he was not pleased. He took the message without remark, and gave it a fairer tone when it was for his lord's ears, being discreet, though his years were few.

After that, Halt told Raoul to be prepared for that charge. Raoul saluted, saying nothing, but he looked loth. Halt would not ask the cause of his discontent, which was no more than that he had much to rule, that the main body of troops should be returned to the camp without clash or broil, and that dispositions should be made for those who were to hold the north gate on the next day. It was an order which Konrad would not have given, knowing how much lay in his hands.

Halt called him back as he turned away. "You need not, if you have other matters on hand. Let Vitelli go. There will be horses needed. It will be far to send back to the camp. There should be some found in the town."

## CHAPTER TWENTY-TWO

THE church grew very still as the great throng watched the group within the chancel rails, who were changing words which it could not hear, but the nature of which it was very easy to guess.

The maire said to Yvonne, "You must go to the Count, for there is no choice. They have taken the town."

Yvonne was slow to reply. She had learnt from childhood to be silent, and to hide her thoughts when she would. Her lips gave no sign of the sudden fear in her heart. She must think what she would do.

Guilbert answered for her with quicker words than he often found. "It is vain to say that. We are four to one, if not more. It were shame to yield to so few. We are not all slain in an hour's time."

He was slow to believe. His hand felt for the weapons which were in the porch. He would have struck there, if he might; but at whom? He could not strike at the maire, and Captain Redwood, be he of what party he might, had not the look of a foe.

The maire answered him, telling briefly what had chanced. He added, "There is no choice but to yield. They are guarding the doors. There is none here but women and aged men. Besides, it is more than that. If we do not yield, they will fire the town."

He looked to Captain Redwood to second his words, and was aware that he had not heard. His eyes were upon Yvonne, and she was looking at him as though she would ask his will.

Halt had no will at that time. He looked into her eyes and their souls met. He knew that he had seen the face that he would love to his life's end. He did not know for a time that the church was there, nor that he was watched by a great throng.

She saw him as well as he her, for his head was bare in that place, and it was not hard to guess who he was, for his armour was of an English make. She knew that well enough, from the talk she had heard in Guilbert's booth. He had known much of armour even in childhood's day. There were no such gorgets hammered on the forges of France or Spain.

But she gave no notice to that. She did not know why she thought at once, "He is an English knight." For a moment her eyes were lost in his own, and her heart beat with love, as it had not done till that hour. But she controlled herself better than he, as a woman does. And the next moment her uncle came to her side, and the spell broke at his words.

He was pale with wrath and his hand shook, but he was of a sense to see that the game was lost unless he could make it good in his own way. He looked at the maire, and at Redwood, who gave him no heed. "At this evil pass," he said, "I would give my niece the best counsel I may."

He drew her somewhat aside, whispering too low to be heard. No one interposed to prevent that. If he gave her a charm that would blast the eyes of the Count, or cause his arms to wither and his strength fail, or vex his belly with the pains of hell, there were few there, if any, who would not be the better pleased.

She came from him to Guilbert when he ceased, taking his hand in hers. "Guilbert," she said, "I must go, lest the town burn. You must leave this to me."

Guilbert felt as one who is cast for a part which he has not learned. What should a man do, being placed thus, and his arms in the church porch? He did nothing at all, and if we blame him, we should be able to point to that which would have been of better avail. "You can tell him...," he began, and then ceased. He had a mind to say that if the Count did her hurt or wrong, he would find a way to get his hands to his throat; but he had the sense to see in time, though his wits were slow, that he would be more likely to reach that end if he had not talked of it before.

He saw Yvonne pass down the aisle at Captain Redwood's side, the maire following behind. He went for his arms in the porch.

## CHAPTER TWENTY-THREE

VITELLI met them on the steps of the church. He said: "They are bringing horses. They should be here now." There were thirty men lined up to be their guard through the town, from which they must pass at a footman's pace, for he had been promised horses for two, but no more.

Halt said: "I shall not need you for this." Had he thought to give her to Vitelli's charge? All men are mad at times.

His own horse was at the pavement. He saw others a short space away. He said: "You can have one of those. It can be returned, having served its use."

Yvonne answered, "I will have that which is mine."

For she had ridden to the church, as was the likeliest way that she should come, being so attired that she would not walk on the streets. For the streets of the town were narrow and unfitted for wheeled vehicles, of which there were few, except such as were used for haulage of goods. The streets were of more comfort than those of a later day in that the houses were built projecting, so that one could walk dry, though there were storm overhead. They sloped down to a central gutter, into which alone the rain fell, cleansing the filth that might be flung out from window or door. But men would walk or ride on a cobbled path that was always dry.

Yvonne had on a close-fitting bridal-gown of white satin, broidered and lined with gold, which came to her feet, but no more. It was slashed on either side to the knees' height, giving freedom to move the feet. She wore a veil that fell from the forehead to right and left, leaving the face clear. She took off this veil as she stood at the church door, handing it to Lucette, who gave her a hooded cape of green sendal, very finely woven and light of weight, such as was fit for the summer days.

Lucette had watched Yvonne as she looked first on the condottieri chief. She had seen how their eyes met. She thought, "It is a lover found at the right time." She had been married to Guilbert in the last hour, but Lucette saw no trouble in that. He was but one man the more with whom Yvonne would be free to play as she would.

Halt had a moment's thought for the things he left. He said to Vitelli, "You will tell Raoul that he is in charge of all till I am back in the camp. He will receive the ransom which is to be paid at this hour." Halt had meant that the gold should be paid to his own hands; but it seemed now to be a small matter, with which Raoul could deal well enough, as indeed he could. He could count, though he could not write, and he understood the weighing of gold, in which he had had practice before.

Yvonne was on her horse by this time, a dun mare, of too slender a build for an armed man, but which might make a good pace with no more than a woman's weight. It looked less than it was beside the blue-roan stallion that had been Konrad's ten days ago, and that Halt was mounting now.

They rode through the town at a walk, changing neither glance nor word, with the escort marching behind and before.

When they came to the west gate, which was held by the Count's men, Halt sent back the thirty who had guarded them through the town, and they rode on at a quicker pace.

Yvonne's mare would have gone faster yet at the first, had she had her will, and she pulled slightly ahead, so that Halt could see Yvonne better than she him. She rode with the hood of her cape thrown back, being in the shadow of the hills, and it being meant only as a cover from the sun's heat, so that her head was bare. Her hair was golden-brown in the light, or black when the shadows fell. It was golden-brown as Halt saw it now for the first time, and curling somewhat where it had freedom for its own will. Halt thought that there was none such in the world's width. He had seen none such, but he may have looked now somewhat better than he had done before.

He saw the profile of a face that was fair and cold, and that looked straightly ahead. He had an impulse to say, "Let us ride on, and the world go," but he knew that it could not be.

As they came to the steeper part of the upward path, and her mare slackened pace to a walk, she looked round and answered him as though he had spoken aloud.

"I must do this lest the town burn. Yet it may not be...." Her voice dropped, leaving her thought unsaid. She added, after a pause, "I am Guilbert's wife from this hour. I am not of those who break faith. We are too late by a day."

It was unreal to him, as though he rode in a dream, but it was a dream vexed by the dull pain of despair which her words gave. He said: "It must be as you will. But there is my sword at your call, and the men I lead. I am at your service ever from now."

They looked up, and they saw the bridge spanning the gorge of the stream, and the battlements of Faucon-haut, with the high corner-tower looking down upon them; but they were seen of none, for Isabeau was no longer there.

She had come down from the tower when she had seen that her brother was riding back from the gate, and she knew that the town was won. She was glad enough when she got to the tower's foot, or rather to that point where she could pass on to the wall and descend by a better stair. For the stone steps by which they had climbed were of more danger to those who must go down, being narrow of tread, and of more depth, so that if a foot should slip, being at the head of one of the long flights, there was nothing at which to catch. It might mean a fall of the whole way, which had once been a boy's death, who had not taken the care that he should. All who went by those stairs would curse him who had built that tower, that he had not made it round, for on the stairs of a rounded turret a fall may be sooner stayed.

Isabeau went with care, and she went last, for she saw that if one should slip she would bear down those who were beneath in a common fall. She saw also that she who fell last would come down on the softer bed.

She met the Count with her ladies at the outer gate, as was fitting when he came back in arms from a triumph won. He was content with that he had done, for he had taken the western gate without the aid of those he had hired, and if they had been first in the town, that had been by the ruse which had been employed, rather than by their own valour. Had the crossbowmen been placed at the western gate, it would have been he who had entered first. There were some of his men who bore wounds, which their scarves bound. There were two dead, and four wounded too sorely to ride or walk, so that they had been left with their comrades who held the gate. The loss was small, and had not fallen among those of gentle blood. It had been a good day.

"Sir Lambel?" answered the Count, when Bernice (who was the third of Isabeau's train, at whom we have not looked before this) asked of the welfare of one of his knights, seeing that he was not there. "He is unhurt; I have left him in charge of the gate we hold." He spoke shortly, having a vexation he was loth to show that Bernice should have eyes that searched for a younger knight. The Lady Bernice was thin, and taller than most. She had light hair and light eyes, and moved in a furtive way. She was the Count's mistress at times, as all knew. It was only she who thought it a secret thing.

Isabeau's eyes searched the train. There was no woman there. She asked: "You have missed the wench?"

"Nay," he said. "Captain Redwood sends her behind."

Isabeau was glad that the sport was not to be lost, but content enough that the woman was not there. The fact was that the technique of the situation was not clear to her own mind. The custom of a dead past cannot be lopped therefrom, and grafted on to a later time as a living thing.

When this custom had first prevailed it had been accepted of all in a willing way. It had its own observances, its ceremonial. It fell easily into place.

But now Isabeau, having brought it to birth, was unsure how she would have it to be. Should the woman be sent to the Count's room, and turned loose in an hour's time, to make her way back to the town?

Or should they have the parade of a bridal feast, and the girl placed at the Count's side, and taken to his chamber at last to be put to bed in the public way that was the custom after the wedding-feasts of that time?

She would do her the most shame that she could, but she was not sure which would be that. If it were made a ritual of banquet and song, would it do her honour, or mock?

Isabeau did not say this aloud, though it was clear to those among whom she talked from the jests she made, and the fact that she would not give her orders for the night in an assured way. She resolved to wait until she should see the bride, which might end her doubt. But she was content that she should not come till a later hour.

It may be thought that the Count should have had some voice in these things which concerned himself rather than her. But he was slow to speak of this matter at all, not being as sure that she had not made him a fool as he would have liked to be for his own peace. He was always one to fancy what men would say when their talk was beyond his ears. He considered that this custom was of a rude age, when lord and serf may have been less far apart than they had since become. A count of that day might not degrade himself, though he took a peasant girl to his bed, if she pleased his eye, or for other cause. But that he himself should so greatly deign to one of baser blood at this day, and one whom he had not seen, and who might be ill-favoured, if not unclean? He cursed Isabeau in his heart, as he often did. Yet he let her go her own way in the ordering of the event, for he would not risk a dispute in which he might not come off the better. He would rather that men should think that she did all to his own will.

# CHAPTER TWENTY-FOUR

THEY rode over the narrow bridge, and took the steep path that climbed to the castle-gate, which they might ride abreast, but with no space to spare.

The ground fell sheer away on each side of the path, and then broadened somewhat as they rode under the shadow of the great tower, and beneath the wall. Halt looked up, and was glad that it had been town, and not castle, which he had undertaken to storm. Raoul had counselled well; yet he had said that the castle could be taken, if the need were. It was true that it had not many men, and its walls were of a great girth, though far less than were those of the town.

When they came to the gate, they were met by the squire by whom Halt had sent word to the Count that he was not coming himself. The squire looked some surprise, but said nothing of that. He took Yvonne's rein, leading her horse into the porch, of which the inner gate was still closed. "Lady," he said, "I am to ask that you wait here, till there be word sent." He gave her a hand to dismount, and led her into the guardroom, which was between the two gates, where men lounged. They stared at her, thinking to see one with whom they could change jests, or who might make boast of the honour to which she came. But they looked, and their eyes fell.

The squire went back to Captain Redwood, who remained at the outer gate. He said: "My lord did not think you would bring her yourself, for I told him another tale. Had he known, he had given a different charge. He will be wroth if it be my fault."

Halt saw that he had brought this to his own door. He said: "There is no fault on your side." Yet he sat his horse without motion, finding it hard to resolve to go.

The squire was unsure what to do. He had had five coins of gold in his hand, which were to be given to the leader of this escort, or scattered among his men if he should appear to be one to whom largesse would be affront. Clearly the coins must go back into his own purse. Should he invite the Captain-General to pass the gate, and expect that the Lady Isabeau would give him thanks? That she would say that he had done wrong if he sent him away was a likely thing, but that she would be more content if he invited his entrance was less sure. The hospitality of those days which the nobles gave, especially to those of their own rank, was wide and free, but it was not etiquette for one unasked to claim entrance till the evening hour, when the toils of the day were done, and rooms garnished, and the ladies clad in the best way.

He knew that the Count had ridden in but an hour ago, and that there was confusion from yard to bower, with grooming and feeding of steeds, tending of wound and bruise, washing, changing of clothes, and eating of meals that were being served in a rough way. He said: "Lord, Count Gismond will be ill-pleased that you should come to this gate, and turn back with no service shown. May I say that you will honour him, being present at our banquet tonight?"

Halt saw how it was. He might say, "I will not go until I have given her whom I brought to the Count's charge." But what use was there in that? She might prefer to face this thing in her own way. He had no part to take, his honour being tied by the fact that he had engaged himself to the Count to bring things to this end; as was hers by the fear that, should she have turned aside, the town had been burned for their failure to do that to which they were now pledged.

Halt did not think that the town would burn, knowing the pledge that the Bishop had asked at his hands, that he should protect it therefrom; but even that he could not say without breach of faith.

Besides, she was wife to another man. He had told her his sword was hers to call if she would, with all else that was his, whether of gold or men, and she had put it aside.

He felt these things rather than thought. He felt also that he would be glad to be there that night, to see what the end should be, though it might bring him no peace.

It was that which the Count might not have proposed, and it might be good fortune that he was asked in this way. He said: "You may thank the fair courtesy of the Count, saying I will be here by the seventh hour after noon; but before then I have much to do."

He went back at a quick pace, which might have brought him to grief on that downhill road, but that he had a good horse which he rode well. He had in mind that he would see this M. Livron who sold charms. It might be that he would soon be clear of this pledge to the dead, bringing it to a good end, or to one that his sword should cut. Ever as he rode he saw Yvonne's face, and he heard her voice: "But we are a day too late." Against reason, against fact, as he rode at that pace through the summer day, he could not feel it was true. He felt, though he could give no reason even to his own mind, that the game was not played to its end.

The young knight, Sir Lambel, whom Count Gismond had left in charge of the gate he won, saluted him with courtesy, and would have had his advice as to what might be done to make it stronger against attack from the inner side, which it was not designed to resist. He was in good humour, being pleased that he was trusted with that command, and more so that he was three miles from Bernice, whose favours he did not seek; but he counted the men the Count had left in his charge, which were a bare score, except those who lay wounded in the wardroom of the gate, and the two dead, and he felt that if the town should change its mind about the holding of that gate, it might go hard with him before the dawn.

He showed Halt how he was making his men to toil, barricading the wall-top both to north and south, and the roadway on the inner side of the gate.

"I will send you ten spears," Halt replied—that would be thirty men—"who would hold that road though the whole town should debate the way."

Sir Lambel thought that that had a good sound. He saw that ten of those spears projecting over the barricade, each in the hands of two men, with a third to deal with any who should pass them between or beneath, would give him a better chance that he might sleep in peace till the dawn; but he did not know how his lord might take it that he should accept of such aid.

"It is kindly said," he replied, "but I know not that I have power to accept. My lord deems I shall hold the gate with the men he left to that end."

Halt would say nothing to that, except that it was little like that any trouble would come, for the town would gain nothing, taking that gate, if the northern one were still his, from which he thought that Raoul would be hard to move. He thought also that half the ransom would be paid by this time, and safely hauled to his own camp. The town would have paid that: it had yielded Yvonne. It seemed an unlikely thing that it would peril itself on a new strife.

He would have ridden on, but Sir Lambel said: "Captain, you would not ride through the town? If you go to your own camp, or to your men at the northern gate, there is a good road under the wall at the outer side."

"But I seek one in the town."

"You should go in strength, if at all, if you would take counsel of me." Sir Lambel would have given escort even from the few men that he had, but he had no horses at all. They had been sent back to their own stalls in the castle-yard.

So Halt rode on through the narrow streets, seeing few either of women or men, except such as turned aside to alley or door, and when he stopped two, asking where M. Livron might live, they said, truly or not, that they did not know. So he came at last to the midst of the town, and met M. Sault crossing the square.

M. Sault was in some grief of mind, having learnt of his son's wound, though he did not think him to be near death, for the leech made light of the hurt, saying if he lay still, and were well bled, he would come through. Beside that, there was trouble over the second half of the ransom, as was common in such a case. Men agreed that it must be paid, but they would not own that they could do much themselves to that end. Those who should have found fifty florins would offer ten, and those who should have found ten would make grudging tender of two.

It would be the town's debt to them, and they must be brought to a better mind in the coming hours; but they were slow to have their wealth known, which might hurt them in other ways.

Also, he had heard report that Guilbert was stirring a spirit of strife among those who were young, and who had naught at stake but their own lives, and it was that which he had set out to quell

Halt drew rein at his side, and asked for M. Livron's abode, which he was sure he would know.

M. Sault did not deny this, but he spoke to another point. "Captain Redwood," he said, "you do us a great wrong, riding thus."

Halt had not thought of it in that way, the risk being his. Yet he could not say that M. Sault was wrong. If he took a bolt in the back, as Konrad had done before, there might be a further price for the town to pay, and yet, riding alone as he did, it would be no more than his rashness asked. Yet he would not turn, having come so far. So he said, in few words.

Sault said: "If you are so resolved, I must be your guide." For he thought that was the safest way.

It did not turn his steps, for he had been going to Livron's door before that. He thought that he might find Guilbert there, or learn where he was, and he thought to appeal to the alchemist's influence over his son. He could not speak freely of this to Halt, for more reasons than one; but he would let his business stand till that of the Captain-General should be got through.

Lucette opened the door, and took them to an upper room, where her father sat. It was a back room, the latticed window looking out over a space of garden ground in which herbs grew of a hundred kinds. Even M. Sault, who knew the town well, had not thought that so much of garden space could be found in that part of the town. Doubtless the herbs were such as M. Livron used in his trade.

The alchemist received them civilly, though without warmth. He thought, or would have them think that he thought, that they had come together thus to collect such share of the town's ransom as it was his part to provide.

"Sirs," he said, "I know the jeopard in which the town lies, and it is such that we should each do our part without wasting of words. I am less rich, in truth, than I am judged in the common talk, as may be said of others as well as I. But I will do the most that I can. If I have a good bond, I will furnish two hundred florins in silver coined, and that by two hours before tomorrow's noon. I say this in few words, for I am an old man who is not well, and who has had tiring hours, and enough grief for one day. I have said the most I can do, and if we talk a week it will be no more."

M. Sault did not believe that, but he knew it for a fairer offer than was being made by most at that time. He said: "If you will do that, we will ask no more, except it be at a great need. But Captain Redwood comes on his own quest, which is not that of the town.

"It may be," he added, turning to Halt, "that you would that I were not here?"

Halt said no to that. He thought a witness would be no harm, and there was no secret in that which he came to say. He sought only to draw the curtain aside from that which had been secret before.

"In a word," he said, "I would know why you made enquiry concerning Captain Wolvenstein's wealth but two months ago."

The question seemed to surprise M. Livron, though whether that was because he had done no such thing, or because he had expected one of a different kind, might be hard to judge. He said: "Enquiry of whom? I know nothing of what you say."

"Enquiry of your agents in Paris."

M. Livron was silent, for he had a fear and a doubt, and they did not point in the same way. Then he said: "I have no agents in Paris. I am an alchemist, not a goldsmith, as you may learn, if you do not know. Will you be plain as to what you mean?"

"I will be plain enough. I seek Captain Wolvenstein's child, of which he was robbed when she was young, and the man who took her, having taken his wife before that."

"To what end do you seek?"

"That is to be said when we shall meet."

M. Livron was silent, as a man who knew nothing of that which was asked would not be likely to be. The fact was that he would have liked to say much, but he saw it might go beyond the point where it would be to his peace.

He saw also that it might be worse that there should be denial by him, and disclosure by another way; and in M. Sault's presence he could not see where the talk might lead.

"You do not think that I am he whom you seek?"

"No, I do not think you to be of that kind."

Halt saw that he was a man fifteen years older than Konrad could have been, or perhaps more. There was no barrier in that, but he did not look to be such a man as he of whom Konrad had told. And there was the witness of the citizens of the town that his daughter was his wife's child.

"Then you must search in another place."

"That is less than sure. I think you know more than you say. There is surely one of your name in the town who can tell me more."

"If I knew, will you say why I should tell?"

At that moment M. Livron had resolved to tell as much as he might without catching his feet in his own net, for he saw that he could not hope that M. Sault would hear further words and not guess enough to expose more.

He was in the mood to say: "If I tell you the man is dead, and that the maid you seek is she who is now my son's wife, will you take my proofs in the right way, not charging me with her father's death, nor to make new evil from that you learn?" That was the substance of his thought, though he might have framed the words to a fairer sound, but as he asked, "Will you say why I should tell?" there was a noise of voices in the room below.

M. Sault said: "I think Guilbert is here. I have a word for him which is one cause why I came. If you will hold me excused...?" He rose quickly as he spoke, and went down.

Being alone with Halt, the alchemist's manner changed. "Captain Redwood," he said, "you have hired yourself to be a foe to this town, and you have brought grief this day on my son, and my son's wife. You are a bold man to come here asking my help, though it were mine to give, which I have not said."

Halt was as plain in his reply. "I did not come as a friend, but as one seeking the truth, whether by steel or gold."

"Then you must come at a better time, when this conflict is through."

"That is to say that you know."

"It is to say less than that. I may give you help if I have your oath that you will use that which you learn in the right way."

"If the man is dead, there is nothing left but to find the maid, and to do justice to her."

"The justice of the gold that is hers by her father's death?"

The question was not wisely asked, nor worded in the best way. It reminded Halt that he had another search to be made. He said coldly: "That is to be told to her when we shall meet. But I let you know that I will take no oath by which he who shot that bolt shall go free." He rose as he spoke, adding: "We will talk again on a near day."

M. Sault was coming back up the stairs.

## CHAPTER TWENTY-FIVE

WHEN M. Sault went down to the lower room, he found Guilbert was there with Lucette, who had let him in. Guilbert was fully armed, and was less quiet of speech than his habit was. M. Sault thought he had drunk wine.

As he entered, Guilbert turned to ask him in an angered tone: "Why do you bring the man here? Has he surety from you or others that he should ride thus in the town?"

M. Sault asked: "Why? Does he harm you?"

"He may be hostage seized to bring all to our will."

M. Sault had had the same thought in his mind, and had put it by. "It would be short gain to us, if it were not less than that. We are resolved that this strife is done. We have lost enough."

"Your loss is other than mine, or you would not speak in so quiet a way."

"I have a son hurt."

"It is a wound that will heal. It is other with me. Were your son dead—"

"God forbid that. Yet it is vain for you to fret over that which we cannot change. We had stood out if we could. But if we had not yielded the maid, they had sacked the town. It had been grief to more maids than one had they done that."

"M. Sault," Guilbert replied, looking at him with an anger which touched contempt, "there are some who think that this town is not taken at all. They had stooped to that which they could not lift had not our shoulders bent to their aid. Think you that we are yet four to one, if not more? They had but died in the narrow streets, had they scattered to sack the town."

"There had been such deaths," M. Sault allowed; "but you must think that the town is built largely of wood. What use were their deaths to us if it should go down, if not by plunder, by fire? And for Captain Redwood, though it be folly that he ride here as he does, yet shall he go safely back, for we are at truce till tomorrow noon, when I trust that we shall accord, and our gates come back to our own hands."

"Well," Guilbert replied, "I will talk with those of another mind." He went out, and M. Sault went back up the stairs.

They had both influenced the other more than they knew. Guilbert had not thought of how quickly the town might be set on fire by those who were already within its gates. He saw that he must proceed with more caution than he had meant to do in the last hour. He put the thought of seizing Captain Redwood out of his mind, for if it should become known, it would wake a strife which would be too soon, they being placed as they were.

In M. Sault's mind it nursed a doubt of a different kind, which had been there before. Might it not be in truth that they had yielded too soon? They had been stunned by the sudden blow of the captured gate, and to know that their foes were within the town. They had been stunned, but not slain, and they were recovering to the knowledge that they had sustained no wound of a fatal kind. Was it possible that Guilbert was right, and that resolute action might even now retrieve the position? M. Sault had a special bitterness in the fact that the crossbowmen whom he had hired and equipped at a heavy charge, and whom he had meant to weight the scale to his own side, had been used as the means to contrive their loss. He had spent thus because he was a good man of affairs, who knew that success can hardly be bought at so high a price as that which failure will take; and, because he was a good man of affairs, he had been urgent to seek terms of accord when he had thought that the hope of success was gone. But being human, he was yet wroth at the way that he had been used to introduce their foes to the town.

The doubt which was in Guilbert's mind and in his, and which caused Sir Lambel to fret least he should be overset in his first command, had not been such to Raoul but a thing seen.

Had he been in Halt's place he would have taken the most he could get in an hour's time, and been out of the town. He saw that the most part of those who had lined the walls had not struck a blow: they had scarcely seen whom they fought. To entangle his men in the narrow streets, or to start a sack of the town before their foes had been beaten down, would be a plain folly to him, he having seen all he had of the defence and taking of towns.

Yet he was well content, seeing how Halt had brought it off in a bold way. There was a good sum that had been already paid, and it had been wise to attempt to hold no more than the northern gate, which he had no doubt that he would be able to do. He gave no thought to Sir Lambel of what force he might have, or what practice in such a charge. That was the castle's risk rather than his. For his part, he trenched and barricaded the street; he made gaps in the top of the wall, where it approached the gate, both to east and west; he threw forward outposts on every side; he left nothing to chance. He thought that if any should try to drive him back from the gate, he would grieve them more than they him.

He was busy at this work when Halt rode up by the town street. Raoul stared, seeing the way he came. He had given orders among his men that none should go more than five yards from their own lines, either to barter, or for such lures as a town may hold. He had seen at times how much may be done by a bold front, when to shrink is to ask attack, yet he wondered how long his captain's life would be likely to be, if he risked it thus.

Halt had no space in his mind for such thoughts, it being full enough without that. He looked round, and knew, as he had not doubted before, that he would leave that gate's defence in better hands than his own. He learnt that the treasure was at the camp under strong guard. He said that he must ride to the castle again, but would be back at the fall of the summer night. He turned his horse for Faucon-haut once again; but this time he rode by the outside of the wall, remembering what M. Sault had said, which his reason told him was true.

## CHAPTER TWENTY-SIX

ISABEAU had not been sure what she would do, and when she had chosen her road at last she found she was too late by an hour, for Count Gismond's squire had gone to him with the word that Captain Redwood would return at the banquet hour, and he had told that the bride was left in the warders' room.

Gismond saw his sister in that, and he thought her fool in more ways than one. He saw that the less he should raise her whom he must wed for a night to his own place, the more he must stoop to her. He had the sense to see beyond that, that the worse he should treat her who had been brought to his will, the more he affronted the town, and that in a foolish way.

Now that they were chastened and bent their knees to his will, he was of a merciful mind. If they would grant him such part of the market tolls that he should have gold enough in the coming days, he would have amity once again.

"You will give order," he said, "that she be shown to a guest-room, where there shall be all that shall meet her need, with change of raiment if she shall so wish, and that she be left there in peace till the banquet hour, when she shall sit at my left hand. You may give order beyond that, that Captain Redwood shall sit at her other side."

(For that place would be vacant, having been occupied by the Bishop, who, being a discreet man, had left but an hour before for his own city of Nîmes, when he had heard that the town was down.)

The Count showed some wisdom in this, and also his fretful care for his own pride, for he would not that one of his own household should sit at her other side, to engage her in talk, not knowing of what sort she might prove to be.

He added: "You will let the Lady Isabeau know that I have ordered this, and that I will that one of her own ladies shall take it in charge, for it is to our honour that we do all in a noble way, it being a thing which will be talked much."

Isabeau heard this, and was somewhat wroth that she had not taken order herself at an earlier hour. Yet she could not say that the Count was wrong, nor was she enough concerned to counter the orders which he had given.

At least, she was not so concerned till it was too late to be done, which was when Louise came with a tale of what she had seen, which was meant to vex Bernice rather than her, though, if it did both, Louise might not be the worse pleased.

That was after Isabeau had had the Count's message, and had looked round at her ladies to say: "Must I find a bridesmaid here? Doette, you are one in three who can play that part."

Doette rose at that in a lothly way, knowing that it would be she in the end, and it might best be done without wasting of words; but she was glad at a later time, having made a friend.

Louise made pretext to go out at the same time, for she would see the bride, and in what mood she was brought.

She came back with a tale which would vex those to whom it was told, as she meant it should.

"It is falcon-gentil," she said, "that you have caught in this trap. She will look in her own place at the Count's side."

Isabeau said: "Your eyes are fooled by a gown of silk which she hath worn for this day. Be she ranked as she may, she is no more than a young wench of the town." She spoke with contempt, but her voice had a note of fear.

"Well," Louise answered, yawning wide, in a way she had when she did not laugh, "you may have that as you will. You will see for yourself, and can call me wrong after that."

"Does it seem that she comes in a willing way?"

"I cannot tell you that. She is one that can hide her thoughts. But it is Bernice's seat she is to have for this night, if not more."

Bernice sorted the silks on her frame. She would have acted as one not heeding the words she heard, but the colour rose in her face. Isabeau had been fool indeed if she had brought one there who might not leave on the next day. She would have liked to say: "She will take Isabeau's place if she take mine"; but she could not without showing that she had understood that Louise's words had a double edge.

Isabeau was less careful to hide that which was in all their minds. It might mean much to her, who had ruled Faucon-haut since the flight of her brother's wife, and something, too, to Bernice. Only Louise could laugh at that fear, as she now did.

Isabeau said, as one who treads down a doubt in her own mind: "It could come to naught. Tomorrow she must back to the town. It could be naught, for they are both wed."

"Oh, well," Louise said, "if you can see that!" She smiled somewhat at her own thoughts.

After that, there was a longer silence than there would often be in that room. Isabeau strove to put the fear from her mind with a strong will. At the worst, she would know how to deal. She would not scruple, at a sharp need, to try the use of a dagger's point, or a poisoned cup. She supposed that if M. Livron were paid enough gold—but then she remembered that Yvonne was his niece, whom he might scruple to poison, even for a full purse. Yet if she should flout his son....

Still, it was folly to vex her mind in advance of a likely cause.

Bernice's thoughts went on the same road, though a shorter way. She knew that the Count cared little for her, though she might be the toy of his listless days.

But to Louise's last mock there was no answer, as they all knew. The Church did not admit divorce, but it would annul marriages among those who ruled upon many grounds. The Count could make pretext to break his bond to one who had long fled: the other marriage had not been consummated at all. And without marriage....

Well, was there not one such woman who ruled a tenth of the French land at that hour?

It had been well said that there are few things that we may not have with a strong will, but to control the price that we have to pay is beyond our power; nor can we tell what it may prove to be till the deal is through. Isabeau saw that she had got her desire, and that Fate was now writing the bill. But she had a good hope that it would be one she could pay with ease. "Falcon-gentil!" she said to herself, with the contempt which it was ever easy to feel. "She will be more like to a barn-owl."

After that, they went apart to dress, as the custom was.

## CHAPTER TWENTY-SEVEN

THE ladies entered the hall at the sound of the second horn, by a side-door at its upper end. After Isabeau, Yvonne came, with Doette at her side. Doette showed her where she should sit, and then went to her own place. The Count entered at the same time, with some of his knights, from an opposite door.

The Count stood by his chair till he saw that the ladies, and any guests of honour, had found their seats. Then he sat down, and after him there was seating of his household knights, and then there was bustle of women and men who crowded the lower board, or who must find space on benches at the far end of the hall, if no better were to be had.

There were all eyes on Yvonne at this time, and a murmur of whispering thereafter, the theme of which it would be easy to guess; but she gave no sign that she saw. She thought at this time—in which she was wrong—that she had no feelings at all.

But all the years of her life had been her preparation for the hour that must now be faced. All her life she had had no confidant of her kind. She had been alone with her own thoughts. All her life, she had learned to conceal them from those to whom they would have been as though she had spoken a strange tongue.

Now she looked at the Count at her side, and was aware that she did not fear him at all. He had dressed himself in that which became him best—silver and black, with a great jewel to close his throat, and a diamond on his right hand that would flash as he carved to the lower end of the hall. He looked a man who would not lightly endure to be crossed, who was accustomed to speak his will, and to pass on without looking back, knowing that he would be obeyed. He had the power of life and death in that valley, till it was lost in the hills, the high justice and the low. He would have had the same power in the town, had it not been granted a charter in older days giving it certain rights within its own bounds, so that it served his lordship in all beside.

Now it had waxed fat and kicked, and this very day he had ridden forth, and it had fawned at his feet. The woman who sat at his side was the tribute of submission which it had sent, in earnest of more substantial values to come.

So it looked to all. But Yvonne thought he was ill-at-ease, as in fact he was. For he was not sure in his own mind whether he should have put on the rich splendour of the black velvet and silver dress, which he wore only on rare occasions of state. Would men jest at him for that when they were sure that he would not hear? Would they smile where they were sure that he could not see?

He was less vexed by this doubt when he had looked on Yvonne. Had the town sent him a slut in her natural dress, and perhaps one who was not overclean.... He saw that he was not to be troubled in that way. But he felt that it was his part to speak when his plate had been piled to his will (for he was a man who ate well, and who would have the best that was served), and he was not sure how to begin.

Yvonne looked at him, and knew that her fear had gone. A plan which had been in her mind before took a steady shape. It was only when she thought of Captain Redwood on her other hand that her heart beat in a way that she did not choose. She had seen him as he entered the hall, and when he took the seat at her side she had resolved to hold him out of her thoughts. Now, to do this, she looked round the hall (which was strange to her), meeting the glance of those around in a confident way, for they had no place in her mind.

She looked down the length of a great hall that would be cold and comfortless enough in its grey ruin on a far day which she could not foresee, but which was now gay with colour and light.

It was nobly proportioned in height and length, and it showed no greyness of stone, either of floor or wall. For though the walls were not hung with great tapestries, as they would be in the halls of princes and kings (though the sala was furnished in this way, as were other of the smaller rooms), yet it was painted richly from floor to roof in patterns and pictured scenes. And the floor was strewn with rushes, fresh and green, and so thickly that it was soft to the tread. Many hundreds of times every year would the ox-team toil up the climbing road, bringing fresh rushes for the castle rooms, and taking down those that were somewhat soiled, that they might be sold in the town.

The table at which she sat stretched across the breadth of the hall, so that she looked down its length. There was a longer table at right-angles to that, the upper part of which was for the household knights, and others of gentle blood, and the far end for those of a common kind. It was a gay scene, for the dresses both of women and men were bright in that sunny land, in a day when the world was not blackened by the curse of coal.

There was abundance of food also, flesh and fruit and pastries, and fish and game, as there has always been in the world, and, at that time, men had not learned to starve while there was plenty for all, for they lived where their food grew.

Yvonne looked at such a scene for the first time, for her life had not been spent in the castles of counts and lords. To her it was strange and great, though there was comfort enough, and luxury of a kind, hidden away in the small rooms of the town, in the houses where the richer citizens dwelt, who did not flaunt it abroad, lest it drew upon them the envy and spoiling of poorer or lawless men.

She looked on it without awe, being of those who are equal to what they meet. But she bent her mind to observe and admire, that it might have the less space for the thoughts which she would not own. Those who watched thought that she looked round as one may who has come at last to her own place, and the fear that had been but a dim shadow in Isabeau's mind grew to a great dread, and a fierce envy and hate toward her whom she had set in that seat.

Isabeau led the talk at the board, for the Count said little, and Yvonne was not likely to be free of speech, and Captain Redwood was as silent as she. She led it with skilful guile ever to matters in which Yvonne could have little knowledge or art, and more than once she appealed to her for advice, or to say what her habit was, to confuse her in subtle ways and to remind those who were seated around of how she came to be there.

When the talk was of the training of goshawks, and to what age they should be left in the nest, she spoke her own mind, and looked across her brother to ask: "Madame Livron, do you not think I am right?"

The name, which had not been used to her before, startled Yvonne in a way that she would not show. She looked at Isabeau, and their eyes met. She knew well that the name had been used to remind her of what she was.

"Lady," she said, "I know nothing of these matters of which you talk, for I am not of gentle blood."

Isabeau's eyes darkened with wrath, and for this time she had no words to reply. There was a moment's silence among those who heard, for it was a rebuke that they could not miss. The rule of courteous speech was very strict at that time, unless it were among friends who would talk in familiar ways. It was written in the manual which was for the instruction of ladies of noble birth that they must use courteous words, even to the enemy of all their friends.

Sir Lanval, who had been talking to Doette in a quiet way, but had been aware of that which passed on the other side, turned to reply, when he saw that Isabeau had no answer to make.

"Lady," he said, "but that we may not doubt what you say, I should have held that there is none here of a nobler blood."

He had said before that to Doette, "She is not such as I thought to see, but I cannot tell more till I hear her voice. For the voice of a woman cannot lie as to what she is."

He had thought: "There is that here which will make me a song, but I cannot tell of what kind it will be." He thought again: "It may be a snake's nest they have stirred. The Lady Isabeau can see that for herself. She is already fearing the sting."

There was a longer silence after he had spoken thus, for Sir Lanval was not one to give such praise in a light way. The Count was not displeased, for he had been vexed that Isabeau should so bait one whom she herself had set at his side, and there was no love spent between his sister and him.

It was after that, when the board was cleared, and there was some passing of wine, but before it would have been time to break up the hall, that Yvonne did the thing she had planned since her uncle had whispered that in her ear which she had scarcely heard at the time, but to which she had given some thought since.

She turned to Count Gismond to ask: "Lord, is it yet an hour from the set of sun?"

The cresset-torches had been lighted around the walls, but it was still twilight without. The summer twilight was long. The Count looked, and answered: "No, it is less than that."

"Lord," she said, "I would speak with you on an urgent thing before then. I would speak apart."

The Count considered what this might mean, which had been so publicly said, for Yvonne had not used a low voice, as though meaning that only he should hear. He was in some doubt as to what Isabeau might have in her mind as to the way in which the evening should end. He cared nothing for Yvonne; but for his own dignity he cared much, and that things should be done (by the standards of that time) in a seemly way. And be knew that he walked on a narrow plank, Isabeau having led him into that which was not of the present customs of men. He saw that Yvonne's mind might be on the same path. He thought: "Does she this of her wit?"

He caught a whisper of Bernice, for his ears were ever alert for that which might not be meant for him: "By the saints, she hath a bold way."

He rose, giving a hand to Yvonne, who rose also at once. He said: "We will retire at this time." They went out of the hall by the door which led to his own room.

Captain Redwood rose to go. He said that he would be needed at his own camp. He bid Isabeau a formal adieu. All through the meal Yvonne had given him neither glance nor word. What of that? It could have done no good if she had. It could be nothing to him. They were held by a fate which neither could turn aside. Still, there had been words he had meant to speak. He had not thought that she would break up the board in that sudden way—to be alone with the Count.

Sir Lanval bade him good night as he passed out. "You have had," he said, "a fortunate day." Captain Redwood did not look like one who is conscious of that. Sir Lanval had no key to his mood, but he added, his words turning to that which was in both their minds: "I would give much to know what will chance in the Count's room in the next hour."

Halt said: "Would you that? I am foreign born. I like not Provençal ways."

The words were curtly said, but Sir Lanval took no offence. "Why, as to that," he replied, "I would not say that I do. But I am not of Provence, nor of Languedoc, having been born in a colder north."

## CHAPTER TWENTY-EIGHT

DOETTE followed Yvonne, bearing a lamp which she had picked up in the hall. She said: "The chamber will not be lit by this time." She entered with them, and gave lights to a room that was lofty and large, and furnished richly and well. She said: "You will have all you can need. There is not aught I can do?"

She knew that it was her duty to wait on Yvonne for the length of this night, of which she was troubled in mind, lest she should do too little, or else too much, and she had not expected the event to develop in this abrupt way.

"I have all I need," Yvonne answered. "I shall want naught. I shall want naught till the dawn."

The Count and Yvonne stood some distance apart, as though waiting for her to go. She said good night and withdrew. The Count barred the door.

He turned with a formal smile, and with words which he had rehearsed in his mind. He had resolved, as he sat at meat, that he would treat this maid of the town as being one of his own rank. He would make love in a formal way. If she should respond well, he might be brought to think better of his sister's plan than he had yet done. He was not sure that Yvonne would have come to that room for the last time. He recognized that she had shown decision in bringing them to where they were. It would be sport to use her to make Isabeau wince, and he might find her of use in better ways than that.

"Yvonne," he began (for he had been careful to learn her name), "were you less fair than you are, you might think that you had been brought here without love, to such honour indeed as my rank can give, but as being required to yield that which a maid values most, to one who would price it low. But such thoughts cannot be for you, who are of a beauty for which a king would give much."

"Lord," she said, "will you hear me first? For I have that which should be soon told."

Count Gismond was annoyed. She should have been absorbed in the pleasure which his words gave. He might not remember to speak them again in so fair a way.

He said: "You presume too far. When I would speak, it is for others to wait their turn, as you would know had you been bred in a better way. If a man should ask me to wait his words, he must be a king, or a prince, having wider rule than the county which is mine."

Yvonne thought, shrewdly enough, that he would fret less for the forms of rank if he were more sure of himself. She felt amused and less afraid than before, though she was alone in that barred room for a purpose that she well knew, and he was a foot more in height, and should be far stronger than she.

"Lord," she said, "I spoke for your own good. But if you would talk first of more trifling things, will you stand further away? It may be else to your grief, which I will save if I yet can."

He looked somewhat astonished at these words, as he might well.

"I know not what you can mean," he replied, "but you have my leave to speak for a brief time."

He did not move further away, as she had warned him to do, nor did he approach. He stood still, as one in some confusion, and ruffled in mind.

Seeing him thus, she was even more assured than before.

"I will be brief," she said, "as the need is. You know that my uncle is M. Livron, an alchemist of a great name, and that I have married his son, though I am trapped here. When my uncle saw, at this noon, that we had no force to resist your will, he said certain words in my ear to which I had no time to reply, it was with such speed thereon that I was hastened away. He said, 'From one hour after the sunset tonight, till tomorrow's dawn, there is no man shall come within six feet of where you may be, but he shall be marked with the pox to his life's end.' You must not blame me for this, for it was not of my thought at all. I would not that any should take aught of me at so dear a price, which I can see that I am not worth. It was to save you from that that I was fretful to speak as the light fell."

"It is devil's trick," the Count said, "or a likely lie. You will find it will naught avail." His face was livid with wrath, or it might be fear, for he stepped back as he spoke. He added: "Were I so seized, I would take vengeance that should be talked while the world stands. I would lay flat the town."

"Then," she said boldly, "you would do mere folly and wrong, for it is your own town. There be many lords that the pox has marked, but none that has made waste of his own town, from which his wealth comes."

"If this be," he replied, changing his ground, "your uncle will need all his cheats, and will find them too few to save. He shall hang on my gallows here by one leg till he die."

"My uncle," Yvonne said, being unmoved by this threat, "has no friendship for me. He must watch his own end. Were you brought to bed with the pox, that you would be wroth could be lightly told, and that you would do him such harm as you might must have been forethought on his side. Yet he might have tricks to overmatch your own craft, he being the mage he is."

"Yes," Gismond replied, with more spirit than he had yet shown, "so he might. I doubt not he hath many tricks, of which this is one, and that of a shallow sort."

He came near with these words to the point of will which had crossed the space which so held them apart, and dared what might be no more than an idle boast. But she answered as boldly as he, and in the way that was most likely to hold him back: "So it may be, for of that I know no more than yourself, or it may be less.

"You may put it to proof if you will; for except you do that, you will never know. But I will tell you this, that if you have the pox it will be less than your death, for when you had that wound on your hand—it may be ten years ago, and it was said that it festered and would not heal—my uncle asked of the stars, and was shewn that you would not die. I recall that there came one who was maire at that time, asking if my uncle would tell when your death would be; but he would say no more than that it would be two years after his own, and that would not be till a far day."

Count Gismond listened to this, and the courage to cross that space was even less than before. There were few men of that time who would have shown a bolder front to such threat. The scientists of that time were more feared than they are now (though there may have been smaller cause), for the knowledge they had was private to themselves, or to their own cult; and men saw what they did without knowing the laws of nature by which they wrought, so that they thought it was devil's work, and would see them burn at times with a good will, thanking God for a safer world.

And as they did not know the source of their powers, they could not guess where their limits lay.

The Count had seen men die of the pox, he had seen the faces of those that lived, he was inclined to stay where he was. Even to hang a man by the leg till he should die would do nothing to cleanse his flesh of that brand, and it would be a poor sport if he knew that it were written in the high stars that his own death must be two years from the thing he did. But after that his mind was vexed with another thought which was hard to endure. Suppose it were no more than an empty threat, and M. Livron should so make it known on a later day? He would be no more than a public jest. Men would tell the tale through the breadth of the Latin lands. It would last longer than he, bringing a laughter that would not die.

It would, he felt, be too much to endure. Even the lazer-bed and the pock-marked face would be less bitter than that.

"If I should stay here," he asked, "will you swear that you will tell to none that I have forborne you thus, and that it shall be known to none but us two?"

She considered this, seeing that which was vexing his mind, and it seemed to her that the bargain was fair enough.

"I will give my word," she said, "which I do not break."

He believed that, for she had a tone that convinced his mind. Yet he would be twice sure.

"You will not tell it even to him you have this day wed?" She had not considered this, but she would not draw back from her word. Besides, Guilbert seemed far away at this time. It was not welcome that he should come back to her mind.

"I will tell it to none at all. I will say that I have no words to speak of this night."

"And your uncle will say naught? How can you pledge that?"

"If I say naught, what can he say? Will he say that his curse failed? It were to make him fool, and not you."

Count Gismond saw that. It had been foolish to ask. He was content at last. He would run no risk of the pox. Men would suppose that he had had his will of his vassal's bride. It would all end in a good way.

Yvonne, having entered first, was standing nearer the bed. He was still not far from the door. He saw that the bed must be left to her. He drew the rushes together that were on the floor, taking care that he did not move nearer to her as he did this.

The bed was of ample size, with massive pillars of cedar, of which wood were also the chests and chairs that the room held. It was curtained in such a stuff that those who might be within could see what went on in the lighted room, but those who were without could not see those in the bed. This was a device which had come down from a ruder time, when men were many and rooms were few, but it had the gain that one might sleep more safely in such a bed, or, at least, would be attacked at a greater risk, for if a man would stab his foe in the night he could not creep up in a safe way, watching his sleep, but he must approach not knowing but that he was observed by a wakeful man, till he should pull the curtain aside, and face one with a weapon raised, or perhaps feel the prick of a blade through his own ribs, which would have pierced the curtain before he could pull it aside.

So Yvonne entered the bed, thinking she had won through much to a quiet night, and Count Gismond slept on the floor.

## CHAPTER TWENTY-NINE

COUNT GISMOND slept but a few hours. He waked with the summer dawn. He was not used to sleep in his clothes on a pile of rushes that would not stay heaped to his will.

He was a wroth man, and in some doubt as to whether he had not been fooled. There came no sound from the bed where Yvonne might sleep, or she might be watching him there. The torches that Doette had lighted had flickered out, as they were timed to do, but the cold clear light of the dawn came through the arrow-slits which were all the windows there were.

As the minutes passed in the silent room, he concluded that it was more likely that she slept than that she had lain awake through the night hours. He began to wish that he were in the bed too. He thought of Yvonne, and the wish strengthened to a desire which it was not easy to check. After all, it was his own bed. It was absurd (or something stronger than that) that a Count should be held at bay in his own room in that way by a woman who was not even of gentle blood.

He thought over the reason for that, and he had a disquieting doubt. Suppose that the disease with which he had been threatened was not a direct consequence of a near approach to Yvonne, but was to be given to him by some later act of M. Livron in revenge for his niece's rape, if he should learn that the Count had disregarded the threat which he had made by her mouth? If that were so, and Yvonne, keeping her pledge to him, did not tell her uncle that he had left her alone, might he not get the penalty of that which he had not done? He might end by getting the pox, without having had the maid.

Feeling that that would be too much to endure, he tried to recall the exact wording of the warning he had received, and as he did this there came a sudden light to his mind. Yvonne was to be left untouched till the dawn. And the dawn was here!

It was not a point on which he could afford to be wrong, but he recalled Yvonne's words very clearly. There was no doubt about them. She might, of course, have misquoted the alchemist's threat. But that was a smaller risk, which he felt an increasing disposition to take. (As a fact, Yvonne had repeated her uncle's words without thinking of the limitation which they implied, and he had spoken in too much haste to choose them with care.)

The thought that he might have been held back, and set to sleep on the floor by an empty threat, joined to that memory which told him that if the threat were of a worse kind, it had only been till the dawn that the spell would hold, and with the fear which was ever in the rear of his mind that his sleep on the floor would become known, and that he would become a mock in the mouths of men—all these, uniting with a fierce desire to possess that which his bed held, which had come to him as he waked, caused him on a sudden impulse to rise and cross the room to the side of the bed.

Well, for good or ill, it was done now. There was no more to fear, let him do as he would. With a quiet hand he pulled the curtain aside.

* * * * * *

Yvonne had sat long watching the man she had fooled as he made his bed on the floor. She did not know that he had been fooled by an empty word. Had she known that, she would have played her part worse, and, perhaps, failed. But she was unsure, as was he. She knew that her uncle had much knowledge of stars and herbs, and of the properties of matter in occult ways. She knew that he could do many things which his neighbours could not attempt. She knew, also, that no scruples would vex his mind.

But she had a doubt beyond that, that he would often cheat those to whom he sold amulet, or potion, or charm. She had seen once, as a child, that he had sold the same thing, with a smile aside, for two purposes of a contrary kind. She would not trust him at all. She saw that to threaten in such a way would have the same effect, whether it should have substance or no, and, should it avail, there would be no proof that it had been false.

All this did not matter to her, nor did she desire that Count Gismond should be marked by the pox. She would have disliked him more had he caused her a greater fear. All she cared was that he should be in such dread as would keep him a good distance away. So it seemed that he was.

After a time she was sure that he slept, though it seemed that he slept ill. The hours are long in the night. There was no use to watch till the day came, while the torches flickered upon the walls, and he slept thus.

She drew off the wedding-dress and laid it at the lower end of the bed. Had she been alone, she would have taken off her shift after that, for in that day it was the custom to sleep bare. The night-garment was an idea of a later time. But she would not do so, being in the place she was. She lay down in her shift, and learnt that Count Gismond slept on a soft bed.

But as for herself, she could not sleep even then. She lay awake, through the night hours, having sombre thoughts. She supposed that she was safe enough for this night, though there came a time when her mind went to the same point that Count Gismond would also see when he waked at the dawn. Did her uncle's threat go to its needed length? Or how long might she be kept here? But she put this aside, thinking that the Count had consented to let her go, and that it would not have to be argued again. But this release left her mind open to the entrance of other thoughts, and they brought her no joy.

She supposed that she must return to the town on the coming day, and she would be Guilbert's wife, for which she had no desire. Her thoughts went to the English Captain who had sat by her that night, and from whom she had turned her eyes, as she had resolved to do; but her thoughts would not be turned in the same way. If it had been he to whom she must go on the next night! Oh, if it had been he! Had she been Captain Redwood's wife, the Count should not have touched her, though she had slain him or herself that she might be unspoiled of his hands!

As it was, she had felt but a dull pain, and a dull resolve to do what she could, which had proved enough. But she had felt it less as her own siege than as one who looks on a play. And tomorrow night she would be Guilbert's wife, and there would be no talk of the pox.

Yet his wife she was, by her own vow, and the Church's seal. Was she truly of wanton kind, as Father Ambrose had said, that she thought thus of another man whom she had known for less than a day, and with whom she had changed but a few words? She was not sure as to this, but she made defence in her own heart, saying to herself, and to such saints as would be likely to hear, that she had not taken Guilbert of her free will, having been snared in her uncle's net. Neither had she seen him at that hour, for whom she now longed and would never have.

For to break her vow did not enter her mind, or, if it did, it was cast out in a quick way, for, she had said to Halt, she was not of that kind. They were a day too late. She would do the best that she could, caring for Guilbert's house, and listening to his talk of his own trade, in which his heart was, as she thought, more than in her, and taking kisses that would bring her no joy. And perhaps, after that…she had heard it said that with the coming of babes there may be peace in a woman's heart even though she be wed in a poor way. Well, it was to be proved, as it seemed, by her.

As for tonight, she was resolved that she would not sleep. She would put on her dress again as the dawn neared, and when the Count waked she would go forth to face what the day might bring. A torch flickered and went out. There was a faint light in the narrow strip of eastern sky which showed in the high arrow-slit on the far side of the room. The Count stirred in his sleep. She resolved that she would delay no longer to rise. She could sit there till the dawn, for she could not lie down again in that dress. As she resolved to do this, the sleep which had delayed so long came unaware. When the Count drew the curtain back she was in so deep a sleep that she did not wake, having watched so long.

He looked down with coveting eyes. Softly he drew back the clothes, thinking that she would be bare. Seeing that her shift was still on, he was vexed, but thought: "It will be soon shed."

As he looked, a gentler feeling entered his mind than he had first felt. "I had thought to take a town weed, and have found a flower. She would be fit for the bed of kings."

She lay still in her sleep, looking younger and of a more child-like mood than she would do when awake, and her mind on guard, which came of the life she lived, for it was in sleep that her soul showed. He looked on her with a fierce lust that put all other thoughts to the door. Would she never wake?

"Well," he said to himself, "she will soon know." He had only to cast off his own clothes. His doublet fell to his feet.

There was a loud knocking upon the door. "Lord, lord," cried his squire's voice, "waken, for you are needed in haste! There is tale of Sir Lambel down and the gate gone."

## CHAPTER THIRTY

YVONNE wakened to the loud voices of men who gave no heeding to her. In her dream she heard the squire's call, and being awake, she heard the Count answer: "I come in a minute's time. Wait until I unbar the door." She saw that the linen sheet had been cast aside in her sleep, as might well be in the warmth of the summer night, with August a week away. She looked through the curtain which Count Gismond had dropped before she opened her eyes. He stood near to the bed, drawing up his trunk-hose from about his feet. Her heart missed a beat at that sight, and with an instinct of vain defence she drew the sheet to her chin; but it quickened again as she perceived by his words that he was not thinking of her.

He had the door open by now and the squire in the room telling his tale. They went out together, leaving the door wide.

Seeing that she was free for the time, she dressed and went forth to a babel of many tongues. There was talk that the condottieri had joined the town, and that they came even now to the castle's storm. It was fact that a body of troops could be seen from the battlements in the broadening dawn, coming from town to castle by the uphill road.

Count Gismond had given orders that a dozen men-at-arms should ride down to the bridge to learn who came, and, if needful, to bar their way, which at that point a small force should be able to do.

In the hall Sir Lanval was being armed by his squire. Doette saw him there, looking on him with troubled eyes. "Lord," she asked, "can you bear arms, your side being so bruised as we know it is?"

"Why," he said, "as to that, I would it were less sore. But it is the left side by the saint's grace, and I can drive a lance none the worse. And I have a charger that knows me well, and is easy to rein."

He had had some words with Lambert before to the same end, but he found that Doette was less easy to still.

"I see not," she said, "that you should take hurt in a quarrel which is not yours."

"As to that," he answered, at more length than he had done when Lambert had asked, "neither do I. But that it is not mine may be less than sure. I am a guest here by my own will, and, beside that, if the castle be in jeopardy of storm and sack, shall I leave you to such a chance? But I will tell you this, that I ride out to learn rather than to do more. For there may be little fire under this smoke."

He saw that they had no certain news as yet, beyond that (if it could be called a sure tale) which had been brought by a fleeing man. He had blood on his head, and a severed lip, in proof that he had not fled without changing of blows. His tale was of the town in arms, and the gate stormed that Sir Lambel held. There had been no help from Captain Redwood, of whom there was talk that he had made league with the town.

Sir Lanval believed something of this, though not all. But if there were a great need, he would not be backward to do his part. His wished he were less bruised in the ribs, and that there were some knights of name on the other part from whom honour might be won.

There could be little for after-boast when those of gentle blood fought with soldiers of fortune and the rabble of towns, let the fight go as well as it might. But there was chance of shame if it went ill, and perhaps of capture, and ransom to be found, which would make him poor for a year, if not two.

So with these thoughts he went down to the courtyard, where his charger stood, saddled and barbed, and took a spear from his squire's hand. Round his neck he hung his shield with the device of the flying swan, that his left hand might be free for the reins. He rode out with the men-at-arms, who were armed and horsed well enough, but in a cheaper way, and with less glitter and show, giving them heart for the work they would have to do if they should find foes at the bridge, as a good knight would in those days.

## CHAPTER THIRTY-ONE

IT had been an early hour of the night when the maire had called on M. Sault at his own house. He was so full of his fret that he gave no heed to the face of him to whom he came ill such haste.

"This Guilbert," he said, "has taken wine till he is like a man mad." (When he said that he went somewhat beyond truth, but so his words were.) "He is calling such men to arms as have naught to lose, and are ready for broils and blood. He does not care that the cost will be ours at the last."

He went on thus for some time, M. Sault saying nothing at all. When he was run down, M. Sault spoke. It was but a few minutes before that he had seen his son die. The maire had not asked of his son, being too full of the thought of his own neck. If there should be riot and strife after terms of truce had been signed, and if it should be put down, as he thought it would, he was in a great fear as to what Count Gismond might do to chasten the town. He had a fixed idea that in such events it was customary to hang the maire, and he valued his neck as though it had been that of a better man.

"What," M. Sault asked, "would you have me to do?"

"I would have us talk sense to these fools. There are those who will hearken to you, whom I might not rule. I would have witness, at worst, that we strove to quieten the town."

"Well," M. Sault said, "I will come." He could see no gain in a riot that lacked force to prevail. He asked: "Where are we to go?"

"They make head in the square that is outside Sainte Sarah's Church. Guilbert Livron is there. He calls on them to storm the west gate, which, as he says, is but weakly held, and so on to the castle walls. He would rescue his bride."

"Then you have called him the right name, for it is a thing that he could not do. I will stop that if I can."

M. Sault, saying nothing of his own grief, got his cloak, and belted on a sword that he had not used, it might be, for twenty years, but that he sometimes wore in a formal way. He said no more as they walked, letting the maire talk as he would.

The maire hurried him on so that he grew short of wind, and he had the sense to see that the sword was a vain toy, but his heart did not change in the purpose that tied it on. Should good men come to their deaths for Count Gismond's greed, and the Count go free of such dole? Were they naught, of a truth, because they were common blood? He summed the men that the town held; he counted his wealth, which was far more than even Michael had known. He thought he would bring it to a different end. Let those who start such strife be the last to pay. Yet he would not that Guilbert should waste the strength of the town in a foolish bout, as it seemed that he was likely to do.

In the summer dusk, the square was crowded with men. There were some who had fought that day, and there were more who had guarded the walls where they had not been attacked.

As they talked, each man became bold with the courage which a crowd gives when it is all of one mind. When the maire had said that they were men who had naught to lose, he went beyond truth. There were many such, for they were men young enough to have vigour of arm, and the mood that desires war, and wealth will ever lie in the hands of those of a riper age; but there were many of those of substance in the town who were there, or who wished them well. For the tax which was being levied to pay the ransom on the next day was a shoe that pinched hard.

There were some murmurs against the maire as they pushed their way through the crowd, but M. Sault heard no jeer at himself, for he was well liked, and when it was seen that he had buckled on his sword, he was cheered as one who came in the right mood.

They found Guilbert with a group of those who had been leaders of the town levies, and who were of like mind to himself, standing round the door of a scrivener's house that was near the church. In the scrivener's office there was enrolling of such men as had had training in arms, of which there were many in the town, as throughout Europe in all parts since the wars ceased.

They would take none but such for the regiment that they now formed, and those who were chosen were straitly sworn, with a pledge to them that, if there should be ransom or spoil won, it should be divided in a fixed way.

The maire was wroth, seeing how far they went without warrant from him, and asked them by what power they proceeded thus. He got a rough answer to that. There was one who told him to get hence while he had a whole skin; and another said they would hear nothing from those who had sold the town.

But the maire did not fear them as much as he feared the thought of Count Gismond's rope, and he stood his ground, though he grew pale at those words. He might have been handled ill, but M. Sault interposed: "Would you brawl, not knowing that which we come to say?"

And when they quietened somewhat at that, for M. Sault was a man feared and of good repute, he added: "You are hundreds to two, and you may do what you will for this night, but I would have you see this. If you can show us that you do well, and you have our word, you will run no jeopard of life more than must ever be in such strife; but if you go in a lawless way, and you fail—as you may be likely to do—then you will all hang at the last, being without the law, and Count Gismond's gallows may creak to a full crop."

Had the provost been there, he might have shown that M. Sault talked no more than a layman's law, for rebellion of vassal or serf is justified by success, and by nothing else that the law knows, and the whole town would be in no better case than a private few, should it fail to make terms in the end; but his words brought a pause, in which one said: "Tell us why you come, in a short way, for the time goes," and another: "You must accept our purpose or go, for, if we stand bickering here, it will raise a doubt among those who are now in a good heart."

Then a third, who owed M. Sault money which he could not pay till the next month, said: "Let us go to an inner room, and the scrivener's work will not pause while we accord, as it is likely we may."

They went in at that, the maire following those of better wits than his own. When they were seated within, M. Sault began at once: "Tell us that which you think to do, for the town must pay if you fail, as I suppose you can see."

The maire, who would have been better pleased that his protest should have been more widely heard, broke in with: "You would attack the castle in time of truce. It is treachery for which there can be no mercy asked. I will have it known to all that I have no portion therein."

"As to that," M. Sault interposed, "it was by such treachery that the town was brought to where it now is."

"Then," Guilbert asked, "you are come to be of our part?"

"I meant less than that. I would hear your plans."

"We go to take the west gate in an hour's time, when the light has failed. It is held by no more than a score of men. We go on from that to the castle walls, which are no better held, for they were few before, and are now a score less by those who were left at the gate."

"Then you go to your deaths, and would wreck the town. I will have no part in that which is a poor plan."

"Will you tell us why?"

M. Sault was glad to do that. He was one of many who think they would have made a name had they commanded in war.

"You may take the gate," he said, "I will allow that. But what use will it be, if the northern gate be still held? You may go up the castle road when you have taken the gate, but its walls are high, and if you would camp there or seek return to the town, you will find that Captain Redwood will have cut you off. He will but march his men so that they close the foot of the castle road, and you will be like a severed stem, for your roots must be in the town from which your supplies should come. Will he care who may hold the west gate, when he has us divided thus?"

"I see not," one of the more prudent of Guilbert's companions replied, "that it need come to that end. We might have force to spare that would hold them back at the place where the roads meet. But will you tell us a better plan?"

"That," M. Sault replied, "is very easy to do. You must attack Captain Redwood's camp in the night with all the force that you have. If you scatter them, you have won all. For you can approach to those of his men who are holding the northern gate, and beset them without and within. It is they who will then be sieged, and must make terms, for they will lack water and food.

"You can then take the western gate, being weakly held as you say, and advance to the castle without dread of a raided rear."

"It has a good sound," said another, "but still it cannot be done. For there is no way by which to surprise the camp while the gates are closed both to west and north. We could go out by the south alone, and should be on the wrong side of the stream when we have crossed the bridge there. And if we should wade the stream, as I allow that we might, it being as low as it is now, yet we must pass close before the western gate, for there is no other way. There would be alarm sounded at once. We should never surprise the camp, but should be attacked on all sides by those who are better trained to fight in the open field. And if we were beaten there, we should have nowhere to flee. We should but go to our deaths by that plan."

There was a murmur of assent, and all eyes were turned upon M. Sault as upon one whose error was laid bare. But he was unperturbed, and instant in his reply.

"That you should think that is a good proof that I am about to show you a sound plan, for if they think at the camp that they are safe from our attack, there will be the better chance of surprise. And, indeed, it is a thing which they are little likely to guess. They will say, 'If the town stir in the night, it is its own gates against which it will fret its strength.' If there were no way but the southern gate, I should say with you that it would be a poor plan. But I would go by ladders or ropes down the river wall, where there is space to pass, now that the water is low, and I would creep up by the Rhône bank, keeping far from the northern gate, so that we may fall on the camp from a side where they will have little watch, and with no warning at all."

There was a thoughtful silence for a moment as M. Sault showed his plan thus. Then Guilbert said: "I do not say it would fail, but to go down the wall will take long with a few ladders or ropes, we being the hundreds we are. I think not that such a plan will be liked so well as that we go straight for a gate that is weakly held."

"But," M. Sault answered, with the patience that he had learnt in the long bargaining of the mart, "you do not plan only to capture a gate that is weakly held. You have a castle to storm beyond that. Do you tell me that your men will storm a wall that is thirty feet, it being lined with their active foes, but will not go down one that is half the depth, or perhaps less, where they will meet nothing worse than a place of stones, or perhaps mud?"

There was no answer to that. M. Sault's plan had the votes of all, unless it were Guilbert, who said no more, seeing that he had no support.

The maire also was silent, for he had come to a better hope that the town might throw off its foes. If it should do this, he would not have it remembered too well that he had been of a poor heart, and if it should go ill, he could call the witness of all that he had spoken to hold them back, which would be hard to deny.

## CHAPTER THIRTY-TWO

THERE was one who had been in Konrad's band since they were both young, and from when, at first, it had been no more than a score of men. He was without folly or vice, and of good courage and wit, one to whom Konrad at times would give missions of trust, yet he remained a man-at-arms still, having no rank, and no more than the lowest pay.

Yet he was not poor, being well content, which was why he got no more than he did.

His name was Iago, and nothing more. That had been given him by a Spanish mother, who had borne him at a camp's tail. His father had been a Pole. He was called Scarthroat, or sometimes Cutthroat, more often than his own name, for a reason that was easy to see. For once, when he was young, he had been in a pot-house brawl, and had been flung by a larger man on to the place where there should have been a fire; but it had died down.

He fell with his throat over the iron bar of the grate and his face was not more than singed, the fire having fallen so low. But the bar had been hot, and before his comrades had pulled him clear, he had so deep a burn across the front of his neck that the scar showed broad and brown, as though he had had his throat cut from side to side, as there were many who thought.

Apart from that, he had taken no wound in all the years that he had followed the trade of war. He had had neither the pox nor the plague, nor had he grown stiff in his joints, as most would at a younger age, so that they must say farewell to their fighting days, and be content to sit by the fire, till they must go to a colder place.

He was a man who talked little, liking to be alone with his thoughts. He would lie awake in the night, so that his comrades would say that he never slept. He said, if he were asked, that he watched the stars, which was the one thing, as he thought, that a man might do forever and not tire.

So he lay awake on this night, in a tent where two others slept, while the twilight went down the sky, and the stars came, and after them a low moon in the east, over the high hills of Provence.

He did not welcome the moon, which he did not like. It intruded, like a thing of earth, to dim the majesty of remoter stars, of which he knew most that his eyes were able to see, and their movements across the sky, though he knew little of the names which have been given to then in the language of men.

As he lay awake thus, from beyond the further side of the camp, where the river-outposts should have been alert, there came the scream of a dying man, which was followed by other cries, and a brief clanging of steel, and then a rush and shouting of men.

Louder than he who died, a trumpet screamed from the direction of Captain Redwood's tent.

Iago's comrades scrambled from where they lay. They caught up their swords, and drew them out, casting the scabbards aside. Half awake, they blundered out of the tent.

Perhaps because he had been awake from the first he was the slower to rise. He had lived through more than one night-attack before this, and he knew them to be fights in which the wrong men would be likely to die.

He was not one who would fail to give the service for which he was paid, but he would keep his wits cool, or he would not have come through those years with no scar but that which his throat showed. He moved to the dark rear of the tent, and lay still, thinking what he could best do. The camp was a turmoil now, and a clashing of swords. He thought: "If Raoul were here…." He had a great faith in Raoul. But how should Raoul know?

From where he watched, it seemed that the condottieri were scattered by the sudden rush of an attack against which they had no time to set themselves in array. He could not know that at the further end of the camp, around their captain's tent, they made better defence. He saw one of those who had been asleep at his side slip away in a crouching style to the bushes which were beyond the camp.

Seeing this, he crept to a place between the tents where there had been a fire for the cooking of meat at an earlier hour. Into the hot ashes he thrust a torch. In another moment he had set fire to his own tent, and to two beyond. After that he could let the fire spread. He had sent word to Raoul.

Halt had been awake too, at that time. He lay tortured of soul. He saw no stars, but a girl's head, which he thought fairer than they.

How had she fared, since she had asked Count Gismond, as it had seemed, that he should take her away? It was torture not to know, nor to guess. It might be worse to know more. Well, his sword was hers, at her call. He had told her that. It might be all he could do. And then the noise in the night.

Being awake, he was swift to rise. So were others, who slept in their clothes, which he did not do. In no more than a loose cloak, he was at the door of his tent. His trumpeter answered his call: "Sound the rally," he called. "Bid them array here as they can. I will be forth in a moment's space." As he spoke, he could hear that the attack had reached the river side of the camp, and was storming its way through. He went back to arm in such haste as he might. He heard the shouts of his men, confident in tone, hailing each other: he heard their officers forming them in such rank as their haste and the night allowed. He came out to meet the rush of the townsmen of Faucon-bas, who had scattered all to this point, and thought to sweep the last resistance aside.

They may have been five to one at that place, they were drunk with success. Those who were in the front were the best men that the town held, those who had former practice in war. The condottieri gave ground to their rush for some yards, but their line held.

The two living lines of men met in a fury of sword-thrust and stabbing spears. There were more killed on that narrow front in the minutes that followed than might have been a regiment's loss in the formal battles which were the habit of war at that day. As they fought thus, the darkness changed to a growing light, which rose from behind the men of Faucon-bas, and shone on the dark faces and shining weapons of the condottieri.

Perhaps it was this revealing light, or because the struggle, in which neither would yield, was too fierce to endure, but a moment came when the weapons sank. They stood some yards apart, looking at each other, as the light allowed, whether in shadow or glare, and at the dead and dying who lay between. But there were two men who fought on.

Halt had taken his place in that line with a bitter thought that the camp was destroyed in the night, though he could not tell how or by whom. Konrad had brought that force to a ten-years' fame, and in his hands it would have been lost in a week. That it was his fault in some way it was easy to guess, though he could not tell how. Anyway, it was what would be said. There was nothing surer than that.

So he felt rather than thought, and it gave the strength to his arm of a bitter wrath. When he found that he was attacked by one whom he did not know, but who singled him out, he did not draw somewhat back into the line, but went forward the more, so that, when the lines fell apart, as though exhausted by a fury which led to no decision on either side, he was left facing this man.

Had he known who it was (and he could have told few of the townsmen by sight, having seen them but for these last days), he could not then have told, for the fire was in his face, and at the man's back; but he had no thoughts to give to such guess if he were wishful to live, for he was attacked with a fury that was not easy to meet.

He had thought himself skilled with the sword, having been taught at Oxford by one who had a great name at that time, and having been equal to most there; but he had little practice in such fighting as this, which was no play, but where an error must be paid with a life's price.

He knew a trick, if he could dare it now; but, if it failed, there might be a sword-point showing through his own back. He could be no better than dead. Could he prove it now, as he had done before with the buttoned foils?

Those who watched in the light of the burning tents forgot themselves and their strife of a moment since. The condottieri saw that their captain fought that he might be worthy of that which had come to him in so light a way. If he failed, it would be the right end. If he won, he would have confirmed himself in the place he held.

They did not think he would win, for he had the light on his face, which made the odds heavy on the townsman's side. But they watched silently, giving no aid.

The men of Faucon-bas might be content to stand still with a good hope. If Captain Redwood went down, it would surely end this stubborn struggle which had come when they thought that they had put the whole camp to flight.

The swords met, and Halt felt that his own was beaten aside. A blade flashed at his breast. Those who stood behind saw its point come out at his back, much as he had feared it would be. There was a cry of triumph from Faucon-bas, and a murmur from the condottieri, seeing their captain slain.

The next moment, Halt's sword drove through the heart of the man who was thought to have pierced his own. He had no more than a grazed rib, having taken the point between arm and side, with a sudden bending away as the thrust came. It was a trick he had practised a hundred times, but not one which he had played before when the price of failure had been so high.

Even then he did not know whom he had slain.

## CHAPTER THIRTY-THREE

IT was late when Raoul slept, and then it was but for an hour. When he rose he looked down from the parapet of the archway that spanned the gate, upon a street that the moonlight showed to be quiet and empty of men. He looked right and left upon the silence of the deserted wall. He might have thought that he would be left in peace for that night, and he could trust the men that he had stationed to watch, that they would not sleep at their posts. But he heard, as he had done at the earlier hour, a distant murmur, a hum from the town which he did not like. At times it was so faint that he thought he deceived himself with his own fears, and afterwards he would be certain again.

Every hour he had ordered that there should be trumpet sounded in signal that all was well, which might not be heard at the camp, there being a light wind from the north, but Sir Lambel would hear it at the western gate, and would give answer thereto. But were either of them attacked, they would give warning with a more urgent strain.

He knew therefore that all was well with Sir Lambel as well as him, and he was too practised in the trade of war to be over-anxious as to what its chances would bring; yet he felt that he would be glad when the night were gone.

As the moon climbed from the east, it seemed that the murmur from the town became less, though it did not die. But there was a sound that the north wind brought, faint enough, being from three miles away, but of a kind that Raoul had heard often before when there was fighting around, which he had been too distant to share.

He stood listening on the height of the wall, and he thought: "There is trouble in the camp, for where else should it be on that side?" and then: "But who should attack the camp? I grow old, and dote."

And then, clear enough, though the wind gave it no help, there came the warning trumpet that told that there was assault of the western gate.

Raoul looked down on a street that was as quiet as before; but there came a shaft out of the night—it might be from the window of one of the houses near—that struck one of the crossbowmen in the groin, giving a wound of the kind which is not overmuch at the first, but from which death is sure.

For some minutes after that, Raoul was so engaged in arranging his own defence that he had neither eyes nor ears for aught lying beyond. When he looked northward again, there was a light in the sky, which he well knew how to read. He said to himself: "The camp burns."

Should he march to its aid, leaving the gate? It was against the orders he had, and might bring to a full disaster that which would be otherwise less. Should he send Sir Lambel help? That was more within the scope of the part that was his, and the trumpet-call from that gate was now urgent in its demand. He was not attacked himself as yet, beyond a scatter of shafts to which his own bowmen replied.

That the gates were so attacked, made it nearly sure that the town had struck at the camp too, though he was puzzled as to how that had been done. Yet he saw that it might be no help to march to its support, if he should abandon the gate and let the townsmen out by that way.

Also, his orders stood, even though he might think of Captain Redwood as less experienced than himself, and less equal to such command, as he surely was.

Losing less time in thought than is needed to word his doubt, he sent above a score of his men in haste to Sir Lambel's aid; he ordered that fire be set to the houses that were nearest the gate; and he sent off one who was light of weight and could ride well, on the best horse that he had, to learn how things might fare at the camp, and to ask what Captain Redwood would have him do.

The man rode as hard as he might, facing a blaze that made his way easy to see; but the same blaze made a blackness to those who looked into the night, so that he was no more than a sound of the coming of hooves that the darkness hid.

He saw a man who ran toward him, and turned aside at that sound. He was a man that he knew. "Ralph," he called, turning his horse in pursuit, "what has chanced"

The man stopped at his voice. "Is that Édouard?" he asked, and then: "We were rushed in the night from the river-bank. The posts must have slept. There are many slain."

"Do none stand?"

"There are some who yet fight round the Captain's tent. I run to Captain Raoul to bear news."

"Then you may go back. It is his message I bear."

Édouard did not stay to see what the man did, whom he thought had run less to warn Raoul than to save his own skin. He rode on, as the fire led, and as he rode he heard a whinny out of the night, and his horse neighed in reply.

He who had set fire to the tents had done one thing that he had not meant. He had stirred panic among the horses that were pastured loosely during the day, but at night were tethered in rows at the outside of the camp, but within the circle of posts that were set to watch. The wind being from the north, and they at the northwest side, they were in no danger at all. But they felt the heat, they breathed smoke; once there came a scatter of sparks.

They strained at the tether-pegs, leaping upward to break them free: they lashed out on all sides, they screamed loud in their fear.

For the most part, they were soon free, with broken ropes and a trailing of loosened pegs.

In a blind panic of fear, they charged through the camp, breaking the townsmen's ranks and doing their masters a service they had not meant. They came to the river-side, into which more than one plunged, so that it must swim or drown, and bunching there, they turned and rushed through the camp again at its southern end, doing more harm than before, and disappeared in the night.

The condottieri who had not been scattered or slain were now drawn in a ring, with their leader's tent in their midst. They were surrounded by those who were not quick to attack again, nor willing to let them go. There were calls on them to yield, to which Halt would have no reply made. He did not only think he could hold his ground, he thought he could break through, and it was his purpose to join Raoul, or to fight his way to the castle walls, if he should find that the town gates had been lost.

But there was the treasure and scrolls which his tent held, which he was not willing to lose. Some of his men had seized a baggage-cart at their lives' risk, and had drawn it within the ring. They had no horses, but it must be pulled by men at the shafts, and who would turn the spokes of the wheels.

The fire did not reach the southern part of the camp, there being a space between the tents which it had not crossed.

This was how the strife stood, when Édouard rode toward the camp, and saw that, if he were to reach Captain Redwood's side, he would have to ride through those who would do him hurt if they could.

He did not doubt that he should attempt this, being of a good heart, though he was not large. He drew out his sword, and spoke to his horse in the right way.

As he did this, he heard the dull thunder of many hooves that were coming behind. He did not know all that had chanced, but he guessed enough.

The men of Faucon-bas turned their eyes from the line of spears that they were not too anxious to feel, to the sound of horses that came again. Out of the darkness Édouard rode. He rose in his stirrups, shouting his captain's name, "Raoul! Raoul!" with all the voice he had. The men of Faucon-bas may have thought that they were charged by a regiment of men. They broke right and left, and Édouard rode through, using his sword once. As he brought his horse round beside the edge of the line of spears, those that followed wheeled alike, and stood for something less than a minute's space in front of them to whom they belonged. Then they broke away in another flurry of flight. They had not come so close to the fire, had they not been led by a ridden horse.

But, as they stood, there had been snatching at rope and mane, and calling by name when a man saw a horse that he knew well, and there were a dozen held, so that there would be means of drawing the cart, with such tackle as could be found, and there was a horse for Halt, for his own destrier had been seized, having been in the front of the rush.

Édouard gave the message he brought. Halt would have written reply, remembering that he had heard Konrad say that many fights had been lost through trusting orders to word of mouth over a wide field, but he saw that time was short, if Édouard would ride back before they should be surrounded again. He remembered also that Raoul could not read.

"Tell your captain," he said, "that we have lost much, but that we can fight through to the town or the castle road. Tell him, if the western gate be still held, he can withdraw from the one he holds, for one gate is enough to keep. He should join me at the west gate; or at the foot of the castle road, if he cannot do better than that."

Then he paused in a doubt. He had better leave all to Raoul, who might judge better than he. He added, "No, tell him less. Tell him I trust his skill. I would have him know what I am aiming to do: to save the west gate if I may, and to have the castle road at my rear, so that we be not more broken apart. Knowing this, he must do the best that he can."

Édouard saluted without wasting of words. He turned his horse, lying low on his neck, with his sword ready to thrust. He did not rise in his stirrups now, nor bluster nor shout, for that ruse was done. He was content that he was a small man. So he came back in a short time to a din of strife that raged at the northern gate, and to tell his tale to Raoul.

## CHAPTER THIRTY-FOUR

THE men of Faucon-bas had not been quick to attack at the northern gate, for that had not been M. Sault's plan. Raoul might have held his post through the night, being vexed with shafts, but no more than that. His men could have lain close, and been nigh to a full count at the dawn. But that dawn would have found him beset both from within and without. He would have had the choice either to fight his way out with a heavy loss, if he could do so at all, or to yield on the best terms he could make.

But Raoul was too old in war to lie quiet while the trap closed, even had his thoughts gone no further than the men that were round him there, and the post he held. When he gave command that fire should be set to the houses at the street's end, he forced a flame of strife also, in which some of the best fruit would be caused to fall from M. Sault's bough.

Faucon-bas could not let its town burn. It came at a run. Men who had been moving to support the attack at the western gate, and many more who would have been down the ladders that had been placed at the river-wall, to join those who had rushed the camp (for they thought, as they saw the fire of the tents, that the strife was done, and that there would be plunder to share), must turn their feet in another way. Raoul did more for Sir Lambel, and perhaps for his comrades at the camp also, when he ordered those fires to be lit, than if he had marched to their aid with every man that he had, leaving the gate for their foes to follow through at their will.

Men who would fight the fire found that their advance was stayed by the barricade which Raoul had raised in the street. They found that, if they exposed themselves, they were marks for the bowmen who were on the top of the gate, or who shot through the slits in the gateway towers. If they were to subdue those fires, it was needful that Raoul's men should be so attacked that they would have no leisure for them. Raoul found that assault came from the street, it came along the wall, both to right and left, it came in a rain of bolts from the windows of such houses as stood, and which were near enough to harass him thus. He saw that if he were beset from the outside he would be besieged indeed, and he could suppose that he would not be long free on that side; but he was resolved to hold his ground till he should have orders from Captain Redwood, and know more of what the position was.

So it was when Édouard rode back through the night, to come to another place that had more light than the moon gave. As he drew near and saw the townsmen swarming upon the wall, he rode the last fifty yards at his utmost pace, and reined his horse closely beside the gate till it should open to let him in, for he feared that a shaft from the wall might silence that which he came to tell. But, in fact, he was not noticed at all till it was too late to do him a hurt, except by him whom Raoul had told to watch his return, at whose call the gate-bars were pulled cut with speed, and its bolts drawn from the ground, so that he could ride in.

He told his tale to Raoul, who said: "Is your horse spent? Can you ride again?"

Édouard may have thought he had done enough for that night, but he answered, "No, it will serve. Give me wine and a piece of bread. Where am I to go now?"

"You will ride," Raoul said, "round the wall, to the western gate. If it stand, you will tell Sir Lambel to show a stout front, for there is strong help on the way. If it have fallen, you will come back if you can, so that I may know what I have to front. You may not have to come far, for I shall follow as soon as I can draw clear."

Édouard rode out again, being vexed by missiles at first, though they fell where they did no harm, and that trouble was soon past, for there were not men on the wall for its whole length, there being no gain in guarding a wall when its gates are gone. Édouard rode as hard as he could beneath a wall that was quiet and bare, though there was noise enough in the night.

He soon came to a place where he drew rein, for though he was not lacking in courage, as he had shown in the last hour, he had no contempt for his own life. He saw that the western gate was beleaguered behind and before. The men of Faucon-bas had descended the wall that they might prevent the flight of Sir Lambel's men. They besieged him on all sides. Édouard walked his horse as near as he safely might, that he should see what he could. It was clear that Sir Lambel had not yielded as yet. It was a simple guess that he soon must if he were not helped from without. Édouard saw that his horse must gallop again.

## CHAPTER THIRTY-FIVE

To him that hath shall be given, and from him that hath not shall be taken away. It is a law that all nature knows. To the victor the spoils, and the laurel crown. Yet there may be less of valour, as there is less call for skill, in those who gain, than in those who must withdraw in a beaten way. It has been said that a leader who has not ruled a retreat has not shown that he is greater than most, though he may win a battle for every week in the year.

Raoul resolved that the gate must be given up, and it was well for his men that he was one who knew the dangers it meant, and who could plan in a cool mind. He knew that if he should begin to withdraw in a confused way, with the townsmen upon his heels, there would be few of those he led who would win free, their numbers being what they were.

He gave orders first, so that each man knew what was to be, and his own part. He loaded wagons, which were for the lifting of wounded men, for he would leave none behind, nor any stores. When they were ready to leave the gate, he withdrew all the bowmen he had, whether from town, or wall, or barricade, and sent them out first through the gate. A short bowshot away, they took the best cover they could, and wound their crossbows ready to let loose a flight of bolts against such as should line the walls when their comrades withdrew.

After that, the wagons came out with a small guard, and were got clear away into the cloak of the night. They could not do this so that its meaning were not clear. There rose a great shout, and the boldest of their foes made a rush for the barricade. Raoul was ready for that. He had not weakened its bristle of spears. The men of Faucon-bas being bolder than before, they gained nothing thereby. They were the worse hurt. When this bustle was stilled, the men who had held that place were withdrawn. Orderly, stern and slow, with a menace of backward spears, the last ranks of the condottieri drew back through the gateway arch.

As they did this, and the men of Faucon-bas ran forward to recapture the gate, there rose a great flame under the arch. Wood and oil-soaked straw had been heaped within it on either side, and Raoul himself, who would be the last to leave, put the torch to these.

When he had lit the one side, he must move quickly to the other, for the flame leapt sudden and high to the archway roof; and having lit the second he was glad to run clear, being no more than scorched by the heat.

Having so hindered pursuit, he formed his men about two bowshots from the wall, for he would not march by the road that went under that, though it would have been the nearest to take. He moved by vineyard and lane, making the best speed that he could, for he would succour Sir Lambel if there were yet time, and he remembered the spearmen whom he had sent already for his support, and whom it was his part to bring free.

Under shadow of night, and being as yet unpursued, he divided his force, giving to Vitelli the charge of the wagons, and about a third of those who remained with him, and fit for the changing of blows, telling him to make straightway to the foot of the castle road, and to strengthen himself at that point, choosing a narrow place, and digging a trench in his front, and to hold his ground there as long as he might against whatever assault, so that when he himself should come, or those from the camp, they should not find that the way to the castle would be closed against them.

He then marched as fast as he might toward the western gate, and attacked those who were upon its outer side with a front which they would not face, so that they scattered to left and right, they being an armed rabble rather than a disciplined force, and Sir Lambel himself (he having two wounds, but not such that he could not walk), and about twenty beside who still lived, and who had shut themselves in the gate-house tower, he brought off, as he had intended to do.

After that, he fell back to join Vitelli, who held the castle road by this time with a line of spears, before which a trench grew, and having seen that this point was secure, and leaving such as were wounded or spent, beside a sufficient guard for that narrow place (for Vitelli had halted upon the road where the one side fell sharply to the gorge of the stream, and there was high and broken ground on his other hand, such as the bowmen could hold with ease), he set forward once more to make junction with Captain Redwood's force, which could be seen making slow advance about half a mile away.

It came on with a great rabble of townsmen upon rear and flanks, making rushes at times, when there would be levelling of lances, and swinging of axe and sword; but in a few moments they would draw backward, finding that they would but die on a line that they could not break, and the close-formed rank of the condottieri would move slowly forward again.

The fact was that the men of Faucon-bas were not eager to die. There were many who would have done well enough in the rear line of such a rush, but few would push hard to be first; and they were not so ordered or ranked that each should have a place that he must not leave, which brought their numbers to naught. And, beside that, they were weary men, having been on foot through the night, after they had spent the day on the town wall.

Had they fought on that wall, with their homes behind, they would have done stoutly enough, but here they were so placed that they might think more of themselves, as most men would be likely to do. When they saw Raoul's men advance upon them, they gave ground the more, and when the two forces joined they were glad to leave the pursuit, and to make way to their own homes, where they could get food and a time of rest, and boast to their wives of the valour by which they had routed both condottieri and castle knights.

## CHAPTER THIRTY-SIX

THE dawn had lightened the eastern sky as the condottieri came to a halt at the foot of the castle road. They had struggled free of their foes, and had leisure now for the counting of wounds, and those that their ranks had lost.

Halt stood with Raoul and Vitelli, having got down from his horse. Sir Lambel sat on a stone, being somewhat faint from the blood he had left behind. They changed the news of the night. Halt looked on two hundred men who had been three, and thought of himself as one who had brought them down. But his mood changed somewhat as he saw that he was not lessened thereby in the judgment of those he led.

It was certain that there had been a bad watch on the river side of the camp; and, but for that, the history of the night might have been different from what it was. But the men who had slept were not there, and were likely dead. Beyond that, it was the chance of war. As things had been, there was a feeling that all had done well, and relief that they had come through. There was heavy loss in the equipment of the camp, beside the horses, which might be hard to find. But the treasure and parchments which were in Konrad's chests had been brought safely away, and were worth much more than all beside that the camp had held.

Raoul had seen the contents of the cart that had been in the centre of the close-formed rank—and his thought was that they had a leader to trust. He had not hoped that those who had fought their way through from the raided camp would have brought away more than their own lives. He knew also—for he had seen it often before—that the loss of men would be much less than at first appeared. They would wander in from a dozen ways, showing wounds, or boasting of great things they had done, or saying no more than that they had been lost in the night.

Now they had cast themselves on the ground, drawing food from pouch or sack which they would share with those who had less, and some were making fire that they might cook, or were already asleep on the barer ground, for the grass was heavy with summer dew.

Halt saw that they could not camp thus for more than a short time, having lost their tents and their gear, and being the number they were. He put from him his own longing for rest, and resolved to march on to the castle at once, taking with him all those whose wounds would stiffen with more delay, as well as those who were sorely hurt, and needing more of comfort and aid than could be given as they then were.

Loading such carts and horses as they yet had, and giving his own horse to the use of one who was less fit than himself, he set out again, taking Raoul with him, and leaving Vitelli with thirty of the men who were least worn—being of those who had defended the northern gate—with orders to hold the road unless they should be attacked in too great a force, which was not likely on that day. Raoul was very sure about that.

"There are few in the town," he said, "being fit for the bearing of arms, who have not been afoot now for a day and night. There will be boasting, and licking of wounds, and much eaten and drunk; but it will be sleep for the most time from now to the next dawn, and they will be stiff and slow when they waken then.

"They must man the walls, and keep watch; but there will be much grumbling, and many yawns, even for that. Had we two hundred men that were fresh and fit, we could have those gates again at the next dawn, or before."

So he said, having lived through the day after such a strife many times before. Yet he warned Vitelli to leave nothing to chance, and to throw his scouts widely out over the rough ground to his left, that his flank should not be turned, or himself surprised from that side.

So it came that Sir Lanval, riding out with the men-at-arms to the bridge, saw a troop approach with no pennon spread but that of the grey wolf which Halt still caused to be carried, showing no device of his own, as most men would have been eager to do. There was no honour to be gained for Sir Lanval here, either with lance or sword, and his bruised side would have somewhat longer to heal before he would be busy with such a bout as would need the best strength that he had. He had said truly that he rode out rather to see than to do. He heard the tale of the night, both from Halt and Raoul, as they told it in simple words, as men not proud of a poor thing. Seeing how it had been, as he had a mind that was able to do, he saw also why the condottieri had become so great a power on the Italian plains, and in the German wars of that time.

As to that man who brought the first tidings of loss, and who had come up the road but a few moments before it was reached by Raoul's men, he made the best tale that he could, and his wounds saved him from the whipping he should have had. But the fact was that that tale had been mostly guessing and lies, for he had slipped off from Sir Lambel's troop to the farther side of the town, to the house of a woman he knew. And when he had been roused in the night with talk of the outbreak of further strife, and he knew he would be a doomed man if Count Gismond should know how he had deserted his post, he had made furtive way back through the town, and seeing how Sir Lambel was beset upon every side, and driven into the gatehouse tower, he had resolved that his chance was to take the news of his loss. For that he had leapt the wall, being the only way of descent that was open to him, and had had a fall which had given him the wounds that he bore.

# CHAPTER THIRTY-SEVEN

THE sun rose over the Provençal hills. It shone down on the swift-moving river, now shallow in its narrower flow. It shone on meadow and copse, and a blackened camp through which the plunderers ranged, stripping the last shred of clothing from the indifferent bodies of the slain, and searching the ashes of the tents for such objects as the fire could not entirely destroy.

It shone through the high window of the garret where Michael Sault had died.

M. Sault stood by the bed. He looked on the death of a score of ambitious dreams, which he had taught Michael to share. He had a younger son who was yet alive, and who was well enough; but it was Michael on whom he had relied, and more largely with every year, as his physical energy lessened, to carry on and extend the far-reaching traffic of which he had laid the foundations in his vigorous youth, and which had now grown even beyond the guessing of his fellow-merchants in the town. What it had been was to have been little beside the future which he designed; and his hopes lay ruined now on the bed in the garret which had always been Michael's, and which he would never change for a better room.

Had his son made a profession of arms, it would have been no worse than a likely chance, which he should not grudge; but he had not thought that he might die in this way. He had been of a quiet, confident strength; quarrelling with none, liked by most, and respected by all. It was hard to think he was dead.

Yet M. Sault was not wholly miserable, though he would not have believed it had an archangel sworn. He had lost his son, but he knew that he had avenged his death. Guilbert might have stirred the town till it had stormed the western gate, though that had not proved so easy to do as it had been thought. Count Gismond's men, being cornered, had fought hard. But with Guilbert success would have ended there. That was plain from the foolish plan he had disclosed. But M. Sault had pointed the way that would spread confusion among their foes. The camp was scattered and burnt. The gates were taken again. The remnant of the condottieri (so it had been represented to him) were in flight to the protection of the castle walls. Perhaps tomorrow he would think of another plan, and the castle also would fall. And, but for him, the town would have been collecting its precious coin, even at this hour, to weigh it over the foemen's scales. Surely Michael had not died unavenged.

As the hours passed, the town boasted and drowsed, as Raoul had foretold that it would; but M. Sault was active with word and pen. He saw that, though the moment was theirs, it was a moment that would not last. There was Count Raymont to fear. There might be other nobles who would come to Count Gismond's aid when they should hear that he was defied by his vassal town. It was at least more likely than that other towns would concern themselves with the fortunes of Faucon-bas.

There was a single chance of success—to capture the castle, or reduce it to such straits that it would make terms of peace before aid could arrive. Seeing this, he sent out posts to Avignon, to Nîmes, and Arles, and to such other towns as were within a day's ride, or somewhat beyond, letting it be known that there was good pay to be had at Faucon-bas by men who were trained in arms, and a castle's plunder in view. He told the maire that there need be no seeking for gold to meet the charges that would arise. They could talk of that on a later day, when the town's freedom was won.

At noon there was order given that the gates both to north and south should be set wide that peaceful traffic might enter again, and those who journeyed might traverse the town

Only the western gate was kept guarded and barred.

As the afternoon came, there was an alarm that closed the northern gate in a panic haste, as we shall see in its place; but that was soon past, and it was opened again.

The Council met in the afternoon, not to discuss means of defence, as it had done in the earlier days, nor to haggle ransom with a captain-general who spoke in a foreign way, and was less easy to move than his aspect had led them to hope, but to decide the terms on which they would offer peace if Count Gismond had learnt enough to know that which would be best for himself.

They resolved that it would be foolish to ask too much, but equally so not to take that which their valour earned.

There were, first, the florins to be returned which had been paid on the last day. Madame Livron also, who should have been back in the town before noon, and whom it seemed that the castle held.

Beyond that, there must be compensation for the charges to which the town had been put. They had the sense to see that it would be useless to ask for gold, which, it was a sure guess, Count Gismond had not got. There must be revision of their charter, with removal of many obsolete clauses therein, such as that which had brought this strife.

Most of all, there must be a clear bargain in regard to the market tolls. As to that, M. Sault showed again that he had a better head than most whether for commerce or war. He proposed to substitute for these tolls the tribute of a yearly sum, which might be equal to, or even somewhat larger than that which they now admitted to be due. He foresaw that the town might grow, as might the stream of merchandise which must pass its gate, but the tribute would not grow in the same way. There was some bickering over this among men of smaller minds, though it seemed that M. Sault would be likely to have his way at the last. The maire, though he was glad he had said no more during the night, was still nervous for peace, his neck not being entirely at ease even now. He would make the terms of peace such as Count Gismond would not be too wroth to hear.

So the day passed in the town; in the castle there was less talk, and more toil. The luxurious, sensuous idle life that had drawled on so pleasantly through the summer days was changed in an hour, as it would often be in those days, to the urgent bustle of war.

It was true that that war had begun on an earlier day, but it had then been no more than a pleasant stir, which was outside and beneath themselves. It was a matter with which they had hired the condottieri to deal, and in which they would take a knightly sufficient part.

It had been sport rather than war, and yesterday it had come to a natural end, with the surrender of Yvonne, and the heavy ransom the town must pay. They might take the town or not, but they had not dreamed that the tide of battle would rise to beat on their own walls. Yet of that, today, they were less sure.

Count Gismond held council of war. Should they continue to hold the foot of the castle road, being three miles away, or should Vitelli be withdrawn from that point? There were reasons to urge on both sides. It was at least sure that they could not withdraw to the bridge, leaving the whole road free, without cutting themselves off from the reinforcements and supplies that must come down the road from the upper valley, which was Count Gismond's domain. Yet, if Vitelli were to defend the post he now held, it would be hard to provide that he should not be cut off by the sending of troops over the low and broken hills that flanked the road on its northern side.

Count Gismond did not like to have Vitelli withdrawn, for it seemed to him a confession that the town had beaten them back. It chafed his pride, which was sore with another bruise, but he did not show this, giving assent to the advice he heard, for he was of sound judgment enough when it governed his weaker moods.

So it was agreed that they should defend the road at a higher point, where there was an overhanging of crags, and it would be hard to assault except by a frontal rush with which their spears should be able to deal. But they need not make withdrawal till the night should come. The town would make no advance for that day, let it plan what it might. They were agreed about that.

"I doubt not," Sir Lanval said, "that in that you are right. They will rest today, having been awake through the night, and content enough that they have beaten us back, so that they can sleep without fear; and those of ours who fought through the dark hours are in no better case Yet we have horses here that are rested well, and men who had charge of the castle walls who have done nothing at all. I would ride out, by your leave with a score of these, or perhaps less, to show that we do not hold them in fear. There may be horses to seize, or scattered men to bring again to a head, or, at the least, there may be one with wounds that a ditch hides."

It was an offer which was not likely to be declined, coming from whom it did. Sir Lanval was a guest of the right kind for the events of this time.

He rode out that afternoon with a score of armoured men, mounted on the heavy horses their weight required, and making a show of pennoned lances and painted shields which made them to look more than they were to the eyes of those who had been born to look up rather than to ride in such guise. He made a wide circuit around the town, causing the northern gate to be closed in a great haste; he traversed the fields where the camp had been, chasing some who still wandered in search of plunder that might be hidden by ditch or tuft, and so beating them with flattened swords that they would have little spirit to learn more of the castle's ways. He showed mercy in that, for most knights would have ordered that they be ridden down, and give sport as they dodged and wriggled to miss the spears.

Besides that, he came back with a dozen horses that he had caught, and half that number of lurking men who had fled the camp in the night and had lain close in the copse. His riding did something also to awe the town, seeing the bold show that he made, and they knowing that they had neither weapons nor skill to face an armoured knight in the open field. But he said himself, as he often would, that he had sought rather to see than to do, which may have been largely truth.

He made it clear, at least, in a courteous way, that he had pleasured himself, and that Count Gismond owed him no thanks.

But after Sir Lanval's offer had been made and agreed, they had gone on to debate what might be feared from the town, and what should be done on their side to bring the war to a good end.

In wounded and slain, including those who were gone from the ranks, and whose fate could not be known, the condottieri had lost about a third of their force, and the castle little more than a dozen men. The losses of Faucon-bas in the storming of gate and wall, and in the night-fighting both within and without the town, were probably much more, and it might be thought that there was little on either side either for wail or boast about that.

But the difference lay in the spirit which the town had shown, for it was more assured of itself.

It had been known to both sides that it had the larger number of men, and that more wealth lay in its walls than that which the castle held; but it had not been shown that it had the valour to face those who were more practised in war, and who were better furnished and armed.

Faucon-haut stood high, and Faucon-bas lay at its feet. That was how it had always been, and there was meaning in that.

Now Faucon-bas rose in its pride, as a tide rises around a rock. Would it rise till the rock would be drowned from sight, or would it be flung back to its own depth?

To Count Gismond it was a thing not to debate. It was as though the world shook under his feet. He controlled a cold wrath that his dignity should not fail, as Sir Lanval talked with Raoul (whom Halt brought with him to that board), as though it were no more than a game of chess on which either side had a mating chance.

Raoul knew much of the warfare of towns, and of their weakness and strength, which he had learnt on Italian plains, and Sir Lanval was one who would ask of all, so that he should learn the most that he could.

Raoul could talk of the siege either of castle or town, and of how their walls could be held or stormed, but of what part he should take therein in this case he had less to say, for that was not to be decided by him. He only said that they had not force as they were to subdue the town now that it had learnt its strength, for though they should cross its walls, they were too few to control its extent. It appeared to him to be vain to risk life or limb that you might enter a town that you would be too weak to sack. So he said. But if Faucon-bas would spend its strength on the castle walls, which, as he thought, it would be unable to take, there might come a time....

Even that was a small hope, and he had reason enough when he said that it was no more than a stalemate as it stood, and that either side must seek allies if it would subdue its foes to its will.

"The town will get no allies," Count Gismond said, in an assured way. "Who is there will take its part?"

There was a murmur of assent at that word. From the nobles around it would have no hope of support. The claims of caste were too strong. There was no town that would give gold or blood for its aid, though it should be put to the sword to the last babe. What was it to them? It was Count Gismond's town, and his loss if he laid it flat.

"They may have no allies to call," Sir Lanval ventured to say, "yet they may find those who will fight for hire."

"They may do that," Raoul said.

"And so," added Sir Lanval, "I think they will."

The Count gloomed at that thought, and the more so that Sir Bertram, one of his household knights (a sagacious man and of good repute, though somewhat growing in girth as the years passed), spoke in the same way.

"There is one there," he said, "who hath his hand on the reins, and who will look clearly ahead. I would we knew who it is. It is not the maire." There was none could guess who it might be, but the thing was plain. It meant that they must look to see the next move as well planned as that which had lost them both camp and gates. There was no comfort in that.

Halt had been silent while the talk came to this point. He had had a letter from Bernardi on the last day, which he had had no leisure to read till an hour ago. He had found it to be in the Italian tongue, which he read with less ease than he should. Being in this case, he had asked Sir Lanval's aid to construe a sentence which was not clear to him. "They are troops," he said, "that I have in the Florentines' hire. He seems to write that he can bring them at any time that I will. Yet they are hired for a set time. I am stumbled as to the reason he gives."

Sir Lanval said: "This is what he would have you know. The Florentines have made new allies; for the time they stand sure. They will release your bond if you so wish. More than that, if you would have your men here, and it be handled with skill, they may pay something to let them go, rather than the full charge for the full time, their use being now done."

Halt said: "It is clear now. I must learn more of this tongue."

Sir Lanval was bold to ask: "Would you bring them into this broil?"

Halt was cautious in his reply: "It is matter for thought, and to hear what the Count may say."

Sir Lanval was about to speak, but checked himself, and became still. Halt had not asked his advice, and besides, there are things that a guest should be slow to say. Halt went to the council the Count had called debating this in his mind.

He debated it still as the talk went on, and the need for further men became plain, if the Count were to chastise the town to his will. He had no love for the Count, nor any quarrel against the town. It was easy to guess that the Count could not pay the charges of the army which Bernardi ruled. Yet he had a strong wish that he should not be foiled in his first war, let the charges be paid how they might.

"I have eight hundred lances," he said, "that are in Tuscany now. I could have them here by the new moon, if I should write for them with speed."

The Count's eyes brightened at that, but he was cautious in what he said. "They would be a great charge. I know not how we could repay you for that." He added, half to himself: "They would be sufficient to scourge the town. They could lay it flat."

There was one who said: "But Count Raymont may be here before then." He meant no more than to shorten the price by showing the Captain-General that they were not dependent on him, but the Count took it in the wrong way.

"We want him not here," he said; "it were better to finish first. At what price," he turned to Halt to ask, "would you take the town? I ask not the number of those you bring. I would pay for a thing done, be it by many or few."

"It would not be done by a few," Halt had the wit to reply. He knew that it was against the general policy of the condottieri to accept payment by results, as they could see that they would fight harder for such stakes, and it would lead to their own deaths. Beside, how could he tell what forces might be hired by Faucon-bas before Bernardi should arrive? Or suppose that this Count Raymont, of whom he knew nothing, but who seemed to be feared of all, should be first on the scene, and claim that he had won the game while Bernardi was on the way?

He would make no such bargain as that, and yet he might be glad to see the shine of Bernardi's spears, for he could not feel that his first bargain with Count Gismond was done, and if he were to remain at his side till a month was through, who could say what strait he might not be in by that time?

He saw again how hard were these bargains to make, that sold the strength and the lives of men, and how difficult they might be to construe. He felt that Konrad would have known how to handle the position, which he was unfit to do. If Bernardi should be told to come, on the chance that his men could be put to use, it would be at a great charge, and what should he do with them here if the need were past? Looked at thus, it was plain folly to let the Florentine contract go.

Yet, above all, he felt that he must bring this, his first war, to a fair end, that he might establish his own name and be justified to himself. He had no lack of gold. More than that, he had made much in his brief command. There was that which Count Gismond had paid. There was that which had come from the town. Even though the camp had been burned, with much scattering of horses and men, it was not all loss.

"I will have Bernardi here," he said, after a pause, which had given time for all to see how much hung on his words, "but I will agree naught. I must see how the strife sways until then. He shall come here at my charge, making the most haste that he may, and we will talk again when he is here."

"But," Count Gismond asked, his dignity being somewhat strained to appear unmoved by the doubt he felt, "you will continue your aid till then? For so I think you are pledged to do."

"Yes. I am pledged to that. I will give you the best help that I can."

It was a reply to content those who heard. The council broke up soon after that. Halt wrote to Bernardi with speed, sending the letter over the hills to avoid the town.

After that, while the Count went to his meat, Halt found a place where he could sleep, being so worn that he could do no more. Even Yvonne had no place in his thoughts. The Count had slept in his clothes for a short night, but he was better rested than he.

It was those clothes which had caused an itch in the Count's mind which would return at every pause of more urgent things. What had his squire thought? Had he noticed that he still wore the doublet and hose that had been his undergarments at the banquet of the night before? Must he not have thought it strange that he should have put them on again, they being unfit for the morning hours? Had he allowed the time that would have been needed to draw them on before letting the squire in? Would he wonder and guess? Would he talk? The thought was torment in Count Gismond's mind. He thought again that he would be a mock throughout France and beyond. He thought also of the evil time that they who have the pox must pass through, and wondered how it would feel. He thought of how they look in the after-days. He thought also of Yvonne, as he had seen her when he drew down the sheet. Why in the devil's name had he been interrupted then as he was? Well, there were days to come.

He had given orders that Yvonne should not leave the castle, the gates of which were now guarded well. He said that she might do the work of a spy for the town. Isabeau heard that, and was ill-content. Yet when Doette went to her, saying that Yvonne would have a place for herself, and where was it to be, she made a fair reply, and ordered that a chamber should be prepared that was near her own, and far from that of the Count, for she would have it clear that Yvonne was not meant to return there.

The knights had held a council of war, to which Isabeau would not have been asked, for what do women know of the ways of war? But before Halt wrote to Bernardi, she had written that which must be sent over the hills by another way, which was to be as potent as his, and more so than the talk they had had.

It was a letter that she would not have had her brother to see, nor to know that it had been writ. She had had it in mind from when she had heard the first talk that they had been thrown back by the town, and when she knew that Gismond would keep Yvonne, and after she had had some talk with her ladies which we must turn back to hear, she had written at once with a firm hand.

After that, she let what she had done go from her mind, which was busy with many things. For there were now nearly two hundred men, and some horses, which must be lodged within the girth of the castle walls, beside those who were always there, and they must be bedded and fed, and there was much that must be decided by her, for in time of peace she ruled as one who must know all, and it followed from that, that when there were new dispositions to make, they would refer all things to her.

## CHAPTER THIRTY-EIGHT

HAVING been roused at the dawn, it had still been at an early hour that Isabeau had ordered that food should be served in her own room for herself and the ladies who were companions to her, as was the way of the time.

It was then that she asked of Yvonne, and Bernice said: "She has had her night. What shall be done with her now?"

Isabeau had no doubt about that. "She has done her part. She must trudge back to the town."

"She will scarcely that, having a good horse of her own."

"Should we let a good horse go, being at war with the town? She should be content that she be not stripped of that gown."

"You are wasting words," Louise said, with a yawn which had more than its usual cause, her night having been shorter than her use was. "You are an hour too late once again. The Count has ordered that she be kept here."

"What," Isabeau asked in a sharp way, "do you know of that?"

"What I have said, and no more. Doette knows. Have you heard the tale that Madame Livron is widow now?"

"Will you be plain?"

"That is plain enough. Her husband was killed in the night. It is a tale of the chestnut-seller, Pierre, who was let through the lines."

Isabeau looked black for a time. Then she said: "I will hear more of this. You must bring him to me."

"That is vain to ask. He will have gone on by the hill road."

"Does the woman know? It should be kept from her till she is sent back."

"I cannot tell that. Doette knows more than I. It was from her that I heard." Doette entered as this was said. She gave more circumstance to the tale. Guilbert Livron, so it was said, had been killed by Captain Redwood himself, when he had led the night attack on the camp. Beyond that, she gave some details which can be left to themselves, for they were untrue, as such talk will most often be. It had been Pierre's tale. Doubtless he was gone now.

"Have you told her of this?"

"No, I was not sure enough of its truth. I would not vex her for naught."

"It must be kept from her, lest she be of a mind to stay here. Was she wroth, being held for a longer time?"

Doette was not quick to reply. She liked Yvonne, to whom she had tried to be kind. She had a sure instinct that she was liked in return. But Yvonne puzzled her now, in more ways than one. She did not wish to do her injustice or harm, but she answered in the only way that she could: "She did not show she was vexed. She does not show much of what she may feel. I do not think she was anxious to go, nor that she will be much grieved at his death. But, truly, I cannot say."

"She hath a mind," Louise said, "to stay where she is."

"Where," Bernice asked, "will she sit at the board tonight?"

"She is a smith's wife," Isabeau answered to that, "or his widow, as it would seem. She can sit on the bench with the kitchen sluts, if they will push close to make space enough. Or else she must find place on the floor. We shall have crowded hall for this night."

"The Count," Doette said, "has given orders for that, that she shall still sit at his side."

Louise looked at Isabeau without speech. Her eyes mocked: "You are too late once again." She said to Bernice: "You will get used to the place you now have."

Doette did not show that she saw how they scratched and spat, from which it was her manner to keep apart. She went on to ask: "There has been nothing said as to where Yvonne shall lodge for this night, if she be still here. The Count has said nothing of that. She asked me that some bower could be found, which may be as small as you will, so that she will have some place to herself. "

Isabeau said: "If she sit at the Count's side, she should lodge in these rooms. I will give her that which I keep for my own guests. Gismond will see that we honour those whom he thinks to be of his own kind."

She did this that Yvonne might be more in her own sight, and that she might have no access to the Count's room in the night. She had brought this event to where it now stood, and it was little pleasure to her. Yet she thought once again to throw dice with Fate, and hoped for a better end. So she wrote to Count Raymont a letter which none must see till it should come to his own hand.

## CHAPTER THIRTY-NINE

YVONNE sat that night at Count Gismond's side, with Halt on her other hand. There was much talk at the board that passed her by, as she was glad for it to do. She had thought at one time that she would say that she was unwell, which would have been less than a lie; but she had put the idea aside, seeing clearly that she must face the issues that snared her life, and that it would be useless to hide away. Beside, she was not of that mood. She had said two days ago that the way over the tiles was not for her. She was not of those who will lightly adventure forth, calling hardship and danger friends. She would be left to herself to walk in a quiet way. But if danger came, she would face it out as she best could. She would neither cringe nor fly. These things were of herself more than her will.

She took her place with a quiet ease, being still in the rich dress of the last day, for it was the only one that she had. Isabeau, looking across at her with a contempt which was partly fear, thought: "Does she count to sit there to her life's end, or so long as Gismond shall live? She may find that one of those times will be short enough, if not both."

There was so much talk of what had chanced in the night, and of what one and another had done and suffered or failed to do, and of what was to be looked for or done on the next day, that Yvonne was less regarded—she saying nothing at all—than had been at a quieter time. But men did not fail to think what it might mean that Count Gismond had placed her there at his side again, their last night having been passed as it must be supposed that it had, and that she sat there in a silence which showed no sign of disquiet, as though she were at peace in her own place, and it was being said on all sides that the smith, her husband, was dead.

As for the Count, he said little more to her than she to him. He was unsure of how much she knew of his approach to her at the dawn, it having been broken off, as it had, by the noise of the squire's voice, and of his hand on the door. Would she tell her uncle of that, if she knew? Did it depend on what she might say to him whether the curse should act? Would she hold—as he saw she might—that her promise to say nothing of how he had made the rushes serve for his bed was made void by that abortive approach? What were her feelings to him—or what might they become if he should deign so far as to let her sit at his side for a lengthened time?

He could not doubt that she would be grateful for that. It was different from being brought to him for a night in a casual way. Was she not one who might take the place of the wife who fled, with a more fitting sense of how great he was than Isabeau could be expected to show?

He looked at her in a speculation stirred by other impulses than the fierce lust which would wake when he remembered how she had lain asleep in his sight, and he had thought to rape her at that hour. He did not mean that she should go back to the town till she had yielded him such pleasure as a woman might, she not being of gentle blood But, beyond that, his thoughts went on to a question they could not solve. There was no doubt she was fair. But her reserve was a veil which he could not lift. What she might be in herself, beneath the fairness of flesh, he was in a greater doubt than Sir Lanval would have been at that time, he being more used and more able to judge of the natures both of women and men. Had he known that

Guilbert was dead, his thoughts might have gone further than they yet did, but, beside Yvonne, he may have been the only one in the hall, except Halt, who had not been reached by that tale.

For the moment, like most who were round that board, he was a tired man. He did not object that Isabeau had found room for Yvonne in the part of the castle which was held private to her and hers. He was content that she should be so lodged, let Isabeau's motives be what they might.

If Yvonne did not speak to the Count, she said no more to Halt on her other hand, and he was as silent to her. He too was a tired man. He had had sleep for an hour, and been awakened again, and felt more tired than before. He looked at Yvonne, and got no glance in return. He felt that the time when she had shown him her soul was no more than a distant dream. He looked at her, cold and serene at the Count's side, and did not understand her at all.

The next morning there came a pursuivant from the town, with a trumpet and flag of truce, for Faucon-bas had no arms of its own, and must show white if it would parley at all. But the pursuivant was one who knew his trade, and he spoke for the town boldly and well, and much better than the maire would have been able to do.

The outpost which Halt had left at the foot of the castle road had been withdrawn in the night, so that the flag came up almost to the bridge before it was stayed, and then there was message sent to the Count who would not ride down himself to change words with those who were flouting his power, neither would he let them ride up through the castle gates, lest they should see too much of the defences which he prepared. But he agreed that Captain Redwood should hear what they might have to say, and Sir Lanval rode at his side, as a friend might.

The pursuivant set out the wrongs of the town with some circumstance and at length, which might have been well prepared for the Count's ears; but Captain Redwood was not concerned with such talk, and when a pause came, he said with less courtesy than his habit was: "When you have done with this, will you say why you are here?"

"I am here to make demand that you deliver Madame Livron forthwith in such honour as you still may, together with the full tale of the florins which you took but yesterday at the sword's point; and on these two things being done with speed, we are prepared on our side to debate what may be fair ransom to be paid for the lives we have lost, and the harm you have done the town both by storm and fire."

"As to the first of these," Halt replied, "I know not that Madame Livron would be stayed if she were claimed by him who has the right to demand, but have you warrant to say that she is held here against her own will? For the rest, you are bold to ask a vain thing, which you cannot think you will get. If it be only asked that you may find pretext for further strife, you may get more of that than you will in a short space. But if you seek peace in a fair way, I will put that to Count Gismond, in as good words as you give, which may be the last chance you will have."

"And that," Sir Lanval added, "is fairly said."

"As to Madame Livron," the pursuivant answered, "if you can show that she would stay here of her own will, I know not that there need be further strife about that he who should have claimed her of right being dead, as you know, but beyond that—."

"Who is dead, as I know?"

"I mean that Guilbert Livron being dead—"

"How should I know that?"

"He having died by your hand—"

"I knew not. Was it he who fought?"

"Guilbert Livron was slain in the night attack on your own camp, he fighting singly in the sight of all. It is said on all side's that he died by your sword."

"I had not heard that, nor did I know it was he."

"Yet, that being so, it may be enough if it be shown that she is free to go as she will. But beyond that, what I have asked may be granted of right, or it will be taken at point of sword, which you will find that Faucon-bas is well able to do."

"If they think that, they may have something to learn. You may tell them that they waste words, as I suppose that you know. I might tell you what we will have from them, but they can ask that for themselves on a later day."

The pursuivant went back with such an answer as he had expected to get, and Halt went to Count Gismond to tell him that Faucon-bas had no will for peace, which was soon done.

But he must think of what he had heard for a longer time. That Yvonne's husband had died at his hand might seem either to remove the most division that held them apart, or to raise a barrier that no love could break, according to what they both were, and to what Guilbert had been to her, of which he knew nothing at all. But was he to think that she had been wedded to one for whom she had no love, and had made accord with the Count, as it seemed to him, in a light way, while her husband waited for her return?

Or did she know that he was dead, and was unmoved, even by that?

What would she feel when she knew that Guilbert had died by his hand? Did it matter, let her feel as she would?

How he loathed the ways of a world which was so foreign and strange! Could he love one who could go so lightly to the Count's bed, and sit at his order as she did, whether her husband should be living or dead? Yes, he knew he could, to his own shame. Her face would not leave his mind. Nor would her words, nor the tone in which they were said. "We are too late by a day." And having said that, she had looked on him no more. Was it too late indeed? It seemed very sure that it was.

Widowed she might be, and unaware, but she was the Count's mistress now. Not one who had given her body to shame that she might save a town from sack, as she would have had him believe, but one who was content to sit at the side of the man who had used her thus, that she might take what she could. For he did not think that she had any love for the Count. It was not reasonable to think that. It was his curse that he should be haunted thus by the face of a woman of foreign blood, and who could walk in such ways. Yet he knew that if she should look again, as she had looked once, he would be hers to the world's end—as he supposed that he was now. But the thought gave him neither pleasure nor hope. He desired a fruit which was beyond his reach, and which he saw must be of an evil taste; but even these things could not change his desire. He told himself that it must be foul at the core; but there was no comfort in that.

# CHAPTER FORTY

RAYMONT, Count of St. Péray, sat at meat at the noon hour, gnawing his beard, as his habit was when he was unsure what he would do. There was none with him but his mistress, Lucia, who did him service at that meal, at which he would be alone, except that there were guests to his mind, which would seldom be, for he had few friends.

He was a man of giant size, and of a great strength. When he was sober, he would be shrewd enough for his own ends, and he would be just in a rough way, and, at times, kind. But when he was drunk there was none who could guess what he might do, and those around would walk in a great dread.

He had power of life and death in his own land, and there was none to care what he did, if he kept at peace with the lords around, and went at times to Dijon, to the Duke of Burgundy's court, to render his homage there. He was a duke's son, by which he came to the land and title he had; but he was of base blood on one side, his mother, who still lived, having been a byreman's wife.

His mistress, Lucia of Vaison, was the third he had had, and the two others were dead at his hands, as none could doubt, though it was not whispered for ten miles round, for his gallows would soon have stilled such a tongue, whether of woman or man.

He had killed the first in a drunken freak, to his own grief, as it is fair to allow.

He had but meant at the first that he should show his strength, holding her over the battlements by one hand, at his arm's length in mid-air. He did this with ease, for she was but a light weight, but he grew wroth when she struggled and screamed, saying that he would let her go unless she was still, and when she screamed again, so he did, whether by error or will.

As for the next, she was found dead in his bed with a twisted neck, and he hanged a groom in the next hour, saying that it was his deed; but the talk went among those who were not under his power that the groom was not of a strength to have twisted her neck like a fowl's, and that what he had done to her (for which they had both died) had been more welcome than that.

Lucia of Vaison had been the wife of Sir Hugo, a petty lord of that place, having a few fields and a little tower of his own. Count Raymont, being less sober than drunk, had made a quarrel with him, and had cloven him through the head, and much lower than that, with his sword. It was a stroke of which men would talk for a long time, being more filled with wonder thereby than to vex their minds as to why Sir Hugo had died.

When his wife screamed, the Count had taken her by the neck, and put her over his horse like a sack. "For such as you I may have a use. I will see more when I get you home. You have naught to hope from a dead man."

That had been three years ago, and Lucia still lived, watching his moods. He was kind at times, and may have come to love her more than those he had had before. He let her dress as she would, for he was not stinting of gold.

Now he looked again at two scrolls that he drew from the pouch at his belt, for he could read, though with little ease.

There was that which had come from the Count of Faucon-haut, telling him of the trouble he had with his town, and that he would have it chastised in a short space, and would then send what was due.

There was one from Isabeau of a later date, in a different tone, and telling much more.

He had once tried to get Isabeau to take the place which Lucia now held, but he was of a fixed mind that he would not wed, and Isabeau would not come to his terms, for she had a pride which rebelled from a public shame, though she cared not what she might do in a quieter way. Also, she thought of the two who were dead before.

So she had stayed where she was, by which Hugo came to his end, and Lucia to what some would call a worse fate. But now she thought to trim her sails for a new wind, for she saw that her brother shook in his seat more than he could see for himself, and if he could keep his, then it seemed that she might soon find that Yvonne was in hers, which she was resolved that she would not have.

"If Raymont call for his debt, I must be his friend," she had thought, not doubting that she could thrust Lucia aside, if she should come to that point.

> If you come with speed, and make accord with the town, you can enter our gates with a double power, and take all for the debt we owe.

So he read, and was not so dense of wit but that he could see that she herself would be in the "all" that she would have him take from her brother's rule.

He looked at Lucia with brooding eyes. There had been a time when he would have given much to have had Isabeau where she now sat at his side.

Lucia did not know what was writ in the scrolls, for he did not offer to tell, and he knew that she could not read. She did not ask, knowing him too well. He was more likely to say if she kept still, for she had found that he would talk in the end, and she could guess much.

When he spoke, it was to ask if the gorget was come back which he had sent for repair to an armourer at Valence.

"It is promised for this noon," she said. "It will surely come. Jean is a man of his word." And then: "Would you ride out? There is a small rent in your tabard that I must mend before that."

"Aye," he said, "I will ride out. I will ride south at the dawn." Then he muttered, as to himself: "Faucon-haut is a fair place. But I will bide here, where my roots are struck."

He did not ride at the next dawn, for he would go south with a large force, and they were not arrayed in an hour. But he was one who would take no rest when he had a plan formed, till he had brought it to fruit.

His castle, which was on a hill-top overlooking the Rhône, and with Valence beneath it upon the further bank, was wide-walled, though not built to a great height, and in this time of peace there were many who idled within its walls.

He had vassals also, who, for their own good, would not be last to be there when his banner rose.

Not at the next dawn, but at the prime of the day after that, he rode south with a great train that was gay with pennons and bright with spears. He rode in the midst, on a stallion which was as great of bone as himself, and could bear him with all the weight of his arms, which he did not wear at that time, for there was peace throughout Languedoc, except for such small bickerings as must always be, one of which he rode out to quell. So his squires followed behind, with his armour and helm and a great sheaf of spears, which he was little likely to use, for he was known as the best knight to ride a course with a sharp spear between Dijon and Nîmes, or perhaps farther than that.

He was in a good mood, having drunk little in the last two days, as his way was when he had business to fill his time, and he had bid Lucia adieu with a rough caress; and a great hand under her back in a way he had when she had done something to meet his mood, and he had the sense to see that he owed her most of his peace.

"Falcon!" he had said, with a great chuckle of contempt. "Faucon-haut will he call his nest, which is mine! I go but to pluck a crow, a pompous crow, and no more. Why, he hath no hand for a sword. Have you seen a falcon, die on a heron's beak, and its pride fall to the ground?"

His own device was a heron's head, so that his meaning was plain to see.

## CHAPTER FORTY-ONE

IT gave no pleasure to the men of Faucon-bas when Count Raymont's banner could be seen from the northern walls. Yet it did not fill them with dread, for it was a sight which they had expected to see. And by the time that Count Raymont was there, there had been much to give them stoutness of heart, and they had come to a great hope that Count Gismond was near his fall.

For it was but a day after they had regained their gates that there had come men from all parts professing practice in arms, and asking that they might be hired for the war.

There were many in the land at that time who were needing such hire, and the deeds that the town had done were told in a growing boast. It was said that they had chased Count Gismond with all his knights for the length of the castle road, and that he had barely escaped with his life. It was said, beyond that, that the castle might fall in a week's time, if not sooner than that, and the chance of wage and plunder be gone.

The town enlisted and armed. It had no stint of gold to be spent, for M. Sault had provided that, and the power of gold was as great then as at any time, either before or since.

On the second day there was an attack made on the castle outpost that held the road. The castle could not afford to lose that, for it was short of supplies, which were being brought down the valley, where its vassals dwelt. It did not seek to recruit men, nor did Count Gismond call those to his banner which he had the right to do, for the condottieri were enough and were better trained for such warfare. They were enough and perhaps more, for the castle was not provisioned for siege, and it was well for it that the time of harvest had come.

Wagons came in a stream down the valley road, bringing grain and fodder, and much beside, and there was slaughter of many beasts, that were cast whole into the brine-pit within the walls.

These carts could come freely in, so long as the road was held somewhere below the bridge, but if the road were lost to the bridgehead, the castle would be cut off, except to those who could come and go by a climbing way over the steep hill which was behind the knoll on which it was built.

For the afternoon of the second day and the morning beyond, there was a fierce and sustained attack on this post, for the castle could not afford to let it go, there still being much to be brought in which they must have if they were to face the perils of siege in a furnished state; and the town could not afford to withdraw, for if it were foiled at this first ditch how could it hope to make good its boast that it would pull down Count Gismond's flag from his own tower, as all men would see?

There was clamour of strife in that narrow place, and the deaths of those who were boldest and best, as must ever be, till it seemed that castle and town would continue to recruit their ranks till there should be none left to be slain either on the one side or on both. But when the noon came, Raoul, having brought on some of the best of his men, who had been rested before, bade that the barricade that had been built should be thrown aside, and charged down the road in such force and with such vigour of blows that their foes gave back for some space, being chased and slain, and more than one flung into the gorge which was below the side of the road.

And when the men of the town rallied anew, and were led backward by others of better heart, they found that they could go on as they would, for the road was clear for its whole length. The men of Faucon-haut had fallen back to the bridge, and the next day, having first done what hurt they could to their foes, they abandoned that too, and Faucon-bas could come to the castle gate, if it took no heed of the shafts and quarrels which would be shot from window and wall.

So on the next day the siege closed. Count Gismond had the strength of his walls, and between two and three hundred men who were practised in war. He would not have had more if he could, for they would take food of more worth than they would add to his strength. The men of Faucon-bas, looking up at those walls, might think that they had the harder part, and were the more likely to die; but their deaths were of less account, for there was large recruiting of those who came from afar, so that M. Sault, who took that into his own charge, could now choose of the best and turn others back as not worth the wage he would pay. He chose captains, too, men who had led others before and were studied in siege and storm. There were also ladders bought of the best kind, such as, being fixed, would not be lightly thrown away, and there were heavy slings that were coming on the road from the south, such as would throw great stones to the wall's height and above.

Before the close siege began, there had been sent away all the women that the castle held who were of a menial kind, for they were mouths to feed, and their work could be done by men. But its ladies stayed, as they must do, they being of gentle blood, lest they should give heart to their foes, as withdrawing from dangered walls.

Isabeau could not be sure that she walked unseen in her garden now, for she had given up the key of the corner tower, on the top of which a watchman was set. From there he could look far over the land. He could see that the southern road would be black at times with those who came to the aid of the town, bringing merchandise for its need, or themselves to hire to its ranks. From his high place he saw a day of fierce strife when men climbed to the height of the walls, and the gate was nigh battered in. But that assault was thrown back as the day failed. And on the next he saw a sight, as it might be thought, of a better kind. He saw the glitter of many spears, and the banner of St. Péray, that came down by the northern road.

## CHAPTER FORTY-TWO

IT was the morning of that day when Count Raymont came. Captain Redwood stood on the wall against which Faucon-bas had stormed till the sun was low, and there were places where its battlements were still dark with blood, and its stones were littered with the debris of the struggle which had risen to that height, and agonized to endure, and been flung back at last to the level from whence it came.

Halt thought of many things which are not of this tale, but which were near and yet distant to him. It was so short a time since he had left a life that had seemed sheltered and sure, to take the adventures of foreign ways, and to be drawn to the trade of war. Now he was brought by fate to a strange power, and he was having a near view of the horrors its glamour hides.

He felt that he had done his part without shame, though there were ways in which Raoul was far better than he. Yet he thought he could bring all to a good end. He did not fear that the castle would fall. They had provision yet for three weeks, and for another with care. They were not so closely invested on the hillside but that a bold man might creep through in the night, as they sometimes did. He thought of Bernardi, perhaps already breaking camp to march to his aid through Tuscany and Provence. That, as he thought, would be the end of this siege, and would bring the town to its knees. After that…well, he would make terms with the town that they should lay bare all that could be known of how Konrad had died, and where his child might be found. They would be active for that, with the fear of sack in their hearts. He did not suppose that M. Livron would be less than his foe now, he having slain his son; but the town would find means. Yes, he might bring that, too, to a good end.

And after that…he did not know what he would. He had no heart for this trade of war, having been thrust into a place where he must use head rather than sword, and bear the weight (as he had come to think) of the guilt of war, as a man does not who takes orders from those above. Well, he could give it up if he would. When he had found the pucelle, and given her that which her father left, keeping only what he might have made in his own time…. But he did not know what he would do. It was not the horrors of war, nor the score of men who lay groaning in the lower hall with wounds of lance and bolt, that so disquieted his mind. He was sick of life, that offered, and mocked, and withheld. Sick for the light of love in a girl's eyes to whom he had not spoken for three days past, having thought that to be best.

For beside the shadow that was at the back of his mind because he had killed the man whom she might be presumed to have loved, and to whom she had pledged herself to give all that a woman may, there was the doubt of how she stood with the Count, which was a problem he could not solve. And as, he rightly thought, she did not know that Guilbert was dead, she must think that her duty, if not her desire, would take her to him, when there would be peace with the town again.

There were only two more that the castle held, except Raoul, with whom he had come to much more than the surface courtesy which is born of a common task. They were Sir Lanval and Doette, who would be often in the safe place, as their occasions allowed. They were both friends to Yvonne; but he thought that they were vexed by the same doubt. Sir Lanval had said to Doette, somewhat as he had said before, and she had repeated to him: "There is a song here, but I cannot tell as yet of what kind it may prove to be."

Now, as he thought of these things he was aware of Yvonne at his side.

She did not avoid him now. She gave him a straight glance, though it did not open her soul, as she had once made it to do.

"Captain Redwood," she said, "you have said that your sword is mine."

"So I meant," he answered. "Will you tell me that it is needed now?"

"Being held here as I am, I would walk in peace, being touched of none, till I can return to him to whom I am wed, as is known to all."

"You can never do that," he said, feeling that he must give her the truth, and that she could sustain it well. "Do you not know that Guilbert Livron is dead?"

She answered nothing to that for a moment's space, which seemed more. She did not doubt what he said. He could see that. She felt as surely as he that they must speak truth if they spoke at all.

She was very pale, but her words were level and cool when she spoke again: "I am grieved for that. He was a good man. I would know how he died."

"He died by my hand when they attacked the camp, and we fought in the dark. I did not know that it was he."

She was paler now than before. She said aloud, but as though she spoke to herself: "That it should be thus!" and was silent again. Then she seemed to put the matter aside with an effort of will. "You must tell me more of this at another time."

"What would you have me do now?"

"I would have you make the Count see that I will not be mistress to him, that I will not be touched by his hands."

Halt considered what this might mean, and how it was to be done. They were both sparing of words. "I can do that," he said, "without use of sword."

"You will be a friend if you do."

They stood silent for a time after that, being both near and apart, and aware of both.

Halt said at last: "You have not always avoided the Count."

It was a fact that she had used him during the last few days, and more than once, that he might give her freedom to do that which she could to aid in the castle's toils, and in the salving of wounds, which Isabeau would have denied. If the Count had taken this in the wrong way, seeing what, as Halt supposed, had been between them before.... They both knew that he meant far more than his words said. To the minds of both there came the time when she had asked the Count, in the full hall, to go with her apart, and he had led her to his own room. What could be more willing than that?

Could she have told all—! But she remembered a pledge that she would not break. She said simply: "I cannot talk of these things."

"Well," he said, "I will do that which you ask."

"You will have my thanks till I die."

She turned away as she spoke, leaving him there in some doubt, but in better heart than before, for he had something to do. And, besides that, he had told her of Guilbert's death, and that it was by his hand. There was no longer a secret thing in his mind which must hold them apart. It seemed less, being told. That she had not loved Guilbert he was now sure. Then was she one who would wed any who asked, and go elsewhere with as light a step? It was not easy to think.

He had heard it said that there is no love without trust. He was not sure it was true. But he was glad that, on his side at least, there was now nothing untold. On her side…he was less sure. But he had something to do. He went, seeking the Count.

# CHAPTER FORTY-THREE

"LORD," he said, in a more formal mode than he always used, "I would speak with you apart."

The Count was formal to all. "You have my leave to speak here. We are heard of none."

"It is a matter," Halt said, "which were not mine were I not asked. It is Madame Livron for whom I speak. She would have it known that she will be touched of none till she be free to go forth."

The Count was dumb for a time between wonder, and pride, and a great wrath. Then he said: "Captain Redwood, I must think that you do not know what you say. She will not go forth at all, except it be of my will. She is a smith's wife of my vassal town, to whom I may deign as I will. But what is she to you?"

"She is one who has asked my aid that she be not wronged, and that she shall have."

"Would you tell me what I may do in my own halls? Or what rights I have, being one hired to my will? Think you do not know what you say."

"I know well what I say. What I do not know are the customs of this land, among which there may be some of a foul kind."

"It is the land," the Count answered to that, "of the most worth in the world, and hath those to rule it who are of the most gentle blood, and who are first in music and song, and in knightly use, as is known to all. Will you teach manners to us, having come from a more barbarous land, and of no rank that I know, and also younger than I?"

"It is a fair land," Halt allowed, "holding much of beauty and grace. I say nothing to that. But I would have the pledge for which I have asked."

"Captain Redwood, it is plain to see that you are come from a barbarous land. You ask insolent things, having no right, forgetting that you are my servant, or guest (as I should have called you an hour ago), and that I am maimed of my hand, so that I could not be fairly met in the field, even though you were of a rank to which such honours are fitly done."

"Count," Halt answered to that, with less courtesy than before, "if you will not give the pledge that I ask, we may get over that ditch, for we can fight with poniards in our left hands, and all will own it is fair."

The Count was not quick to reply. He was resolved that he would give no pledge. It was not only that he had planned, as he had told Yvonne, that she was to be honoured that night by that which might raise her to the place which Isabeau had feared would be hers to take.

His pride was too great to endure that he should be so constrained by one who was no more than a hired soldier to serve his will. Yet he did not wish to fight in so strange a way, in which he was almost sure to be badly hurt, if he were not killed.

The pause gave Halt time to remember that he had said that he would have no need of the sword.

"Lord," he said, "you should think of this. There are three hundred men in these walls, of which two hundred are mine. There are three times eight hundred more who may be marching here at this hour, and who will storm castle or town with an equal will, and they are sworn to my rule. Shall we be friends or foes from this hour?"

"It is but a small thing that you ask," Count Gismond answered to that. "It had been granted at once had you asked in another way."

"Lord, if I asked ill, you must consider that I am come from a barbarous land." The Count saw that there was reason in that.

## CHAPTER FORTY-FOUR

IT could be seen from the high tower that Raymont had halted in front of the northern gate, which had been closed as he came. It seemed that Faucon-bas must face such an attack as would weaken its siege of the castle walls, even if it were not equal to take the town. But St. Péray did not attack at once, as he was not likely to do. If he thought he could storm the wall, there must first be unloading of carts, and he must set his strength in array.

On the high roof of the tower, before a parapet which was little more than a foot high, Count Gismond looked down the vale that was his, and on the town with its girding wall, and the width of the Rhône Valley beyond.

The Rhône shone, a twisting band of silver and blue, in hill-shadow and morning sun. Brighter than that, many-coloured, bristling with spears, in the low meadows beside the Rhône where Konrad's camp had been, he saw the army his cousin brought, and there was a fear in his heart that he must not show.

Sir Lanval also had climbed the stairs of the tower, and Captain Redwood, and Raoul, and one or two more, for it was of great moment to learn what Count Raymont purposed to do. Isabeau stayed in her own room, braiding her hair in a new way, that Raymont would not have seen, or, at least, not on her head.

"They should have got message here," Raoul growled, "so that we should know what they are meaning to do."

"Well," Sir Lanval allowed, "so they should. But they may think that they have. It may have been cut off, or lost in the hills."

"Yet," Halt said, "we shall see what they do well enough, having so high a watch."

Raoul was not appeased. "We should know sooner than that."

He was vexed in his mind, seeing a chance spoiled such as any captain of battle would like to have. Why should St Péray break his strength against that of the northern wall? He spoke of that with contempt. "Would you stick a knife in a pig's ham?"

What he meant was easy to see. Count Raymont should not have halted there. He should not have halted at all. He should have made camp a few miles away, and come on at speed, with his force in array of battle, and when he came near to the town he should have passed it by, making straight for the foot of the castle road. That was the neck, where Faucon-bas might have felt a wound that it could not heal. And they of the castle should have known before what he would do, so that they could sally out at the right time upon those who laid siege to their walls, and had become aware of a threatened rear. They would have been cut off from their root. Raymont would have driven them up the road, and Gismond have chased them down. They must have leapt down the gorge, or climbed the cliffs, or else yielded or died. The castle siege might have been raised in an hour, and the town have closed its gates on a great loss.

Count Gismond heard this talk, and said nothing thereto. He was not likely to talk to Halt after what had passed between them so soon before. He took some comfort from the plea that Sir Lanval had made. A letter might have failed to get through. But he feared Raymont, who had an ill name, and he was a man in his debt, and one who could not rule his own town. He saw that it would have been ruin to quarrel with Captain Redwood now. Yet silence was the most he could do. He needed friends, and was alone in his pride.

They watched for an hour, and went down, leaving those who would give quick warning of any change in the panorama of war that the valley showed. They made ready to sally out on those who were round their walls, if there should be a movement of Count Raymont's force which they could help in that way. But when the noon came they had done nothing, for the Count stayed where he was, though it seemed that there was parleying between him and the town, the meaning of which they could not guess.

The sun was descending the western skies when the news was cried that Count Raymont was on the move, and it seemed to those who watched that he aimed to do that which Raoul had talked of before. For he marched round the town, leaving it on his left hand, and advanced to the valley road. But the men of Faucon-bas had had notice enough, and, whether by bargain or fear, it was plain that they did not mean either to be caught, as they would have been at first, or to oppose his advance.

They could be seen to be drawing back to the western gate, leaving his way clear, and those who were camped under the castle walls, and the approach thereto, and around the bridge, began to withdraw, so that when Raoul sallied out with a third part of those that the castle held, as he had been eager to do, he fell upon men who were already in act to flee, and who did not go down the road, where they must have met Count Raymont as he came up, but further away by the upward paths, scattering among the hills.

So it came that the Count of St. Péray marched up to the castle gate without stroke of sword, and with the gay front of his ranks undimmed, except by the summer dust.

He came to an open gate, for Count Gismond must call him friend. He had foes enough without him. He was a cousin who came to save. Yet Gismond counted his men, and had been better pleased had they been less than they were. They crowded into the great courtyard as though they had come to their own home. The castle was full enough as to humankind, but its horses were fewer than they had been had not most of Captain Redwood's men come on their own legs. There were many stalls built along the inside of the outer walls, so that there was shelter for three hundred horses, with good space for each, or for many more if they were tied two in a stall.

St. Péray did not ask his cousin's will as to this. He had horses that needed grooming and food, as was easy to see. He told his own men to see that this should be done.

He said to Gismond: "You will be full here, but my men must bide, for where else could they be? They can lie hard, if they must; but we can talk of this at a later hour."

The castle was in poor form to receive guests, having been under such stress of strife in the last days; but Isabeau had been active to prepare all in the best way that she could. She had said to her brother: "Gismond, we must give your chamber to him, for there is no other that is now fit, or can be so made in an hour's space." Gismond agreed to this with an ill will. He saw that they must show courtesy to one who came to their aid and was of power over themselves for the gold they owed. He hoped that he would be soon gone.

Raymont was shown to his cousin's room, where he was served with water and napkins that he might cleanse himself from the day's dust, and offered choice of the best clothes that the castle held; but he was one who must bring his own, being the size he was, so he sent them back with no thanks.

He was asked if he would take food, but he said no to that. He would have wine of good strength. His squire said that he would rest in his own room till the banquet-hour, and so there he remained.

It was an hour after that that Raoul came to his captain to ask: "Shall we stay here, or shall I draw my men out to the hills?"

Halt was surprised to be asked this, though he was troubled as to what St. Péray's coming might mean. He had seen a man that he disliked at the first sight, and one who, he thought, had a hidden mind. He had heard him speak to the Count his cousin in a curt way, which was not that of a friend who had ridden far to his aid. And as to what talk he had changed with the town, or what would be done next, he had put all question aside. They would talk of that, and again of that, at the board tonight. So he had gained his room, where he would stay by himself till the meal be called.

Only to Isabeau had he spoken a little, and that apart; but it might have been of no more than of the dispositions which she would make for his own ease, or for that of his knights, and she had not seemed displeased as she turned away.

In fact, what he had said had been: "They must sit high. I must have those near who are friends. You must not fail me in this."

Isabeau had called the seneschal after that, and had urged that St. Péray's knights should be so ranged at the board that they would be well content with the honour they had. "If our own must sit low," she had said, "you must tell them why."

The seneschal was of a mind to accord with hers, for he knew the power that Count Raymont held, as did those to whom he must speak. They would all wish that their guests should have no cause for wrath, and should go out in a quiet way.

Halt, having nothing to do at that time but to look on, had seen Count Raymont's eyes upon Isabeau as she turned away. He thought that they held contempt, and yet that they regarded her with intent, as though he would know her worth. It was such a glance, up and down, as a man might give to a horse of a bad repute, which was sleek and fine, and which he was tempted to buy.

Halt saw that Count Raymont's coming, be he a good friend or a bad to his cousin's cause, would be likely to push his own condottieri aside, unless the town should be of enough heart to defy their united strength, and he should be asked to aid again in storming its walls. The town, he thought, might be bold enough to do that, but, even so, he would have a less part than he had thought to take when Bernardi's troops should arrive, and he could put himself at the head of an army indeed.

Such was his mood when Raoul asked: "Shall we stay here, or shall I draw my men out to the hills?"

"Why," he asked, "should you do that?"

"Well," he said, "the castle is overfull. We could say that when men lie too close, being strange, and of different tongues as they are, there may be broiling and blood. "

"So we could say. But for ourselves you will have a better reason than that. The day is late now. We have much to move, and few horses. And we have no tents for the men, if they lie out."

Raoul looked as one who was not sure what to say. "I may be wrong, but I hear talk.... The Count's men have no love for ours, though they hold them in fear. Had they dared, they had pushed us aside, so that they would have held both the outer gate and the inner wards. There had been strife about this, had I not been there at the right time. Vitelli's dagger was out, and I could not blame him for that. I have them ranged now so that I can draw out in a rapid way, and I think they will see us go with good will. Perhaps I grow old. But I can tell you one thing, which is not to be said aloud, though it is known by some of his men, for Count Raymont charged them that they should say naught. He has made his own peace with the town."

Halt saw that if this were true, it was ominous that it should have been so done in a secret way. He had a great trust in Raoul. Yet he had a doubt as to what his honour required, and he knew that he was unwilling to leave the castle for other reasons than that.

"I doubt," he said, "that I should so withdraw, being pledged to Count Gismond's aid."

"We are not hired for strife with Count Raymont's men."

"We are hired to fight against those who may take part with the town. Yet you may do this. You may tell Count Gismond what we purpose to do, and if you have no denial from him, you may withdraw with fair words to all. But for myself, I will stay where I am for this night."

"Then I will do naught."

"You will do what my orders are. I have had ill words with Count Gismond this day, and if I say that I withdraw now, he will think that which is not meant. But if I stay here, he may see that the two things are apart. Besides, you must get my own chests and the treasure free.

"After that, I can say at the morn that I go to order the needs of my own men, and I can return or not as I will."

There was sense in that, as Raoul saw, though he was loth to obey, as at last he must. He went to Count Gismond, telling him that they could camp in more comfort outside the wall, except his captain, who, being well lodged, would stay where he was.

Gismond may have felt a doubt about this, but he said little, as his habit was. He would not show suspicion of those around, whom he had lost the power to control. Of his cousin's purpose he had an instinct of fear. But if he were false what could avail?

He asked Raoul of how soon Bernardi might come. Raoul thought well to talk of that as a near thing. Bernardi would come by the coast road. He was known to be swift to march. He might be in Liguria now.

Gismond may have wished he had accorded with Halt over Yvonne in a readier way. He cared nothing for her, beyond a carnal impulse which was forgotten in the stress of these anxious hours. But he said no more, being held back by his pride.

Raoul drew his men out through the castle gate. Those of Faucon-bas, who had been besieging its walls, had been scattered about; but some of them had returned, as though to resume the siege, but with more thought to retrieve their tents, and much gear that was theirs.

Being as few as they were, they fled with speed when Raoul's spears showed through the gate. He took such spoil as he would, and camped about half a mile up the stream in a secure vale which had a brook in its midst, doing well enough with what he had got in that way. He would have been better pleased had Captain Redwood also been there, but he looked to see him on the next morn. When Bernardi should come, they would be able to talk of what was due to themselves in the right tone, even though the two Counts should be in accord, and the town as well.

Halt stayed where he was, for which he had given Raoul a reason which might be good enough in itself, but he knew that it was not that which had ruled his mind. He stayed there because he would be near to Yvonne.

## CHAPTER FORTY-FIVE

COUNT RAYMONT stood in Count Gismond's room, with a grim smile on a face that was flushed with wine. He took up a heavy mace which few would have cared to wield, and which was as light in his hand as a child's toy. The smile on the bearded lips broke into a chuckle of joy as he thought of what would be said in the next hour. But he laid down the mace. It was not usual to go to meat carrying arms of offence. The dagger at his belt was his table-tool. To carry that mace would be to spoil the surprise which he had in view. And there would be no need. He could have his will in a quieter way.

His squire gave him a banquet-robe of fawn velvet, ermine-collared, heavy with gold, and he cast it about his shoulders in a way he had, as one who owns the world and thinks it a small thing. He strode out of the room.

The banquet-hall was thronged with ladies and knights, and with those of Count Gismond's household for whom space could be found on this crowded night. The ladies were few, being no more than Yvonne, and Isabeau and her train, for it was only they who had faced the siege. But to find space for all of Count Raymont's party who had claims to the rights of a gentle blood, or of office held, had not been easy to do.

The hall was already full, for the Count of St. Péray had lingered the extra minute which would assure this, and there was none seated at all, for they stood in his honour till he should come, as Count Gismond's example caused them to do.

St. Péray strode up to where Sir Gismond stood at his chair's side.

"Gismond," he said, in a loud voice that could be heard even by those who stood round the lower doors, "is the gold ready to pay?"

He did not speak as one wroth, nor as one asking for that which he hoped to get, but as one who meets a jest in a jovial way.

But Gismond's wrath as he heard was a thing dreadful to see. To be so contemned in the hall where for fifteen years his word had been life and death! Men saw that his left hand went to his dagger's hilt, and his eyes were dark with hate in a face from which the blood had been withdrawn. But he answered in a controlled way, though in a harsh voice that could be heard as clearly as the boisterous challenge he had received: "It is not ready as yet, as you well know. But it will be counted out on a near day. It is for that we are taming the town."

Count Raymont's lip was raised in a sneer, and there was ridicule in his eyes. "Aye," he said, "you were taming the town—or the town you. Then till the gold be paid, you will see that my place is here." As he spoke, he shouldered Gismond aside, and sat down in his chair.

Gismond stood where he had been pushed, while the hall watched in a tension that gave no sound. Then he stepped forward, and with his maimed hand struck Sir Raymont across the mouth.

Raymont leapt up with an oath of rage, and so that the chair of state, which he had filled from side to side with his bulk, fell backward upon the floor.

"Now, by Mary's womb," he cried, "and the God it bore, if you did not for that."

"One of us," Sir Gismond answered, "will soon die. There is nothing surer than that."

He spoke in a hall in which tumult woke. St. Péray's knights were pushing to gain his side, and were jostled back by those who would not help their way through. There were few but had hand on a dagger's hilt, if they were not showing the blade.

Sir Lanval's voice sounded clearly above the din. "Sirs," he called, "let this thing be done in a seemly way, lest men speak to our shame."

Sir Raymont turned on him, and met a glance that did not fall. "I know not whom you may be," he said, "but you must stand back from, this, or your neck shall pay."

Sir Lanval wondered in a cool mind whether he were bringing himself to a quarrel with this half-drunken giant which might well be the end of a life he would be sorry to lose. But he answered in a quiet way, which brought reason to the minds of many who stood around: "I am Sir Lanval, the trouvère of Rouen, of whom some have heard, though it be a name of less power than your own. But, by the knighthood which we both have, I would plead that this matter be brought to no less than a knightly close."

"Shall he strike and live," Sir Raymont asked, in a somewhat less voice than before, "having no hand for a sword?"

"If, as I see it," Sir Lanval answered, "he be challenged by you, he must knightly reply, either by his own body, or by such champion as he may find for his part. He must do this, though his hand were shorn at the stump, having used it as we have now seen."

It was not a judgment that seemed to give Sir Gismond much hope, he being maimed as he was, though it might save his life for a day; for against Sir Raymont, he being so huge, and of such repute, a champion would not be simple to find. But it stayed the threat of a common brawl which might have drenched the banquet-hall with blood; for though there were few arms at hand but the daggers which all must wear, being needed to part their meat, they were deadly weapons to use in a crowded place among those who had no armour at all. To St. Péray's friends, it seemed that Sir Lanval had delivered his cousin's life to his hands, yet none on the other side could object that he had said more than the law was.

"If I be so challenged," Sir Gismond said, "I have the choice of arms. There is none can deny that."

"Of any in knightly use," Sir Lanval agreed.

Sir Raymont did not object to that. Whether with lance or sword, he did not doubt that he could put Sir Gismond down without loss of breath, and could have done so had his hands been as they first were.

"I will challenge him now," he said, "to mortal combat, either on horse or foot, either with lance and sword, or with axe or mace, or such weapons as he may choose, they being of knighthood's use, within seven days of this date, for this despite he has now done, and if he fail to meet me within that time—"

"Cease your talk," Sir Gismond said; "it is now we meet, in this hall."

"With what weapons," Sir Lanval asked, "would you have it to be?"

"With the poniards which we now wear, they being held in our left hands."

There was a doubt in Sir Lanval's mind whether that might not go beyond what could be required of Sir Raymont, that he should give assent thereto. To claim the right to say in which hand a weapon should be held…. But he was silent, not being asked, and he may have felt that he had said enough then.

Sir Raymont took his dagger in his left hand. "Stand apart," he said, "that we may have space; and tell them to keep back the meats for a short time, which will be enough. "

There was a good space at the top of the hall, between the wall and the table where those of most rank should have been seated before now, which was like the top of a T, crossing the long board that ran down the lower hall. Those who had been already at the top of the hall, where their seats were, stood back round the wall, making a clear space in the midst, and the crowd that were below surged forward to the lower side of the table of rank, but did not come beyond that, which they were not accustomed to do.

Count Gismond was a tall man, standing alone, but he looked small as he faced him who now sought his death. Men thought at first that he had but a slight chance, and were then less sure. For the idea which Halt had put into his mind in the earlier day, which had seemed murderous then, might have given him an advantage against any of no more height than himself, as he had since thought, for he had been used for years to wield his dagger in his left hand. He did it three times a day at the board. Being brought to bay as he was, the thought had come back to his mind, and had given more hope than he would have otherwise had, though he was in such wrath that he would have fought Count Raymont with any weapon he must, or with bare hands on the hairy throat, which had been a poor jest for him.

Now Count Raymont rushed forward, and thrust, as one who would make an end, and not be kept from his meat. Count Gismond made a quick guard, as he stepped back and aside. The blades met and came apart, and there was blood on the giant's wrist.

Gismond turned in the same movement by which he had bent aside, and made a downward stab, which Raymont was not quick enough to avoid. It was clear to all that they were in such anger and hate that the strife could not endure, each being in less care for himself than in haste to kill. They had been in such haste to close that they had not thrown off the banquet-robes that they wore, which may have saved Raymont's life, as for that stroke, for it slit the loose velvet robe a foot's length over the heart, though doing little damage beneath.

"Now if that stroke had been up...," Sir Lanval thought, for he had seen men fight with knives in a tavern brawl, who were more used to that style, and in a warier mood. But his thought changed as it came, for there was an end to that strife.

Raymont had been warned twice, by the blood on his wrist, and by the slit in his robe, that he might soon come to his death, which he was not eager to do. As he saw that, some of the wine left his head, which he had drunk during the afternoon. He became more wary, though his lust to kill did not cool. He stepped back, pace after pace, catching Gismond's blade on his own, and watching for a chance to strike, when he might do it without having a blade in his own ribs. As he did this, they had come to those who were lining the wall to watch, not backing into them, but moving along their front. They came where Isabeau stood, and as Gismond passed her by, following his foe, he stumbled forward so that his head bent. Whether he would have fallen to the ground there was no time to decide, for Sir Raymont's dagger came down on the shoulder, nigh to the back of the neck, and Gismond sank, with his face in the rushes that strewed the floor, and the dagger's hilt showing behind his neck, for it had been let go as he fell.

Isabeau looked down in a cool way on her brother's death. "There was a bone," she said, "on the floor." So there was. Everyone could see that. In the stress of the siege, the rushes had not been changed as they would have been but for that, nor had they been cleansed as they should. Bones will fall to the floor when men eat, or the dogs will draw them about. It was a chance from which either might have suffered alike.

But Sir Raymont smiled grimly behind his beard, for he had seen her foot move.

"Take him out," he said, "and let the banquet be served. I am lord here from this day." He looked at his wrist, which still bled. "Bind me this," he said, looking at Isabeau as one who orders a dog which he does not trouble to see. So she put her napkin around his wrist.

## CHAPTER FORTY-SIX

COUNT RAYMONT sat down again in his cousin's chair, not heeding the sound of those who were raising the body from the floor, which still twitched somewhat as they bore it out. He turned his head only to call, as it went through the door by which he had entered the hall: "Put it not in his room, which is now mine. There are kennels for living dogs, and they are better than he."

He pressed his bulk between the arms which had been ample for Count Gismond, who might have sprawled at ease had his dignity so allowed, but which would scarcely accept the breadth of their new lord. He looked round the hall, to see that men were taking their seats, and the aspect which they might show. He saw little to rouse his ire. It was a time when men were used to violence and death. They had seen it, even to yesterday, around their walls. They thought first of themselves, as men ever will. Those who had been Gismond's men had quick and anxious doubts as to how they would now stand, and whether they would be retained in the offices which they held. St. Péray's followers were merely glad that their lord had had the best of the strife. Those who had been waiting to serve the meal brought the dishes with speed, as the crowded hall settled itself along the tables, and on the benches that lined the walls at the lower end. They offered joints of boar-meat and beef, and wild-fowl upon the spit, that each in turn might cut from it the piece he would as it passed his chair.

Yvonne had seen the duel of the two counts without greatly caring how it might end. She was not likely to take Count Gismond's part in a warm way, for he was one whom she had no reason to love. But he had never caused her as much fear as it might be thought in reason that she would have felt, and since she had had Halt's promise to take her part, she had not feared him at all. But she had looked at St. Péray as he had entered the hall, at the great wine-flushed bearded face with its sneering joviality, half cruelty and half contempt, and at the wide-hanging fawn-coloured cloak, which made his giant bulk seem even more than it was, and her heart missed a beat with a sudden dread. As she looked at him, she had a premonition of ill which she could not rule. She watched the quarrel, and that which followed therefrom, with little care or hope as to what its end should be; but had it rested with her, it is likely that Gismond had lived, and his rival sprawled his great bulk on the floor.

Now, as the seats were taken along the board, she stood back from the chair which would have placed her beside that of the Count.

Her eyes sought Halt in appeal. "Will you take it for me?" she asked, in a voice which none heard in the bustle that was around. So he took her place by the Count's chair, and she sat on his other hand.

She had left off the rich bridal gown in which she had been brought to this place, having had Doette's help to provide a dress which was better fit for the day, and for a stress of strife when all must join in toils which they had not touched at another time. Often, of late, Isabeau and her ladies had come to the meal without changing of dress, doing no more than to wash their hands in a quick way, but for this night, when they would appear before St. Péray and all his knights, they had become splendid again. Yvonne would not put on her bridal dress, which she did not love. She came in that which Doette and she had changed to her shape—an old dress which had been fair once; but its colour was faded now, and it was soiled with the tasks of the recent days, and stained in one place with the blood of a dying man whom her arm had held. Being so attired, and sitting somewhat back as she did, might she not hope that the lightning would pass her by? And what had she to fear?

The Count ate with a good will. He called for wine. That of Provence was brought, and he sent it back. He would have Burgundy wine. He commenced drinking again. He was in a jovial mood, and inclined to show that he would be a good lord.

He looked at Halt for the first time. He would know those among whom he came, and make friends if he could. He was somewhat puzzled by what he saw. Halt had not quite the look of a knight of Languedoc. Yet he sat in a high place. Also, he seemed at his ease, as one who was not over greatly concerned by the change of lords which had come at that hour. And he was younger than most who sat at the upper board.

The Count decided that he must be a young man whom Gismond's favour had raised, so that he must sit by his own chair. Perhaps a steward, who had control of servants and land. Shrewd enough in his own way, he thought that he had the look of one who might be left with such a trust by an absent lord, which there are not many who can.

"I would know," he said, "what you are, and what trust you have held." The tone was gracious enough, but he spoke as one who sits high. It was less a question than a command.

"I am not of Count Gismond's train," Halt answered. "I have hired him certain troops which I have, that he might show a bold front to the town."

St. Péray looked at him in doubt. He thought he knew what bands of Free Companions were in France at that time. Probably he was a young man with no more than a dozen spears. But he noticed that he spoke in a foreign way, though his words were clear. "What device," he asked, "do you show?

"That," he said, when he heard, "is Konrad Wolvenstein's blazon, as all men know. But he is older than you."

Explanation followed. He had not heard that Konrad was dead.

"Well," he said, "you will not be needed from this day. But you shall be paid what is due. You shall be fairly paid for all for which you can show seal or bond, or a fair claim. Roland," he called down the board, "you will see that this be done at the morn."

He had a feeling that he showed to all in a royal way. Now that he had come, there would be no stinting of gold, no rebellions of vassal towns. He was a lord who could rule—and pay.

His glance went on to Yvonne. He saw a demoiselle who was fairer than most, but dressed in a poor style, as one who should have sat at the lower end of the board. She puzzled him, as Halt had done, being another whom he could not place. He saw that Gismond must do honour to Captain Redwood, he being now the chief of the army that Wolvenstein had made to be famous through the width of the Latin lands; and so it would also be needful to be to one who was wife or *amie* to the condottieri chief. He supposed that Yvonne sat where she did by such right, and he spoke of her to Halt in that way. Halt answered in a vague phrase that neither told nor denied, and had he been left in that belief he would not have looked at her again. But Isabeau would not be still. "That is the smith's wife," she said, in a voice that was meant to go further than him, "whom Gismond brought to his bed. It is a shame that she should sit longer there, now that we are come to a new time."

She thought that Count Raymont might tell Yvonne to go to a lower seat when he heard that, putting her to a public shame, such as might often fall on the mistress of a dead lord, with less reason than might appear in this case. Had she seen Lucia of Vaison, she would have thought as little of her as she did now by report; but Lucia would have had too much wisdom to talk thus at that time. For when Raymont was flushed with wine, or lifted above himself by some wild deed he had done, Lucia had learned to say nothing unless she must, for none could tell where it would lead.

He turned his eyes on Yvonne when he heard that, in the brooding way that he had at times, so that men could see that he pondered something that he might do, though they could not guess what it would be. He got no glance in return, for Yvonne kept her eyes down, nor was it easy to tell that she was aware that he looked at her thus, and that other eyes followed his own.

After that, he looked at Isabeau for a time in the same way, and she looked back boldly enough, for she was not faint of heart, and she had not thought that it would be easy to tame this ruffian knight to her will, as she was attempting to do. Besides that, she was confident in the beauty of that which he must behold when he looked her way.

He took his eyes off her at last, and a rumble of laughter stirred in the bearded throat. "Give me more wine," he said to the page that was behind his chair. He drank deep.

He began to speak, as though he were thinking aloud, but in a voice that could be heard by all those in the hall, they having no ears or eyes to spare except for him, as might be easy to guess.

"There be women," he said, "of two kinds, and no more. There are those that will lick the hand of him by whom they are whipped, and there are those who will cut his throat in his sleep. Now I wonder"—and at this he turned his eyes on Isabeau again"—I wonder which you would do."

"Raymont," she answered, still showing him a bold front, "I cannot jape, my brother being dead in this hall."

"Whom I thrash," he laughed on her, "with jovial, cruel eyes, "finds it no jape, as you may yet learn, if you will. Isabeau, I have not done with you yet."

He reached his hand to his goblet again, and drew it back. He rose heavily, lurching somewhat, and the table would have risen at that signal, though the meal was not done. But he stood with one hand on the board, by which he steadied himself, and with the other waved them down.

"I will walk," he said, "while I yet can. You shall drink to a new time, for the night is young."

He put a great hand on the shoulder of the page who was behind his chair. He walked halfway to the door, and looked back. "There shall none leave this castle from now without order from me, till I have seen all. Let all heed, for to let one through were a fault that their necks should pay." His glance swept round the hall, and came to Isabeau again. He added: "But I sleep with none. I have done that never at all. I bar my door at the night."

He went out, leaving those who were slow to speak their thoughts, for men felt that they walked on a narrow edge. There was little talk after that, nor were they of a mind to sit long. There was no mirth in the hall, for there were no jongleurs now, they having gone to a quieter place.

## CHAPTER FORTY-SEVEN

YVONNE said: "If you would get me clear of this place!" and her eyes said more than her words. She stood with Halt on the battlements, where they had met before, and where, though they might be seen, they could not be overheard by those whom they did not see. She had been slow to ask him for aid against Count Gismond the day before, and if her eyes said more than her lips at this time, it was because they were harder to rule. For she saw what he must think of her, and she would not make it worse than it was.

The widow of a man just dead—one who had been slain by his hand—the mistress of another who was not yet in his grave—what would he think of her if she should appear to say that she would be his in turn, if he would take her to his own place? And it was all so false, with a falsehood she could not tell!

Yet though they were parted by silence and troubled thought, there was a love which was far stronger than these, which made them one against the menace of surrounding things, and held him there at her side when Raoul would have had him forth to the safer hills, and which had impelled her to speak his aid against the threat of Count Gismond's lust, and now against the vaguer shadow of Raymont's power, and Isabeau's envious hate.

Halt knew, as he heard her voice, that she was his from now, and he hers, be she what she might, and whether it might lead to an evil end or a good. He had a great joy in that thought, and a fierce resolve that he would not fail. Yet it was not easy to see what he could do.

"So I will," he said, "for I must. Yet I see not how, except that I ask it of the Count in a frank way, and if he refuse, you are worse held, for he will be warned of what we would do."

"But why," she asked, "should he hold me at all? I was but pawn in a game which is now done."

So it seemed, from what Halt had learned since the dawn, and had told her in the last hour. There was free talk, now that Count Gismond was dead, of the new peace with the town, and it could be seen from the walls that it had opened its gates, as having no further fear. Already the southern road, that led down to Avignon, and the coast beyond, was thronged with those who were leaving the town, now that there was an end of strife, and of the gains which may be made therefrom.

The town had been promised a sure peace if Count Gismond were overcrowed, and now he was dead, and there was no more to be thought of him. M. Sault had contrived the terms of that peace, showing once again that he was shrewder than most, for Count Raymont thought that he had got the better, and M. Sault knew that the beam was touched by the other scale.

M. Sault had said: "We will make no peace till Count Gismond is down, for he has caused this war, and my son's death."

To which Count Raymont replied: "Let him be down to the grave's depth. But what peace will you make then? What was due to him will be due to me. I may read your charter to the same end, and I have more spears to enforce my will."

M. Sault answered to that: "I would have such peace that it will stand till the skies fall. I would have it so that no debate can arise at a later day. I would pay a fixed sum instead of tax on the market tolls, so that both will know what it would be."

"That," the Count answered, "has a fair sound, if you will bid to the height you should. But what sum will you pay?"

M. Sault named a sum which was somewhat more even than that which Count Gismond had claimed. So he explained. He said that a lasting peace would be worth that, and he desired friendship between castle and town.

Count Raymont asked: "Is that all? Is there no bicker about a bride who must have more husbands than one?"

"That is past. As to her, we can ask nothing now. What is done is done, and he to whom she was wed is a dead man. Her uncle also, who was father to him, has cursed her for the cause of his son's death. He would not take her again, though her knees pled."

"Then," Count Raymont said, "there need be no more talk as to her. For the rest, your provost can draw a bond, and I have a man of law in my train who will see that it is done in the right way. As to Count Gismond, I will make such sport that you will see him no more unless it be to beg at your gates."

That was how it had been; and M. Sault had had hard work to make maire and council see that he had done well. It was not till he said in wrath: "Let me have the tolls, and I will pay this tribute with a glad hand," that they began to see in his way. For he looked ahead. He saw that the town would grow. The day came when it was a small sum to that which it would have been had all been left as it was.

Now it had become clear that the war was done, and all men moved as they would, except only that Count Raymont lay late, as he would when he had drunk wine, and till he rose none could go out of the castle gate.

Halt had tried that, before meeting Yvonne. He had said: "But such orders are not for me." He had not meant to leave her alone, but to test whether he could get free. Had he done that, he would have sought Raoul, and come back, having seen his camp, as a captain should. But he had found a strong guard at the gate, and was met by the crossing of spears.

"Lord," they said, "that the order was not for you we can well believe. For how should it have been? But our lord may not have thought of all, and if we do not obey, it is at our necks' risk. Will you not forbear to a later hour?"

Halt said yes to that in an easy way, for what else could he do? He did not care for himself, nor think at he should be longer held when the Count should rise, but he saw that Yvonne could not be got out at that time. He went to Sir Roland, who was the Count's bursar when he rode abroad, and made a fair bargain enough, getting an order on a goldsmith at Dijon for as much gold as he could expect to have. And then he climbed to the high wall where he thought that Yvonne might be by that time, as he found she was.

Having thought what he could do, he said, though with little hope, "I will see Sir Roland once more. It can be no loss, and if we gain we gain all."

Sir Roland was a knight who was past the wars, though he was not old, for he had taken a wound in the leg which had left him a limping man. He was yet one of good courage and heart, though he had taken to inkhorn and pen. He was the one man who showed no fear of the Count, even when he was stirred with wine, and it was said that the Count could be ruled by him, when he would listen to none beside.

"I would ride forth," Halt said, "to my own camp, and am stayed at the gate by an order which, as I suppose, was not intended for me. I might have gone through with a bare sword, which the Count could not have blamed overmuch, for such orders should be given with care; but I would not bring the warders to shame, or the Count's wrath. I would go to visit my own camp, as I should surely be free to do. I thought, having warrant from you, they may let me pass."

Sir Roland saw a man he could trust, and he answered in a frank way. "I will speak for your ears, knowing that it will not go beyond. The command, which yourself heard, was given when the Count was disordered by wine, and I am assured that it was not intended for you. I think I know what meaning it had, though I may be wrong about that. I will own that the warders would let you through, if they had my word, for it was I who gave them the charge. If you have no great cause to ride out, I would ask you, of courtesy, not of right, to stay awhile till the Count shall rise, which may not be long. But if you have cause of weight, I will give order to set you free. For I will say to the Count that, as he gave me charge to settle that with you which I might find to be due, I must conclude that I was to send you forth with Godspeed when I had done that."

Halt said: "It is cause of weight, or I had not asked. You have met me well, as I thought you would, and I would have said no more had it been but a light thing."

"Well," Sir Roland said, "as you still ask, I will give order that you shall go. Have you squire or groom who should go too? I will ask you this: that if you go now, you do not return. For you will see that it is one thing that you should leave, your charges having been met, and your bond closed, but it is another that there should be passing in and out of the gate, the order being what it is, and all others being held back."

Halt thought that this had a good sound, he being offered that which he had been thinking how he might ask.

"There is but one I would take, if you would make order that I may pass the gate, having one in my train,"

Sir Roland said: "I will give order myself, for it must be clear beyond doubt. Is it woman, or man?"

"It is a woman."

"Will you tell me her name?"

"Yvonne Livron."

"It is a name I have heard."

Sir Roland looked at Halt, and his manner changed, though his tone was as friendly as before. He went on: "You ask me more than I thought, or than you are likely to get. What is Madame Livron to you?"

The hope that had risen died as he heard this, but he saw that his best chance was still to answer in a frank way. He would make Sir Roland a friend if he could. Beside that, he saw that he was not a man who would be easily fooled.

"She is this to me: that I have promised her escort that she may ride safely in her own way. You will know how the roads are likely to be at this time. She is one, as I see you know, whom Count Gismond held through the siege; but he is dead now, and there is peace with the town, and there is nothing that should hold her here for a longer time, being a place where she has no friends."

"Yet it would seem that she has one." Sir Roland pondered his words. "She may not be long without friends, if she stay here. If you are wise, you will let her be."

"I see no reason for that. She will take nothing which is not hers. She has her own horse in the stalls."

Sir Roland smiled at that. "Why," he said, "you can have the horse, if you will. But for the widow, if such she be, you must ask the Count when he wakes, and if you are as wise as you look, you will leave it unsaid then."

"Will you tell me why, in a plain way?"

"I will tell you, perhaps, more than I should. When the Count gave the order of which we talk, it was, as I think, to one end—that Madame Livron should be held here that he might have his pleasure of her. He would not that he should wake to hear that she had slipped away.

"If you ask his leave that you take her now, it will come back to his mind, and he will surely refuse. But he was in wine at that time, and he may have other thoughts when he wakes. He may not recall that he gave such an order at all, and she may be no more to him than an old shoe that Count Gismond has left to be cast away. You may get her quietly forth at a later hour, and if your mind is set on this, I will help you the most I may."

"The Count would not hold her against her will? By what right could he do that?"

"I said not against her will, which would be to prove. But he would have little scruple for that. She is a woman of common kind who has been Count Gismond's mistress, and he is slain. She is one to whom his slayer has the best right. The town has no will to claim her again, and her husband is dead. It should be good fortune for her, as you may find her decide. But we talk beyond that which we know. The Count may not regard her at all."

"It will be best so. For I must stay here till I take her free, being so pledged; and I am pledged beyond that, that there shall be none do her wrong here, so I must have some words with the Count if he will not let her free without that."

"Is she worth that which may end in the shedding of further blood?"

"I am well assured that she is."

"Well, you should know better than I. But few are. I can do no more for you at this time."

Sir Roland went to the gate, to give them orders which were more strict than before. After that, he thought how he might turn the Count's mind when he awaked to another way. For he would be Captain Redwood's friend, if he could.

## CHAPTER FORTY-EIGHT

HALT went back to Yvonne to tell her that he had failed, and as much of what had passed as it was needful for her to know.

"It will be best, as I think," he said, "that we wait, saying nothing more, and it may be that the order will be withdrawn, and we can ride out. The Count cannot keep the gate closed for a long time, the castle being as full as it is."

Yvonne saw that it was best. It could be no gain to draw attention to herself by clamouring to get free. As Sir Roland had said, the

Count might wake in another mood. She might be overthought if she kept still.

"But you will need," she said, "to go to your camp. You are here alone."

"No. I will stay here. We go neither or both. Raoul has but two hundred men. I could make no head against Count Raymont with those, he now having castle and town, and his own strength beyond that. If there be mischief meant, we must face it out as we best can till Bernardi come."

She felt a gladness of heart as he spoke thus, which covered her former fear. She said: "You would do that for me! But there may be no trouble at all."

She saw that he meant to fight the Count with all the strength that he had, if it should be needed to get her free; and that it showed much, both of valour and love, that he should elect to stay at her side, he being able to ride out if he would. She felt that there would be more light in her life, and that she would be strongly held in a good way, if she were once freed of those walls, as she had good hope that she might soon be.

After they had stood there for a short time, she said: "I will go to my own room, for it is there that I shall be noticed of none. I can send word to you, or you to me, if there should be need, or the gate be free." For she would not go into the great hall at that hour; nor to the larger garth, which was free to all of gentle blood, whether of the household or guests; nor would she stay on the battlements, not knowing who she might meet, for they were much used at that time of the year, in the hotter hours of the day; nor would she go into the sala, where Isabeau and her ladies might have welcomed her ill, even disallowing her right, as not being of their own rank. In the great girth of those walls there was nowhere that she might be at ease but her own room, and no surety of that, for it was hers by no more than Isabeau's will. Yet she went in good heart enough, feeling sure that Halt would find a way, and thrusting down a worse fear which would rise at times. She said: "We may be fretful with little cause, and before night we may be free to go where we will.

She did not think beyond that in a clear way as to where she should go with Halt, or what they should next do. She was of a mood to leave it to him. It would be enough to be free of those hateful walls. Yet the thought that they might be together for future years was a joy that beat ever beneath her fear.

The hours passed, and the Count still kept to his own room, where there was taken meat, and more of the Burgundy wine that he most loved. Halt went down to the stalls to see that his own horse would be groomed and fed, and fit to be brought out at his call, and that Yvonne's mare would be in the like case. Then he played chess with Sir Lanval upon the battlements, where he had told Yvonne that he would be for the most time. He lost three games out of four, for he was ever listening to the talk of those who passed up and down, seeking to learn what he could. Doette came at times, watching the games, and at others she would go down to Yvonne's room. That was after there had been some talking between themselves, and she had understood Yvonne in an hour somewhat better than in the past weeks.

It was in the later day, after the noon meal, that Sir Roland sought the Count in his own room, and after that he found Halt, and said that he would speak to him apart.

"Count Raymont greets you through me," he said, "and would have you know that you are free to ride out at any time that you will. He had no thought to have held you back, and he prays your pardon that his order was taken in a wrong way."

"That is of little account," Halt replied, "for such errors may often be in times of battle and siege. Is the gate now open to all?"

"It is free to all, except Madame Livron, and a few others I need not name."

"Then I must stay where I am."

"Captain Redwood," Sir Roland replied, "you are young, and should value life. You are alone here. Would you tell the Count what he shall do with a woman on whom you have no claim?"

"I have this claim, that she is the one I will wed, when I have her free of these walls."

"Then you must let the Count have his pleasure first, for against that you have neither right nor power."

"He will first meet me in what manner he will. I will see him now."

Halt would have gone at that word, but Sir Roland stood in his way.

"Captain Redwood, would you hear one who is not a foe, if you do not call me a friend? The Count would not meet you at all. By your pardon it must be said, you are of no known rank in this land. Were you here with a great force, he would show you such regard as your spears should ask, but you are alone in his power. He would throw you over the wall, if he made no worse sport for you than that. Would you fight us all with that toy?"

He spoke of the sword that Halt had belted on when he would be ready to ride, for his hand had dropped to its hilt. It was a one-handed sword of the English make, such as were not used in Provence, or in Languedoc.

Sir Roland faced the fury in Captain Redwood's eyes, thinking that he would be swept aside in a rough way; but he stood his ground nonetheless. He added: "She may be all that you think. I know nothing of that. But no woman is worth a life."

As he spoke, he saw that Captain Redwood calmed himself with a strong will. He said, as though to himself: "It would do her no good." He looked at Sir Roland, and said in a quiet way: "You have been friend to me. It was a plain folly I would have done."

Sir Roland looked at him still in some doubt. He asked: "Will you ride forth to your own camp?"

"I may do that in the end. I would think awhile. But I shall not seek the Count. You may trust that."

Sir Roland stood aside, and Halt walked quietly away. He found Doette, to whom he said a few words. She went with troubled eyes, seeking Yvonne. Halt sat at the chessboard again, and played worse than before.

## CHAPTER FORTY-NINE

THERE came a page to the sala door. Being told to enter, he looked round, and when Isabeau bade him speak, he answered: "It is Madame Livron for whom I look. I have a message for her."

"She can be found, if you show need."

"It is the Count's message, and I must give it to her. It is that he will come to her room in the next hour, and that she be ready to do him what pleasure she may. But I know not which her room is."

Louise spoke, before Isabeau had resolved what she would say: "That is soon found. It is but two doors beyond this."

The page went, hearing a voice which was raised in anger, and one that jeered, as he turned from the closed door. He went on to that which he had been told. He knocked on a door that Doette opened, and he went in to Yvonne, to whom he said as he had been charged. She looked at him with eyes which he could not read. She asked: "Is that all? You said in the next hour? It will not be sooner than that?"

"I will tell the Count that you will wait his will in an hour from now."

"You will tell him what I have asked."

The page bowed, and withdrew.

Yvonne looked at Doette when the page had gone. She said: "It is more soon than we thought, but there is no difference in that. There is time enough."

"I will let Captain Redwood know. Sir Lanval will make that sure."

"You must have no part in this. You must go now. If you are suspect, you could not help us again."

She said that for Doette's sake, rather than in sight of any further help she could give, but it was plain sense. Doette went to the sala, where she told of the message the page had brought, and how Yvonne had said that she must be left to herself after that.

Isabeau thought: "Will she mock me again? Am I caught twice in my own snare?"

Louise answered, as though she had spoken aloud: "He may throw her out, having had his will. She may be gone in an hour." The words were well enough to Isabeau's ears, but the tone was of one who would give comfort by talking of that which is little likely to be.

Bernice said: "Or he may wring her neck. He has done that before now."

Isabeau raged to herself. She would have had the Count come to her room, and not that of the smith's widow, as she would call Yvonne. After a time she got up, hardly knowing what she would do, and went to Yvonne's room. She had a hate which must find relief in words which she well knew how to speak in a wounding way, if it went no further than that.

She was quickly back. There was relief in her voice, as well as a puzzled doubt. "She is gone away. That is sure."

Louise laughed. "You will find she will be soon here. She will not hold the Count back from his joy. Where could she go?"

"I know not where. But I tell you she is gone. That is sure."

Louise got to her feet from the cushions on which she lay. "If she make practice to foil the Count, we may see sport ere the day close. He is a wild beast, having had wine. So it is said." She followed Bernice and Doette, who had gone with Isabeau back to Yvonne's room.

Some of Yvonne's things, which had been few enough, were still there, but some others were gone. "See," Bernice said, "she has taken combs!" Such things had a point that they could not miss. It was simple guess that she would not be there when the Count came.

"Where can she hide?" Louise asked. "She cannot get past the gate. Be she in what hole she may, he will drag her out by the hair, if he be in his wild mood."

"I can tell you that," Bernice said, with a cruel joy in her small, colourless eyes. "I can tell you where she will hide. It will be in Captain Redwood's bower by this time."

"Pah, Bernice!" Louise answered to that. "She is not so simple a fool. She would be caught there at the first look. Besides, she would be seen to go in."

That was a likely thing, for Halt had one of the small rooms which opened from the sides of the great hall which were for the unwedded knights. It was seldom that the hall was so left that one could go into one of these bowers without being seen: it made them very safe for guests who had gold or gear, for they could not be entered or robbed in a private way.

Isabeau had made up her mind what she would do. She would take the chance as it came. She said: "Let her be for the time. She will keep, for she cannot fly. You shall leave me here, and I will tell this to the Count in my own way. It may be good times for all, if I do that which I hope."

Her ladies went back to the sala, where they ate sweetmeats and talked, till they were roused by a woman's scream.

## CHAPTER FIFTY

ISABEAU stretched herself on Yvonne's bed. When the Count came he would find something better than the cold reluctance or unpractised art of one too young, and of too common a blood, to be more than clumsy in the high mysteries of a game that Isabeau had played often before, and believed that she could play well.

Sleek and smooth she lay, like a splendid cat, satin-soft, and supple, and long of limb. Her hands were behind her head, and her eyes were distant and hard, as she planned that which she meant to do.

She lay on the black coverlet of the bed, that its contrast might better show the gleaming whiteness of the body with which this game must be played, and won. She heard his hand on the door, and her eyes softened and smiled, as she knew well how to make them do.

He had the great robe of fawn velvet around his shoulders, still showing the slit where her brother's dagger had ripped it down. He threw this off as he came in, being as naked as she.

Her lust awakened at what she saw, and she looked at him with lazy, amorous eyes, in a way she had at such times; but there was the wrath of a savage beast, sudden and fierce, in those with which she was met, as he looked down on her, and saw that it was not she to whom he had thought to come.

He was at her side in three strides, and as he came she turned over, whether by feint or fear, as one who would shrink away. Yet her face was still raised to his own with eyes that mocked and allured. Did she know already that it was not her honour (of which she had none to lose), but her life, for which she fought at that hour, using the best weapons she had?

She laughed low in her throat. She raised her nearer leg from the knee. With her foot on his thigh, she feigned that she would have pushed him back, as it had been well for her to do; but she had no strength against his. He looked down on the pushing foot, with a cruel sneer on the bearded lips. He took her ankle in a great hand.

"It was with this foot," he said, "that you wrought his death."

He looked down on the splendid body that lay at his will, and there was that in the wine-glazed eyes by which she thought she had won.

Holding her ankle still, he put his left hand to her upper arm, and jerked her over on to her back. There was a moment when they were very still. She did not doubt she had won now, and was not sure that she did not like being handled in that bruising way. His eyes were upon her in a drunken doubt that she could not read. But how could she doubt the end, knowing as she did that there was none fairer than she? She showed the lithe grace of a cat, of a sleek, amorous cat, as she lay thus in his grasp, and there could be but one end. "Lucia," he said, "is a slut to you. But I sleep safe."

He held her still in the same way, looking down as though still in that drunken doubt of what he should do next, and in that pause a great fear came to her heart.

He looked round. There was a small table beside the bed. There lay on it her own dagger, small, sharp, thin-bladed, having a jewelled hilt. He loosed her, and lurched somewhat as he turned to pick it up. He muttered: "This will do well." It seemed so small in his hand. It was then that she screamed, as she strove to rise from the bed, and his arm swung round, sweeping her back. He caught her again by the foot which she had put to a use that they both knew; only, it was now with the other hand, for he had the knife in his right. There was a moment's flurry before he could get her down with a great foot on her neck, and then he drove the small, keen blade into her belly, to no depth, and ripped her up for half a foot, or perhaps more.

"It should serve," he said, with a great laugh, as he let her go. "I would have you know that you die."

Isabeau had screamed again as the knife cut. Now she lay still, as one dazed, watching the spreading blood.

The Count turned to an open door, at which Louise and Bernice stood in the front, and behind them a growing crowd. He put on his robe again, though without haste, throwing the dagger back on the table where it had lain before.

He drew himself to his full height as he faced the frightened faces that thronged the door. His voice had a more sober sound: "It is justice done to my will." He walked out between those who gave way before him to right and left.

An hour later, he took his place in the banquet-hall, seeming sober and unashamed.

## CHAPTER FIFTY-ONE

YVONNE had left her room a few minutes after Doette. She wore more clothes than she would often do in the summer days, but, beside that, she took no more than a bag would bear, for she would not risk by delay, and, indeed, she had little to take.

Halt had done better than she. He had had his saddle-bags, which were of a good depth, packed with such things as would be of most use, since he had first thought of what might be done at a sharp need, which had been while he talked to Sir Roland, and mastered a wrath which had but led to his own death.

Hearing from Doette that the time had come, he had gone down to the yard and found a groom, whom he ordered to follow him with the bags, which he was not likely to refuse to do, being told by one who was of such command but a day before, and whose honour was not shorn by Count Gismond's death.

The groom may have wondered as he was led, not to Captain Redwood's own bower, which had been a more likely thing, but to the door of the great tower, which stood wide in these days, its roof having been used to watch, as they had had enough reason to do. Here he took the bags from the groom, and laid them down on the floor. "You may go back now." Wondering somewhat, the man went.

Halt sat down on the bags, with his sword near to his hand. He had not waited long when Yvonne came. He took up the bags, and they began to climb the narrow stairs of the tower. They could not close the door, having no key; but he cared little for that.

When they got to the roof, they found a man there who had been set to watch. That was because none had altered an order which had been routine till the last day, since the siege had commenced. The man, knowing that there was no longer cause that he should watch well, and thinking that none would climb to see what he did, had gone to sleep in the sun.

Being stirred by Captain Redwood's foot, he went down, as he was told, and was glad to do.

Halt looked at Yvonne then, and the look she gave him was good to get. "Well," he said, "we must stay here, if we can, till Bernardi come."

"Here?" she asked, looking round, and there was some wonder, though without protest, in the tone of her voice, for she had not known what he had planned, but only the place where they should meet, and that she should bring what she could for her own needs.

The roof, as we have seen it before, was square and flat, with a parapet which was so low as to make it appear that the builders had tired of bearing stones to that height, which was likely enough. There were no chambers within the tower, the space being filled by the thickness of walls which they had thought it would need to make it firm at so great a height, and by the stair, and a central shaft which went down to the level at which the tower rose from the wall; and over this shaft there was a low roof of tiles to throw off the rain. At one side there was the door by which they had come. Its porch rose not more than three feet from the flat roof of the tower, being sunk so that those who climbed must come clear of the stairs in a crouching way.

Yvonne looked on the wide scene of river, valley, and stream, at the great hills around, and the further mountains beyond the Rhône. It was a fair scene in the light of the summer day, and she had not stood there before. The sky was blue overhead, and the sun shone in the west, but there was black cloud where the Rhône Valley opened toward Avignon, and the more distant sea. She said: "There is storm in the south."

The words brought to his mind the fear of what life must be on that roof should the weather change from the summer peace which he had known since he had come to these parts, so that it had seemed to him like a settled thing. What must she think of a plan which had brought her there to drench and shiver on the naked roof till Bernardi should come? "Well," he said, "we can go down, if we will."

"Oh, not that! Are we safe here for the time we will?"

"We should be safe, if I can make defence as I have thought to do."

He moved round, looking narrowly at the great stones which formed the top of the tower. He asked: "Is your dagger good?"

"Yes," she answered, in some wonder of what he might mean, "it is good enough."

She wore a knife, as all did at that time, for it was needed at every meal. But she had not thought that she would have to fight with her own hands, though she would do that if he asked. "What am I to do?"

"I would get this stone free, if I can."

He looked at one which was looser than most, having been mortised ill, and slackened further by time, and the storms which must beat on that height in the winter days. He said: "I would save my sword, if I can."

Her dagger was better than good, being of Guilbert's gift, who had known steel, and his also was good enough. They both worked as hard as they might to get the stone free, with few words as yet, but with the joy of a common task. It proved to be greater toil than might have been thought, and when it could be somewhat tipped from the corner of the parapet to which it belonged, it was of such weight that it was not easy to get it clear, nor to draw it across the roof. Yet, with their double strength, it was done at last, so that it lay across the front of the low doorway, making it harder to pass than it had been before.

The sun was low by that time over the western hills, and when they looked down on courtyard and garth and battlement, which were spread below them like a pictured scene, they were almost deserted of men, for it was near the hour of the evening meal. They became conscious of their own hunger and thirst, which were increased by the hard work they had done. Halt unpacked one of the bags, which was stuffed with food and some bottles of wine. "We shall not starve for this week, or perhaps longer than that." It seemed long enough to think that they would stay on that roof, even if they should be left there in peace, which it was easy to doubt. But if they should be there longer than that? Who could say how long it might be before Bernardi should come, or what he might do to set his new captain free, when he should learn that he had thus put himself on a tower's roof?

Yvonne's mind stirred to a nearer need. She looked down on her hands. She had never eaten without washing first, till it had become a strength of custom which was not easy to break. And her hands now, after their labour with mortar and time-soiled stone! Yet she would not fret for a small thing. She found a napkin in which food had been wrapped, and did the best cleansing she could, passing it to Halt when she had done. She looked again at the southern sky. "We may yet be glad of that storm."

While they ate, they talked of the need of water, which might be greater than that of food, and sooner felt if they should be long there. There was a little gutter which ran round the roof of the central shaft, and then turned outward to join that which was round the inner side of the parapet, under which it emptied at the last, so that the roof should no be flooded by rain, or the melting snow. They saw that if this gutter were blocked they would have water enough when the rain came, and when they had eaten what they would, they contrived to block it well enough to delay the water, if the storm should come, as it seemed likely to do.

So the time passed, and they were too busy with what they did to regard that there was some bustle below, such as there had not been before that. For the Count had not asked for Yvonne till he had sat at the board, and saw that the two places were empty at his left hand. The thoughts of others, and the whispered talk that men will dare at such times, had been turned to the room where Isabeau lay, being not yet dead, though she was nigh to that with the blood she had lost, and having a wound that no leech would heal.

But when the Count asked, and it became clear that Yvonne had left her room at her own choice, and not, as he had thought at the first, by Isabeau's violence or craft (for it was not easy for him to think that one of a common blood would be slow to accept the honour which he did by deigning to share her bed, and still less that she should have thought to resist his will), then it was soon told that she had been seen to talk to Halt more than to most, and the Count asked: "Has he passed the gate?" And when he learned that neither of them had ridden forth, though their horses had been in readiness all the day, then he called that full search should be made, and so, as the day waned, and they could be found in no other part, and the groom who had borne the bags having said something of that, though not all, it was seen that they were most likely to have climbed to the tower's height.

"Then," the Count said, "they are surely trapped, and it should be simple to bring them down."

"By your leave," Sir Roland answered to that, "if Captain Redwood be in a mood that he will not come of good will, it will be less simple than might be thought at the first word, for it can be seen at the tower's foot that the steps are narrow and steep."

The Count chewed his beard for a time. He was one who would face facts, though it might be in a brutal way. If he were told that Captain Redwood were in a strong place, he would not bellow to fetch him down, though his men die.

"Had he told me," he said, after this pause, "that he would have the demoiselle for his hire, it had been accorded with ease, for there was a debt due, and what was she to me?" (As to that, we may think as we will.) "But," he went on, "now that I am so contemned in my own hall, it must have other ending than that. Yet if he will yield her in peace, it is in peace that himself may go."

Sir Roland answered: "I cannot say what he may do, but if I go to him alone, he may take it in the right way, and I will make peace if I can."

So, at a time when it was dusk below, but when there was still some light on the roof of the high tower, Sir Roland ascended the stair.

It was such toil, he being lame as he was, that he may have wished that he had been slower to speak, before he came to the last bend of the wall; but he was there at last, and had enough breath left to call aloud that he came in peace, and had a quick answer from Halt that that was well if he came alone, and they had some talk after that.

But he came back to the Count to say that he could not prevail. Captain Redwood would not come down, except on a sure oath being sworn that both Madame Livron and he should go free. Beyond that, he had said that it would be at their own peril that more than one should ascend the stair from that time, for if they came in more force he would grieve them the most he could. He had also said that it would be to Count Raymont's gain to let him go quietly forth, for there were those who would have him free in a different way.

"Now, by the two Sainte Maries of the Sea," the Count said, when he heard that (which was the greatest oath which could be sworn in those days, either in Languedoc or Provence), "if they come, it shall be for no more than the bones of a dead man, and there be few of these troops, that are hired of all, who will hold their ranks for a dead chief."

He laughed somewhat at that. Then he bit his beard again in a thoughtful way, and said at last: "But it shall be left to the dawn. They shall have the night on that roof in the best comfort they can."

There was a sound of rain as he spoke, which stirred his laughter again.

## CHAPTER FIFTY-TWO

THE next morning the Count ordered that all the troops he had brought, with those who had been of the household of Count Gismond, should be arrayed in the castle court.

He spoke to them of the late master of Faucon-haut, who had died by his hand, and who was to be buried in Ste. Sarah's Church at the noon of the next day. He said that he had had great wrongs at Count Gismond's hands, but that he had been killed in a duel himself had sought, as was known of all the knights who had been there, of whom Sir Lanval was one, being a trouvère who would tell that tale in the right way. And if there had been treason astir, it had not been of his will (for whom his own hands were enough), and he had done justice for that.

There were many who could not guess what was meant by the last words. Nor did all know how Isabeau had come by the wound from which she was dying now. But they knew that Count Raymont had made his seat strong, and it was not for them to reply. Also, those who were of the castle, and had known the Lady Isabeau's ways in other matters than this, could not be sure in their hearts that the Count might not have a good case. And when he added that if they were true vassals to him they would find him a good lord, but that he was one who would be mocked of none, either in castle or town, they thought more of themselves, and of places they might gain, or that might be still held, rather than of him who lay dead in the castle chantry, or of her who died in Yvonne's room.

When he had finished these words, he called for twenty men who would volunteer to bring Captain Redwood, and the woman who was with him, down from the tower. He said that there would be peril for those who should go first, for it was a narrow upward way, where there was not space for two to go forward abreast, and Captain Redwood might hope that his sword would make it secure, whether against many or few. But as to that, they could draw lots as to who should be first, so that the chance would be equal for all. He would give five silver crowns to every man, be he first or last. But they must not come down alive, having failed, lest they meet a worse fate at his hands than could lie in the danger of Captain Redwood's sword, for he had no value for cowards, nor was he one who would be defied in his own towers.

There was a quick offer of more than twenty to take that risk, so that he could choose those of the better kind, for there was a chance to each that he might be the last, and the crowns were for all. At the worst, there would be no more to face than the sword of a single man. At the best, they would have nothing to do but to climb a stair, looking at the backs of those who went before. It was not to be thought that Captain Redwood could deal with twenty men pushing upward against his sword, though he might give wounds or death to some of those who should be at the front.

So the silver was paid, and the lots drawn, and he who was to be first took a good sword, and the second a ten-foot spear, which could be pushed up at his side, to vex the legs of one standing above. They wore helms and gorgets of steel, to take the thrust of a downward sword, and they told each other that they would do well enough, even if Captain Redwood should make defence, seeing the coming of such a regiment of men, which he might be fainthearted to do.

To approach the foot of the tower, it was needful that they should traverse the battlements for a space that could be seen from its top, and though they would pass out of sight after that, so that it could not be certainly known that they were ascending the stair, yet it would be easy to guess. Yet there might be no loss in that, for they could have little hope to surprise those who would be alert to the noise which such a party of armoured men would make on the stone steps, and the sight of the strength in which they came might incline him to yield with less trouble than there would otherwise be.

There were curses enough when they saw how steep the steps were, and how narrow of tread, but they went on, as they must, and when they came to the last turn but one, above which there was no more than the few steps which led to the door at the top, they saw that Captain Redwood stood far above, in a faint light, having come down to that place that he might give them warning before they died.

"Go back," he called, "while you yet can, or your deaths will be on your own heads."

There was a roar of curses at that, and of ribald threats, such as men of their kind will shout when there is death in the air, and Halt was quick to withdraw, for there was a risk that there might be some who had bows which they would bring into use, which there was no light for him to see.

He went quickly up, and pushed through the space which was left by the great stone which had been moved to the stairhead, and he bent his strength to heave it forward on to the steps; but he could do no more than move it a few inches, while the seconds passed, till he called Yvonne to his side, and together, with all the strength that they had, they moved it, as they had done before, so that it toppled forward and fell.

They saw it bound down the short flight in two leaps, and had it stopped there at the turn, they had been in worse case than before; but it was too large, and the steps too steep and too narrow for that. It leapt again out of view, and as it did this there was a cry of terror that changed as it began into a scream of a different tone, and after that there was a mingled sound that was dreadful to hear.

For it had struck the first man, who was then nearly at the top of the flight, with a force which had swept him back upon those behind, so that they went down in a heap, with the great stone pounding them as they fell. They choked the next turn at the foot of that flight, and some fell further, and some stayed, but as those struggled who were underneath, some of whom were least hurt, the stone, that was on the top of the heap, started again. Those who had fallen further it smote anew, giving wounds or death where there was hurt enough before that, and then, being no further stayed, it bounded on from flight to flight to the foot of the tower, where it was shattered upon the battlements into three bloodstained fragments, one of which struck a man who stood there to his death, after which it lay still.

Then a little crowd gathered round the foot of the tower, but not approaching too near, so that none dared to lift up the dead man at that time. They watched for what more would come down, which was no more than a thin trickle of blood that dripped and curdled upon the steps. And then, as the crowd grew, a man came who slid rather than fell, and rose at the foot of the steps, and stumbled, and fell again. After him, there came several with different wounds, as of him who had the rim of his morion driven into his skull, and yet lived till they drew it out, and others which may be left untold, which were not pleasant to see.

There were but seven who came back from that climb, even in such fashion as that, and the rest might have lain as they were till they died (if they were not already dead), or gained strength to descend, had not Sir Lanval said he would go up, if no other would. He took no arms, but he had a white scarf in sign of peace, and a great shield over his head, and he was a glad man when he had passed the wounded and dead. He called who he was in a loud voice, and had a fair reply, and was bidden to come up, if he came alone.

He returned in a short time, bearing one with a broken leg, which was hard to do on those steps, and bringing assurance that any might climb in peace, if they went only to succour those who were hurt, and no higher than that. So Count Raymont was able to number the dead, which he did with a black brow. It was after that that Raoul came to the gate with a strong bevy of spears, making demand that he should speak with Captain Redwood. The Count answered with fair words, saying that he could enter, and could speak to his captain to his content. He may have thought that he could use Raoul as hostage if he should get him into his power, or he may have meant what he said in a literal way, thinking that Raoul could go up the tower if he would, and there stay, where he would take his share of what food and water there might be, which could not be much, and be of less harm than if he were in command of two hundred men who had made their camp in the hills. But it mattered not what he meant, for Raoul said that he would stay where he was. He said, beyond that, that if his captain were not free within two hours of that time, he must judge that he was held in duress, and do the castle the most grief that he could, till he should be set free.

After saying which, he rode off at a good pace, lest he should be answered by a flight of bolts from the wall.

## CHAPTER FIFTY-THREE

"As to that," Sir Lanval said to Doette, "that which I did was of no merit, and is unrequiring of praise, being that to which I was vowed, so that it was beyond choice.

"For you must know that the order of knighthood does not only require that those who take its vows should serve God on the field of war, when it would be a less thing than it is, for there are few men who will not fight when the battle joins, whether they be knighted or no. But the service to which we are vowed is to all weakness and need, so that we do no more than we must at such call, even though it may be at times with faintness of heart, or a lagging will. But as to this, there was no danger at all. If I feared as I went up—as I will own that I did—it was for no cause.

"For when I had made known who I was, and Captain Redwood called to me to go on, I found that they had no other stone ready to roll down, though there was one that they toiled to bring, which will be in its place before now."

"You may say as you will," Doette answered to that, "but I have never been in such fear."

"Yet," Sir Lanval observed, "you heard what I would do, and said no word which would draw me back."

"I had said no word had I thought you would heed, nor should I have had boldness to presume that, for my mother taught that it is not the part of ladies of gentle birth to hold back any knight by their own weakness or fear, to make him less than he would be without them. But I know myself to be coward, which is a weakness I cannot change, and, soon or last, you must know that, if you would know me at all."

"But that," Sir Lanval said, "is what I shall never know. I should say—if you cared at all for my life, which you will not have me to doubt, as a friend may—that you had a larger courage than I. For it is ever harder to wait than to do. And I know now of what it is that I will make you a song in the spring days."

Doette made no answer to that, though there was a hidden light in the fawn-brown eyes, over which the lids fell, of which light Sir Lanval might have been glad to see somewhat more than he did.

But he went on to say: "But for now you will not take it amiss if I would that you were gone from this place, and that you will not delay, even until you can have reply from Poitou. And I would have you tell the Lady Bernice that I will escort you both to wherever you will to go, if it can be so agreed, as I think it should."

For, of Isabeau's ladies, Louise was already gone, not having waited for her to die. She had ridden out to the town, taking more things than Isabeau would have said to be hers; and, after lodging there for the night, had hired service enough, and was even then going north on the Dijon road, with a company of merchants who had a strong train.

Doette had done less than that, but she had seen that the castle of Faucon-haut could not be longer for her, and had written to her mother at Poitou to make provision for her return to that place, or where else she would, and to send gold for her charges upon the way.

Bernice was less willing to move. She lacked friends who were wealthy and strong, and who would be glad to see her again. She nursed Sir Lambel, who still lay ill of the wounds he had had when he fought for the western gate, and she was more loth to move from his side than he would have been to have seen her go.

"I must wait," Doette said, "till my mother send, and Bernice is in no haste to be gone, nor is she sure where it will be."

She would not own that she was short of gold, knowing that Sir Lanval would be quicker to lend than she to take at his hand. Besides, it should not have been, for her mother supplied her well; but she had lent to Bernice, and others, of whom Isabeau had been one, in the days when gold had been short for their needs, and each had said: "Tell it not that I borrowed this," and she had been still, so that each thought that they had taken no more than a part of her store, when they had had all.

Beyond that, she had had a doubt in her mind that if she should take Sir Lanval's escort, even with a maid in her train—who must be hired for that—her mother might not be well pleased, unless Bernice should also be with her for the whole way. So she said: "I must do what my mother will, unless there be more need than. I now see. She is not one to delay, after the plain words I have written to her. She will send in haste. It were a likely thing that she send spears. And, beside that, I would be glad to see that they are free of Sir Raymont's power. How did you find them to be?"

"As to that," Sir Lanval replied, "I could say naught did I not know you to be a sure friend who would not give word to their foes, for it was on that pledge that I was let to climb out to the roof of the tower.

"They seemed in good heart, and in good accord, and are resolved to endure, but they have many needs, and they had to stay for some hours on the upper steps, which are narrow on which to sit, while there was storm in the night, for they had no shelter but that.

"But now they are making shift to pull apart the roof which is over the central shaft of the tower, so that they may build of timber and tiles, if it be no more than a screen from the wind."

"There were some old cloaks, such as could be spread on the floor, and some cushions on which to lie, which we had when we watched from that tower, which Isabeau would not have brought away, it being so much toil to bear then upward a second time, and she saying they would come to no hurt in the summer days.

"They have those, as I think. But they will lack food in a few days, and water now. They have wine, and have caught rain in one bottle which they had then drunk. Had it been cleaner, it had been more gain, but it had been drained from the tiles of the roof."

"Then if they stay there, we must give them such aid as we can."

"That," Sir Lanval said, "it would be a sore peril to do. Nor is it clear to my mind that I should be free to do that, who am too like to Sir Raymont's guest, if I stay here. As I see, I must stand aside, doing what in honour I may, as the time comes."

Doette said no more on that point, seeing the view which he took, on which she could not say he was wrong. But she thought: "I am no guest of Sir Raymont, having as good right to be here as he, if not something better than that." For her mother had paid a large sum that she should be where she was for two years, of which the most part was to come.

So as the days passed, and there was no sign from the tower, and Sir Raymont jested at times: "Let them shiver and starve. There will come a time when he will be fain to barter all for a good meal. He will be glad of a worse paramour than he now has, should she lie in a better bed." And as she heard this, the thought grew in Doette's mind that what Sir Lanval might not in honour do must be done by her, and that, if her courage could rise to that point, she could do it as well, if not better, then he.

So there came a night when she rose at the darkest hour, carrying a satchel of good size, which she had packed with such things as Yvonne would most need (which she thought that she had chosen much better than Sir Lanval would have been likely to do), and went out of her room, to the larger garth, by the private way that the ladies had so that they need not cross the great hall.

So far, she had no fear that she would be heard or seen, for now that Isabeau was dead, and buried in Ste. Sarah's Church (which had been done with enough pomp, for Sir Raymont did not stint gold, though he did not go to pray at her tomb), and Louise had gone her own way, there were only Bernice and herself who slept in that part. But when she had got clear of the garth, and was beneath the steps by which the outer battlements might be gained, she found that her troubles were still ahead. For there was such watch on the walls that she could not hope that she could go the distance she must without being seen and stayed.

She had not forethought that it would be so hard as it proved, for there had been no guard at the foot of the tower during the daylight hours. They could come down if they would. It was what they were meant to do. Having come down, they could go where they would, till they should be seized and held, for where could it be? The walls were too high to leap, the gates too guarded to force.

She had thought that she could wait till the warder should have passed on his rounds, and go unseen to the foot of the tower stair.

But it was Raoul who had prevented that, though it had been far from his thought or will. He had so harried Sir Raymont's power with ambush and raid, with the two hundred men that he had, that there was a doubt that he might not even assault the walls in the night, and Sir Raymont had ordered a closer watch, being one who would be careful in all devices of war, when he was not sodden with wine.

So she had turned back perforce, seeing that what she did must be in the daylight hours, and having hidden the satchel behind a seat, where it would not have to be carried far.

The next day, choosing the hour of the midday meal, from which she had made excuse for herself, she drew the satchel, with a hand that shook much, from the place where it was hid, and made her way to the foot of the tower, being seen of few, and hindered of none. Very quietly, she ascended the tower.

She was halfway up the last of the long flights which were of the full length of the wall, when the thought that it was about there that she was in the most danger that she would be heard; and that those above, hearing a noise so near, would loose a stone which would dash her to dreadful death, made her heart beat for a time in a mad way, and then pause, so that she felt that she was about to swoon, and what hope would there be then? For she would fall down those steps which were so cruel and steep, and that would be hurt enough, before the noise she would make would call down a worse fate from her friends' hands.

And so, thinking that she would swoon at each step, which she did not do, she struggled on to the last turn, and as she came to that place where she could sit leaning somewhat against the wall, she called as high as she could: "Yvonne! Yvonne!" making no effort to do more, and in a moment Yvonne came.

## CHAPTER FIFTY-FOUR

YVONNE wore a dress which was much soiled, and there was a scar on her cheek, where it had been cut by a flying fragment of tile, as she had helped to break down the roof which was over the central shaft of the tower, so that they could build something which would be more useful to them. She was thinner than she had been, and the bones in her face showed, as they had not done before, which was from the lack of water rather than food, of which what they had was not yet done, having been rationed with care. But, except for what rain they could catch at times, they had no more than a little wine to drink for each day, and that also was almost done, so that from thirst they had suffered much.

But the quiet courage which she had always had was now more sure of itself, and her eyes had the light of a great joy. For the love which had come at once when those two had met (which is ever its best way) was now brought to an equal trust, and the peace which will follow therefrom, and, beyond that, they had good hope to defend themselves where they were, and to endure till Bernardi came.

Yvonne took the satchel's weight, and gave her also a hand, so that they were soon out on the roof. She said: "You are friend indeed! But is it not at a risk which you should not take, even for this? If Count Raymont should know...."

"No," Doette said, "there is little reason to fear, if I do not linger too much, and am heedful as to leaving the tower. I am safe now. But it was the dread of what you might do, should you hear my coming before you should know me friend."

When she said that, Yvonne knew how great a thing she had done, though indeed there had been no danger such as Doette had feared. So she said: "We had not done that dreadful thing had there been any choice left. Nor should we do it again unless there were those who came in strong force, and were plainly foes."

And when Doette knew that she could come again without dread of a fearful death, she made light of the risk that she should be seen to come, and of Count Raymont's wrath.

"There is little peril in that. I can be secret and sure. Let me know your needs, and I will come tomorrow again at this hour."

"It is water more than all else, though the white wine you have brought is a priceless boon." She named some things, other than water and food, that she would be glad to have, and Doette said that she would remember all. They kissed—which they had not done before—and parted at that, for Doette would not wait. She said: "I will tell Sir Lanval—who is your friend, as I think you know—that I have found you less soiled and worn than I had feared to see. Also, you have a glad look. I think you have come to your joy."

"You may say that. Though we think not to wed till we are free of this land, for Captain Redwood will go to England again, which he has heard that he can, for the matter which sent him here is a dead thing. But I must not hold you to talk of that." For she saw that Doette was restless to go.

All this time Halt was asleep on the further side of the roof, for they had divided the day and night, so that each of them should watch for eight hours—but not all at one time—while the other slept; and they had eight hours also when they would be together, and talk of their past lives, which had been so widely apart, and of the future they thought to share, and forget the thirst that they felt when they watched alone.

Doette went back, and was not observed, and so, getting bolder by that, she stayed longer the next day, finding that Yvonne was very willing to talk, and they had both much to tell. She returned, as she thought without being seen of any whom she would rather miss, and told Sir Lanval all, as they sat over the chess, and he sought to teach her to play, which she never would.

"I would," he said, "that there were word from your mother brought, or that you would ride forth in my guard, which there may be few ladies who would not do, they being placed as you are."

But she answered: "I know not that I would go now, unless my mother should send with a strait command. For I give aid to those above, which it would grieve them to miss."

"Well," Sir Lanval said, "all things end. You should not move your knight, being so placed, for it threatens much, but if it be once advanced on whichever square you may choose, it has lost the most of its power. It is often thus on the field of war, for war and chess are brothers of the same blood." They went on with the game.

Sir Lanval saw that she would not go, at the least for that day, and he said no more. But he had a sombre fear that there was more sorrow to come. He had told his squire to be alert at all times, and ready to ride forth in an hour. And he had ceased the making of songs.

## CHAPTER FIFTY-FIVE

THAT night, at the banquet hour, Count Raymont sat in his chair of state, which had been Gismond's before, and he poured the wine with a freer hand than he had let himself do in the days since he had used Isabeau's dagger the way he had.

For at last he was sure he could bring all to the end he would, without further peril or strife, and he planned that he would ride back to the place that he better loved before the next moon should appear.

For he had made peace with the town, giving them a new charter which pleased them well, and had made dispositions as to how Faucon-haut should be held and ruled when he was not there, and the menace of the condottieri, which had been one that he could not flout, was now passing away.

For it had been much as he had supposed in Raoul's camp. There had been menace from it at first; for though Raoul had been too weak to assault the walls, and had lacked ladders and much else that he would have needed for that, which had been lost on the night that the camp was burned; yet he had harassed the roads, and caused the gates both of town and castle to be closed more than was the habit of peaceful times.

He had sent over the hills and released those forty bowmen whom M. Sault had first hired. He had paid them well, and enlisted most in his own band, and would have been the bolder for that; but there was a tale that he had had trouble with his own men, which grew as the days passed.

For they said that Captain Redwood was dead, and why should they stay there? Why should they wait till Bernardi came, if he ever would? They did not seek to quarrel with Raoul. He was a leader with whom they would be content. But there was a great treasure in the chests which were now in his tent, which they claimed to belong to them, now that Konrad and the new captain were dead. And it would be much for each man, they now being as few as they were.

If Bernardi should come, he would say the same as themselves, and either take the gold with a strong hand, or he would divide it among the whole army, and how much would there then be for each? Let Raoul make a new band for himself, or, if he would not do that, let him divide the gold in a fair way, and they would each go where he would, as was often the way when a captain died.

There were different tales as to what had followed from that. Some said that after riot, and some spilling of blood, Raoul had divided the gold, seeing that there was no other way. Others said he was dead. But it was a sure fact that the band had gone.

Count Raymont could say that it had been as he first foretold. And if Bernardi should come now, would he make a private war of his own on all the strength of Faucon-haut and Faucon-bas—with St. Péray beyond, which was far stronger than both—for a dead captain whom he had never seen? It was foolish to think. The condottieri fought for hire. They did not make their own wars in the land.

And he had little doubt but that Captain Redwood was dead, or too weak to be any further fear. There had been none seen to look over the parapet of the tower (which, indeed, both Halt and Yvonne had been careful not to do, for a crossbow bolt could rise to that height, and their lives had become dear to each other and to themselves), and it was known what supplies they had, which Halt had

had packed into the saddle-bags he had taken up. And there had been no rain for five days.

Now Count Raymont had offered twenty crowns of gold to the first man who would climb the stairs and bring news of what the roof held. There were many who were disposed to go up, dividing their minds between a fear that they should venture too soon, and be crushed by a leaping stone, and an equal fear that they would delay too long, and another be sooner than they, and the crowns go into the wrong hands.

There was a woman at the lower board who sought to tempt a man to be first to go up, caring little for him in her heart, whether he might die or live, but thinking that it was she who would spend the crowns. "I would," he said in a doubt, "that I could feel more sure than I do that Captain Redwood is not yet watchful and strong."

And another woman, of a different mood, who had seen more, answered, "As to that, you should ask the Lady Doette."

Before the man could reply, the great voice of Count Raymont, for whom the words were not meant, but who had overheard something of what was said, silenced the hall.

"What is this which should be asked of the Lady Doette?"

"Lord," the woman said, who had meant no mischief to her, but had seen her come down from the tower, and who now had no courage nor skill for a likely lie, "whether Captain Redwood be yet alive."

The Count wasted no more words upon her. He turned to Doette to ask: "When have you been up the tower?"

Sir Lanval, sitting at her side, would have stayed her from any speech, but she had a courage of her own kind, and was not of those who will lie.

"Lord," she said, "I took food to my friends." Her eyes, which were often veiled, were now lifted to his, showing no fear, and they looked at one another for a long moment, while his hand went to his beard, and the hall listened, and became still.

Then he asked, in a quiet way: "At what hour have you done this?"

"At the hour of noon, or nearly to that."

"Well, tomorrow you shall do it again."

That night Sir Lanval said to his squire: "Lambert, I will knight you in seven days from this time, if we both live to that hour."

# CHAPTER FIFTY-SIX

"As for that," Sir Lanval said, "the Count means you no harm, for it would be the loss of that which he aims to do. And I think that you must go up, for there is no better way. You can take water and food, and you can stay there for a time, which, as I think, will not be for long. It may be that Captain Redwood's army will come, of which I have more hope than the Count fear, or if you should see the arms of Poitou at the gate (and you can see all at that height), and know that your mother has sent her word, I think that you might come down, if you were in a sore strait, for the Count would not dare to do you great wrong, knowing the power of Poitou, and it being allied to Burgundy as it is, the Duke being his own lord. And before that you may hear from me."

"Well," Doette answered to that, "I was in doubt, but I will do it if you are sure that it is the best way. But I am in sore dread of the part you take."

"Lady," he said, "you must not doubt overmuch, for though I am a maker of songs, I have used a sword before now. And I have a plan beyond that, which there is no leisure to tell."

Sir Lanval spoke thus to give her the best comfort he might, and to be assured that she would go up the tower, which he thought safest for her. For though there was truth in what he had said that Count Raymont might fear to wrong one of the great house of Poitou, yet that could only be when he was not maddened with wine, for what he might do then against one who had roused his wrath, there was no guess that could tell.

The Count had a simple plan, by which he meant to end that which made him less than lord in his own towers; which, now he knew that those above were not starving to death, he was resolved to do without longer delay. He chose six men who were active and young, and who could be trusted to climb those steep and narrow steps at a faster pace than Doette, when they should know that they bought their lives with their speed.

They were to follow her at some distance behind till they came to the last bend, and to that point they were to be as silent as they could; but when she had taken that turn, and would be seen by any who looked down, they were to dismiss caution for speed, so that they should catch her up at the top.

The Count rightly thought that, even if they made more noise than they should, Captain Redwood would not loose a stone from above till he should be sure that Doette was not there, it being the hour at which she would be likely to come, and when he should first see his foes he would see her also upon the stair. After that, if they could not win to the roof, being six against one, and with the girl's body for shield—well, they would be no loss when they died.

It was not long from the matin hour when Sir Lanval rode out with his squire, as he often would, so that his horses should not spoil in the stalls. He wore a surcoat of silver and blue, very gay to regard, and beneath it his coat of mail, which he did not change when he came in, from which time his squire was not seen after he had stalled the horses well. Sir Lanval strolled here and there, but he did not speak to Doette, nor regard the talk of what was to be tried at the noon hour, but he also was not seen—nor was he missed—for a time before then.

So the noon came, and the crowd gathered on the battlements to see what was about to be, the Count being there, and his own and the castle knights, but they stood a wide space from the foot of the tower stair, for they remembered how far the first stone had leapt as it struck the pavement that was as hard as itself, and burst into three parts.

Doette came, making no protest, and carrying food and wine which she feared the Count would forbid, but he took no notice of that. He was content that she should play her part on such terms as she would, and his eyes were for the six he had chosen to follow her steps. They were men-at-arms of the best he had, lightly armoured—for who could climb those steps in an agile way being encased in a weight of steel? But four of them carried bucklers and long one-handed swords, and two others had spears which might be pushed past a comrade in front to a deadly end. They saw Doette start on her way, and followed at the right distance behind.

It was when they were halfway up the third flight, and Doette was higher than that, that they saw Sir Lanval stand at the top, with his sword bare in his hand. They knew that they were in no danger of the flying stone that they most feared, seeing who were above them now. They were not men to turn for a drawn sword. They came on at a better pace than before.

Sir Lanval let Doette pass. He said to her: "If they come near to the door, you can tell Captain Redwood to send a stone down, for it will no longer matter to us."

She said: "He would never that, as you know."

"Then it is the more needful that we do not fail."

She passed Lambert, and went on. Sir Lanval thought: "She will be safe now, be the end to us as it may."

He did not doubt that he could hold the stair; but he looked beyond that.

He stood on the level space which was where the stair turned at the bend, which was not more than two feet at its most width, and Lambert stood somewhat behind and at his side on the higher stair, and a halberd was in his hand. Sir Lanval called to those who came up: "You will halt, if you are wise, for I have something to say."

The man who was first slackened his pace, but answered in a bold way: "Sir Lanval, we have no quarrel with you, but we must do our lord's will. We pray you to let us pass."

"It was that which I wished to say. If you will pause enough to give the Lady Doette time to get clear of this dangered way, then you may go as you will, either up or down. It is nothing to me."

"Lord, it is that which we may not do, being against the orders we have. We must follow close, and there is danger in this delay."

"Then you must get past if you can."

The man said no more. He came on at the most speed he could, with his sword ready to thrust, and his buckler over his head.

Sir Lanval saw the long spear of the man behind come up at the side, seeking his legs. He must step aside as he smote, and his blow was no better for that. He felt a sword-point at his groin, where he would have taken an evil wound but that it was on the right side of his mail, and the links held. He struck again, severing the shaft of the spear.

Lambert thrust with his halberd at the man who was first, who was overset by the blow. He swayed, letting his sword drop, and caught at the halberd-head lest he should fall backward on those behind. Lambert fell on Sir Lanval, who came to his knees, being saved by the corner of the wall from a further fall.

The man who was first regained his balance with the aid of the halberd, to which both Lambert and he clung; but those behind had a worse fate. The man who had the spear had taken it in both hands when he thrust, and his balance was lightly lost. As his comrade swayed upon him he fell. Having nothing but each other on which to catch, the five went down the full length of the steps to the next turn, where they lay heaped, and must struggle with caution, lest they fall a like distance again.

The first man had dropped both buckler and sword. The point of the halberd was near his breast. He must cling to that, and was at the mercy of Sir Lanval's sword. Sir Lanval asked: "Is it enough?" The man was grateful for that, for which he had cause.

"Then," Sir Lanval said, "we will go down."

He had no mind to add two to the mouths which must be fed on the tower roof, but he could not guess what Count Raymont would say or do, when he learnt how he had been foiled.

## CHAPTER FIFTY-SEVEN

THOSE who watched at the tower foot saw the minutes pass, and they heard no sound. The silence lasted till there had been time to ascend to the roof, and more, and they thought it a likely thing that there would be fighting there which they would hear, and perhaps see.

And as there was no sign of this, they said: "It must be that they have yielded, being weak, as they doubtless are. They are on the way down." And then there was a noise of one descending the stair, and a man limped out with a twisted leg, and sat down with a groan, and after that there came the man who had been first, who was little bruised, and then Sir Lanval and his squire; and then—after a time—two men who were helping a third who was worse hurt than themselves. And that was all, for there was one who lay where he fell, having a broken neck.

The Count looked, and understood. For a time it seemed that he was made dumb by his own rage. But when he spoke, it was in a quieter way than he often would, though it may have been of no less menace for that.

"Sir Lanval, being my guest, and having taken the part of my foes, will you tell me good cause that you should not die?"

"That I am your guest," Sir Lanval answered, in a tone more quiet than his own, "is a point to which I have given much thought, but it is one on which I am not yet clear; but that I have taken part with your foes is not true. I did no more than there was clear need, that I might save the Lady Doette from being placed between swords, as my knighthood bound me to do."

The Count said to one who stood by: "Call a strong guard." For he observed that the knights around him were, for the most part, unarmed, or wearing no more than their swords, and Sir Lanval was sheathed in mail; also, he was one who was well liked, and that he was a trouvère of such fame made him a privileged man. So that, in the sight of many, he could scarcely do wrong.

Sir Lanval did not hear the words, but he could guess what was said. He knew that if he were once in the castle dungeons he might have a heavy ransom to pay, even if the Count should let his life go. But he could not hope to fight his way out, seeing how strongly the gate was held, even should he get so far, which was not easy to hope.

But, beside that, he did not aim to get free, leaving Doette where she was, and with no surety that any rescue would come. He must bring this thing to the point he would before the guard came.

"I have no will," he said, "to be guest of yours, and I stay here no more than my honour needs, that I may succour those ladies who are abused at your hands. You may render that which I cost for this time, if you will, like a tavern score, which my squire shall pay."

"I hold no ladies abused," the Count answered to that, "for she who is on the tower is not one of a gentle blood, be she abused or no, and the Lady Doette could have ridden forth at any hour that she would, till I knew that she was here to comfort my foes. And, for the rest, you will be glad to get free for much more than a tavern score, for I have broken men on a wheel for less things than you have now done."

"That you have done such things," Sir Lanval said, "so that knighthood is shamed in you, I should believe without words." As he said this, he pulled off a leather glove from his hand, which was backed with steel, and threw it straight and hard, so that it struck Count Raymont between the eyes. "If you have honour left that you may still lose, you must now fight with one who is not a woman that you can stab, nor a man with a maimed hand. For you may put me in what dungeon you will, but there is a mark of shame that you will bear to your death if you let my glove lie."

The Count wiped the blood from his brow, and took up the glove. He said: "You have chosen your death, which I might have spared without this. I will meet you on foot at tomorrow noon, in the courtyard of this castle of Faucon-haut, whether with axes or swords, and when you lie at my will, I will give you space to remember before you die."

Sir Lanval heard, and he would not show that his heart sank. The Count had choice of the weapons with which they should fight, and of whether it should be on horseback or no, so that no more could be said about that. But Sir Lanval had thought that the lance would give him what hope he could have against a knight so famed, and so much larger than he, for he knew that he could tilt well.

While this quarrel had run its course, it had drawn the eyes of all who were standing round; but now there was one who chanced to look out to the town. He could not see as far as he would have done on the roof of the tower, but the battlements of Faucon-haut were high, and he saw much. He saw no glitter and shine, for the sky was a sullen grey, and there was no light from above, but the road that came down from the hills was dark with Bernardi's spears.

## CHAPTER FIFTY-EIGHT

IT was but a short hour from the sight of Bernardi's spears that his trumpet was at the gate. It came with the wolf's-head banner and a flag of truce at its side; but the note it sounded was brief and high.

Those who looked from the walls saw but three who rode up to the gate. They were sheathed in steel, and their horses were good, but they made no show beyond that, for the condottieri had little love for the tossing plumes and glow of colour with which kings and princes would go to war. For they made a trade, and not a pastime, of what they did on the field.

Short and defiant, the trumpet-summons rose and ceased, and echoed among the hills.

The message, when it came to the Count, was as brief as the trumpet-call. Offering neither terms nor threat, the army demanded its chief.

"Roland," the Count said, "you shall speak them fairly in this, and it should be easy to make accord. I will make no strife with such force as is now here for a man that I do not want, or a woman of the town, who has been Gismond's mistress before. Let them give a good pledge that they will part in peace, and those they seek shall go free."

Sir Roland went to the gate with this tale, but it was a pledge that he could not get. There was parleying after that, and it was agreed that Sir Roland should meet Captain Bernardi himself upon the bridge at the third hour after noon.

The Count said: "You will speak him fair, making peace if you see a way that with honour you can." For he saw that if he should overthrow Sir Lanval upon the next day, there would be enough honour for him, and if he should fail to do that, there would be an end in another way.

The condottieri lined the road on the far side of the bridge, and Sir Roland and Captain Bernardi met in the midst, both being on horseback and unarmed, and having but two companions, as had been fairly agreed. Sir Roland could ride well enough (having been helped at the horse's side), though he walked ill.

Bernardi rode with his head bare. He had been black, but was now grey, a man somewhat tall and thin, with dark eyes in which there was seldom mirth, and a beard cut to a point in a formal way.

He greeted Sir Roland courteously, though without warmth, showing that he had heard his name, and of his wound, and that he knew that he had been a good knight before that. Sir Roland was pleased, for he had not thought that his name would be known to one who had spent his life in Italian wars, and he answered in the right way.

After that, they came to the point for which they were met. "The Count asks a pledge," Bernardi said, "to which he has no right, and which I could not grant if I would. For if I say that, the Captain-General being released, we shall retire in peace from this land, and you release him thereon, and he, being so freed, should give orders of a different kind, where would my pledge be?"

"It might be thought," Sir Roland replied, "that those you lead would obey your will."

"It might be so thought with truth, but I must take orders from him to whom all belongs at the last."

"As to that, it might be thought, Captain Wolvenstein being dead, and your power being what it is— But I will not talk of that. I will only say that you cannot ask for Captain Redwood's release if you will give no pledge that we shall have peace when it is done. If you wish to have his assent, would you take a letter from him giving you power to make terms?"

"I would take neither his hand nor his seal, for, to be frank, I do not know his hand very well, and his seal may be in your power. More than that, I should not know himself, should you let him free; but I have those who would, among whom is Captain Raoul, whom I think you have met before, and who is now holding the road at its lower end, that the town may know that this matter is not for it."

"I know Captain Raoul, and am glad to hear that he lives, for there have been tales of another kind. But if you cannot make terms of peace, and the Count will not release him whom he hath now in his power without that, must we have war for so little cause?"

"There is no need for war that I know. But you must speak to Captain Redwood himself, as it should be easy to do."

"Then shall we make truce for a day, while we learn what his will may be?"

Sir Roland had seen from the first that it was to Captain Redwood that they should have gone, had they been sure—as he now was—that Bernardi would take his orders from him.

"I will wait no day," Bernardi answered, "for I know not how great his need may be. I will wait an hour, but no more. For the order I have is not to parley, but fetch him forth. And I will tell you this, which may help you to make accord if he should require terms which you do not like—I will take this castle in three days with the force which I now have."

"It may be more easy," Sir Roland said, "to boast than to do."

"I make no boast, but speak of that which it is my business to know. I have come over the hills, by ways which Captain Raoul had already found, so that I should not approach by the town road and have hindrance therefrom. Being where I now am, I can hold them back for a week with no more than hundred spears. The Count's vassals among the hills are cut off from his support on the other side. They will not make head, lest we burn and plunder them, house and byre. While we leave them alone—as I have given orders to do— they will be content to lie still. And I have such strength of ladders and storming-tools, and of men trained to their use, that I can assault without pause, either by night or day."

Bernardi spoke as one who gives reason, rather than in a threatening way, for his one passion was for the science of war, and had all men been as himself, there would have been little fighting to do, for they would have agreed what its end would be, and made peace at first on such terms as its strife must bring.

"Well," Sir Roland said, "you may be right or wrong. Yet you might storm our walls in the time you guess, and have failed then, for your Captain might be dead by that."

"If he be so, I will hang Count Raymont on his own gallows, as you may tell him from me."

"You would never that, be your quarrel the most it might, for it is not a death for a knight to die."

"I should not be moved by that thought. He may have hanged those who are better than he. I am one who is not knighted myself, nor, it may be, the less esteemed for that loss."

"There are those," Sir Roland courteously allowed, "who are themselves, and have no need of the honours of men, as there may be knights who bring no honour to the order they join, yet is the order not lessened thereby, though it be too hard for them to attain thereto. But as for Count Raymont, though he may do such things at times as his friends are not glad to see, yet I would say this, that the fault may be at times more in manner than deed. For there may be others who do worse things in a better way."

Captain Bernardi was not concerned to dispute this, thinking only that Sir Roland did well to say what he could for his own lord, but it had a kernel of truth. There were men of better repute who would have harried Gismond for the gold he owed a year sooner than he had done, and then only when Gismond's town was in riot about his gates. They would have done as much in another way, though they would not have taken his seat at the meal. If he had killed Gismond thereafter, he had been challenged thereto, and had had no choice but to fight, and if he had arraigned Isabeau as the cause of her brother's death and could have proved a fact that himself knew, she would have had pity from none, and her end would have been the stake. But he would become heavy with wine, and must then do things in a coloured way.

Now Sir Roland went back, and told him what had passed, and he said: "An hour is a short time. Let it be proved at once what Captain Redwood will say."

Sir Roland went to Sir Lanval, and asked: "Will it be death to go up those stairs, or can you tell me a safe course?"

"There will be no danger at all, as I know that there will be no stone passed again till they can see who ascends. But you are lame, and if you will trust me in this I will do the best that I may."

Sir Roland agreed to that, and Sir Lanval again ascended the tower.

## CHAPTER FIFTY-NINE

SIR LANVAL went up the tower, and called out who he was as he neared the top of the steps; but he got no answer at all.

He went on, and came out on to the roof to see the backs of a glad group who did not know he was there.

For having seen that Bernardi came, they had taken courage to eat and drink from the store that Doette brought with a freedom that they had not otherwise dared. It was many days since they had had such a meal, and having done at last, they stood looking over the low parapet at the great host of those who had marched to their rescue from the Tuscan plains.

From their high place, they saw the growing strength of their friends, the long ranks of the fighting-men, and the mule-drawn baggage trains coming downward between the hills as even those on the castle battlements were unable to do. Could they have a great fear, seeing this, even that their rescue would long delay?

Yet they were roused to an instant fear by Sir Lanval's voice, and to understand how great their folly had been, before they turned to see who was with them upon the tower.

"Yes," Sir Lanval said, as Halt asked him what news he had, "it can be peace, if you will. It can be peace in an hour." He told the message he brought.

"I might ask," Halt replied, "that the cost be paid of the army which has been brought here, without which I know well that I had not gone free with my life, nor would Yvonne have been in a better case, and, as you know, it will be a great charge. I might ask much which I will not do. But if we go in freedom and peace from these walls, which I hope to see never again, I will ask only one thing. That M. Livron, the alchemist of Faucon-bas, be given into my hands, that I may do with him as I will."

"If your asking goes no further than that, and you will withdraw your arms when you are free, then you can have your will without doubt. The Count will not vex himself for an alchemist's life, who is not of his blood."

"I said not that I sought his life; but he must be in my power, that I may do all that I will. If these things be agreed, we will come down, having such oath from the Count as you will tell us that we can trust."

"If you will be guided by me," Sir Lanval answered, "you will not be backward for that, but come down, as having no cause for fear. For I am assured that the Count is of a will to accord in this way, not desiring so great a war for a little thing. And, beside that, he is not one who would seek to cheat with a false word. He is too violent of mood."

"Then we will come now, as you say. It is clear that Yvonne will be free to ride out at my side, having first taken all that is hers."

"She will need more than that," Doette said, "which I can supply. So they picked up such things as they would carry down, which were not many, and as they did this Doette spoke to Sir Lanval aside: "Lanval," she said, using his name in a way which she had not ventured to do before, "I am afraid to stay longer here. If you will take me in honour forth, I will go, or else with Yvonne, even though Bernice stay and my mother's word is not come. I will hasten that we may ride out no later than they."

"You will do well to go with them," he said. "I know not whether they be of gentle blood, but they can be trusted well. But for myself, and as for this day, I cannot come."

Doette looked as one who had been struck by a friend in a strange way. Her voice was toneless and low as she answered: "You must pardon me that I asked that. I had been less shameless and bold had you not urged me thereto at another time."

"You do me wrong with your lips," Sir Lanval said, "which your heart denies. You know well that I would come by my own choice. But I must tell you the truth, which I had thought that I would not do. The Count holds my gage, and, till I have fought with him, I am held here, as you are not one who would fail to see."

Doette looked up with anguished eyes in a face from which the blood had drawn back. "Oh, Lanval," she said, "you have done this for me! I had rather died. The Count is—. But there must be way of accord. Captain Redwood can make such terms that it cannot be. Why did you not wait for an hour?"

"As to that," Sir Lanval said, "it seemed that I had little time. Though I will own, had I looked over the wall, I might have brought it off in another way. But, for the rest, you must ask Captain Redwood naught, if you would be my friend, and my honour is worth your care. Nor must you fear overmuch, for I have told you before that I can use a sword, and not only a song."

And as he spoke Doette remembered what her mother had taught, and she sought to hold down her fear. She looked at him with brave eyes, and said: "I am a coward, as I have told you before, which you must not heed. You will bring this to a good end, and we will ride out on the next day."

Sir Lanval kissed her hand as she said that. He answered: "Could I fail now that you have said that? I will have the scarf that you wear."

But in his heart he knew that his chance was small, for the Count was skilful with axe and sword, and was far stronger than he.

## CHAPTER SIXTY

SIR LANVAL thought: I must win this, if I can, for in the sky of my life the sun is not yet high, and there is the promise of a day that would be fairer than most. Beside which, it will grieve Doette if I die, which I would be loth to do. Yet I shall have no mercy from the Count if I fall, for he is not of that kind. It is a good omen that I have slept, as I must have done, for the night has not seemed long, and the dawn comes.

He turned his thoughts to decide to what arms he should trust, which was not easy to do. Nor was it easy to keep this question before his mind, which would ever turn to Doette.

Then the lines of the song came back, which he had begun to make when he had first seen the high towers of Faucon-haut, on what seemed a far day, though it was no more than few weeks before.

> Oh, mignonne mine, though parting be
> The end of every love, ma mie...

He had not finished it then, nor could he now, though he tried anew. Lambert came, bringing food and. wine.

"Lambert," he said, "I will trust the sword."

The squire looked the doubt that he felt. He said: "The Count will have axe and sword, so I hear. It is said that he has fought thus before. He takes the sword if the axe fail, but not else. You cannot meet axe with sword, being set against one of his reach, and who is armoured in plate."

"Nor could I meet axe with axe, as you know well. It is a weapon with which I am not practised at all; and it is one that will honour strength rather than skill, in which I am unequal alike."

"So you will say," Lambert replied; "but you think yourself to be less than you are." Had he brought his full thought to light, he had added to that: "You would have been a great knight had you given less heed to the making of foolish songs, which is jongleurs' work, and not fitting for gentle blood." But he said aloud: "The Count is older than you, and of greater girth; he will sooner tire. Beside that, he is gross with wine."

"He may tire first, if the fight be long," Sir Lanval allowed. "But that is not simple to bring to pass."

"The barriers will be ten yards by ten. They were putting them up as I came through the courtyard but now."

"Ten by ten is not much, but is well enough. I would have had it twelve."

"It had been less had I not been there. I told them that I would hew down with my own hands any that were less than that."

"Well," Sir Lanval said again, being unchanged in resolve, "I will trust to the sword." After that he had another thought. "Yet I will bear an axe. Get me one that is well-balanced and light, and of a most keen edge."

Lambert went on this errand, and returned with one of which his master approved. Sir Lanval stayed in his own bower at this time, thinking to rest the more, and having a better will to abide with his own thoughts than to talk to those he would meet if he went forth.

Now that Lambert returned, he said: "Find me whether Captain Redwood is here, and if he be free of his time; for, if so, I would go to him, having that which I would say."

For the Count, having made peace, had done so in the large way that he had, whether for evil or good.

"You shall abide here as my guest, if you will, till you have dealt with this alchemist of the town. For why should you dwell in a tent when there is space here with a better roof?" He added: "If you make him dance on a hot plate, there will be few to care. But it will be at your risk, for they call him one who can curse well." He might have said more, had he known the trick—if it were no more than that—which had put Count Gismond to sleep on the floor of his own room.

He said also that Captain Redwood and his friends might like to see the fight, which was to be at the next noon. He may have been thinking of this first when he offered a roof to his recent foe. He would have all the witness he could to a duel which he did not doubt he would win, as few did.

But when Lambert enquired, he found that Captain Redwood had ridden out to the town. Sir Lanval could observe that other men would have minds for their own affairs, even though he were to fight for his life at the noon-hour.

Halt had gone to the alchemist's house, having been well assured that, if he would see him alive, it was his best chance. Fauconbas would send him with a good will. They would send him in a litter, or dragged at a horse's tail, rather than have another war against such force as Bernardi brought. But they could not say that he would be delivered alive, for he was a sick man. Old, and weakening before, he had been broken up, as it seemed, by his son's death.

So Halt rode into the town, not being alone for this time, but with Yvonne at his side on a dun mare that was hard to rein to the pace she would, and behind him an escort such as asserted his power.

When they came to the low-ceiled shop in the narrow street where Yvonne had lived for the most of the years she had, Lucette met them therein, and led Halt up to the room where her father lay, after which she returned to talk to Yvonne, having so much to wonder and ask that her question could not wait for the answer of that which had come before.

Halt saw a man who was sick to death, unless he acted a part, which, with such as he, cannot be set aside as an unlikely thing, and he confirmed much that he had guessed before, and learnt some things that he had not known.

For he had seen, since he had talked to Yvonne upon the tower, and had learned that she had been reared by M. Livron, and had been known as his niece, that she must surely be Konrad's child. He blamed himself that he had not guessed this before; but he had had no guidance thereto. For why should Guilbert have married a cousin, or one who had been reared in the same house as himself? He had known Yvonne only as Guilbert's bride.

But Yvonne had told him of her dim memories of the wanderings of childhood days and of her mother who died, and of how her father—if such he were—lodging in a mean den, and being hurt in a brawl, had come to her uncle's house—as she had supposed him to be—and had lain there for many months, till at last he died. So there could be no search for him now.

She had told also that her uncle had had a servant for many years who had had awkward walk, having had a foot hurt which had long healed. She would not have called him lame, but there could be little doubt that it was he whose footmarks had been traced after Konrad was shot, for he had disappeared from that day.

There was little doubt that M. Livron had planned to marry Yvonne to his son so that Konrad's wealth could be claimed at his death, and it seemed that he must have contrived that death, either through fear of what might come when they met, thinking that Konrad was on his track, and that, at least, he would lose the marriage that was so near, or else with no more purpose than to bring Konrad's wealth to Yvonne's hands, which would be his son's at a quick day, and while he yet lived to make good her claim.

Most of this M. Livron allowed for truth, but as for Konrad's death, he would not admit that he had had any part. He said that the man had been a servant of Yvonne's protector before, and that he had had a hate of Captain Wolvenstein which must have waited its chance. He gave Halt papers in proof of who Yvonne and her mother were.

Halt came down from that room feeling that he had done all that he could, and that Konrad might say that he had brought it to a good end. He did not propose to spend his life following a man through the world who walked with a maimed foot, though, if they should meet, it might be an ill day for him. But he had found Yvonne, and it was a sure thing that he would give her all the care that he could, and she would have the wealth that Konrad had left in his hands.

He came down to find that Lucette was loth for Yvonne to go, having more love for her than she had known till they came to part, but it was a parting which could not lag, for they would be back at Faucon-haut before noon, when the duel was to be fought.

Sir Lanval was arming himself with his squire's aid, when Captain Redwood came to ask what he would have of him, having heard that he had been sought while he was in the town. Sir Lanval was in a gayer mood than before, now that the conflict neared and there was something to do. As he drew on his mail, he hummed the song he had made in the first days when he came.

Swords, swords again, for Isabeau!

Was he fighting for her? It was a queer thought, but, at the root, he was not sure how far it was wrong. He lifted his shoulders somewhat at that. Yet he had had no wrong from her, and she had purred at her song. "The saints rest her for a sleek cat," he said, half aloud; "but they must watch for her claws." And then to Halt, as he came in: "Captain Redwood, those who fight should be hopeful to win, and you must not think I am less than that; but it is known to both that I am meeting one who will be hard to bring down, and I may be dead in the next hour.

"When I look round and afar, I have many friends, both in France and beyond, but he who has many friends may have few of the closer kind, and it is so with myself, as I had not thought until now. You may think that you have had enough of the charges of dying men, but I would ask that you do a few things that would not be heavy or long, and which you will find written here. And I have told Lambert to render all to your hand. And I would ask more than that, that you will not leave without care that the Lady Doette has come clear of these walls, and is in sure escort to her mother's court at Poitou, or where else she may choose to go. Do I ask more than I should?"

"I would do more than that for those who have been our friends, even were it less clear than it is that you now stand as you do through that which you did for us. But I think that you will come through to a better end, and Raoul, who has seen more of battle than I, is of the same mind."

"Well," Sir Lanval replied, "that is what, of course, you should say." He went on with his song.

And then Captain Redwood withdrew, for Doette stood at the door.

Doette had been praying to many saints of a kind repute, but to the Madonna in chief, as one who might have the most pity, and certainly had the most power. She had thought of many things she would say, but now she stood mute till she saw that the scarf she had given was fastened upon the helmet which he was about to put on.

"Lanval," she said, "does that mean that you are really my knight?"

"I am yours only, till death, be it near or far, if you will honour me to that height."

"Then I will give you one kiss, that you will know that you cannot lose."

She kissed without tears, as she had vowed to God she would do, and laughed as they came apart from their first embrace. "Now we have done more than they, in all the time they have had."

"If you would tell me of whom you speak?"

"I speak of Halt and Yvonne. For she told me that they held themselves apart by a strong will, they being placed as they were."

"Then they are surely of gentle blood."

Doette had a thought that those of a gentle blood did not always act thus, having seen something of other ways; but she said nothing of that.

"If you say they are of gentle blood, it is a good guess, for Captain Redwood—which is not his real name—is a great lord in his own land, from which he came because he was called to a trial of state, where his witness must have brought a friend to death, which he would not do. But that is past now, and he is going back to take the place that is his, and Yvonne is Captain Wolvenstein's child, which he came to seek, and the wealth that he left is hers."

"Well," Sir Lanval said, "that is a good tale, and such as I thought to hear. Lambert, I will have my helm, for it is time we should go for the bout."

## CHAPTER SIXTY-ONE

SIR RAYMONT was the first to enter the barriered space which had been enclosed at the centre of the courtyard. There were chairs set, and benches and stools, for those of gentle blood who would sit at one end or other to watch the strife; but, beyond that, there was little of show or state in the ordering of the day, which came of the haste with which it had come to head, and the fact that it took place in Sir Raymont's own castle, and he was one who cared little for any pomp. Also, the order of heraldry was yet young, and had not brought such events to the control which it would soon do.

Beside those who sat, there was a great crowd of the castle household, and some who had been allowed to pass the gate, that they might look on. They filled the courtyard, and lined the top of the flanking walls on their inner sides. Most were of Count Raymont's part; but Sir Lanval had many friends, especially of those who had been of Count Gismond's household before, and the leaders of the condottieri were there—Captains Redwood. Bernardi, Raoul, Vitelli, and a dozen more that it is needless to name, for they are not of this tale.

Sir Raymont was of a giant bulk, which showed huger to most there than they had seen it before, for he was clothed in plate armour from head to heel, and had a great plume of heron feathers rising from the top of his helm. He did not think, as Sir Lanval did, that he might be slain in the next hour. He was too sure of his strength, and he had brought more than one of such duels to a quick end before men learnt that he was one to be left alone.

"You will take fair ransom when he is down?" Sir Roland had asked, at the last. But he made no answer to that. He did not lack gold.

Sir Lanval came very soon after him, looking less than he was, as they stood face to face, waiting the signal of noon, for the mail he wore fitted closer than any plate.

They were both armed with axes and swords, and had shields which hung from their necks, so that they could have both arms free for the wielding of weapons, if they should wish to fight in that way.

Raoul said: "Sir Lanval will have quicker feet, and will last better, being less gross. I would bet something on him."

"Then you should bet," Bernardi answered, "what you can lose, and no more."

Sir Roland was near as they changed these words. He said: "You have not seen Sir Raymont when he is roused. It is like a tempest going to war."

Raoul felt more doubt after hearing those words; but he would not draw back from what he had said, only he thought he should have better odds than he would have been willing to take before.

"I doubt not," he said, "that the Count may have vantage enough, but there are times when the weaker wins. I will stake twenty florins of silver against one hundred, which should be fair odds on what yourselves say."

"I cannot take that," Sir Roland answered, "being a poor man, but I will take you fifty to ten."

"I will make no bet," Bernardi said, "against him whom I would see win, but if I did I should call the odds fair. For the world has many tales in which the giant rolls in the dust; but, when I have watched, I have seen that which has a more likely sound."

As they spoke, there was a trumpet-flourish, brief and high, which was sounded by one who had seen that the dial moved to the point of noon. Sir Raymont, who had stood leaning upon his axe, like a figure of steel, raised it thereat, and rushed upon Sir Lanval, whirling it aloft as he came.

It was like a bull elephant's charge, clumsy, and yet a wonder of lightness and speed, he being of such bulk, and wearing the arms he did. He made no guard for himself, trusting to the armour he wore, and that his opponent must defend his own head. The axe came in a sloping downward sweep as though for the left side of Sir Lanval's neck, and then turned in the air in a sudden way, by a trick that Count Raymont had practised long, so that it came down on the other side from that where it would be expected to be.

Sir Lanval did not wait for it to come down on one side or other. He knew that he faced such a stroke as he could neither turn nor endure. He went to his knee as he swerved aside, hearing the wind of it over his head. It shore off a part of Doette's scarf from his helm, so that it floated toward her feet.

At the next moment they faced each other again, having both turned their backs from where they first stood. They were both un- harmed to an outer view; but things were not quite as they had been before, for as Sir Lanval had stooped he had swung his axe at the side of the giant's knee.

The blow lacked the power which was needed to do harm. The axe-blade slid down the greave. But Sir Raymont knew how near he had been to a laming wound, and he was more cautious for that.

After that, they moved round each other for some moments, keeping somewhat apart. Twice Sir Raymont rushed, and Sir Lanval avoided the blows, being more nimble than he, and after the second of these Sir Lanval struck back before he could recover his axe. Sir Raymont leaned away to avoid the blow, which grazed his gorget, over the top of the hanging shield. There was a murmur of voices at that, for it was seen that the stroke had come with such force that Sir

Raymont might have been slain, had he been a second slower to lean away.

They saw that Sir Lanval was quick both to avoid and to strike back, if the chance came, before the Count could recover balance and guard. Those who had been seated began to rise and stand at the edge of the wooden rail, that they might see that battle the most they could. They said that Sir Lanval was doing well, but he could not last; the Count's fury was too great for that, the sweep of his axe too wide.

But having been twice warned that to forget defence was a fault for which he might dearly pay, Sir Raymont changed his axe to one hand, in which he could still wield it with ease, and took his shield on his arm. Then he advanced again, thinking that the bout had endured enough, and that he would end it now in a safe way.

Sir Lanval saw what he would do, which he liked ill. He had not such strength of arm that he could wield his axe in the same way. He thought that he would bring an end, if he could, by other means, of which he had thought much in the night; but he had seen that it was a great risk.

Now he drew away as fast as he could, till the barrier rail was against his back. Then as the Count advanced he lifted his axe in both hands, whirling it twice in the air, and threw it with the most might that he had.

Sir Raymont saw, as he thought, the act of a desperate man. He raised his shield, thinking it was at his face that it would come; but it was aimed at his knee, as it had been at the first. Men saw it strike. It fell clattering on the stones. They could not tell whether it had done any great hurt.

Sir Lanval leapt aside, and away, wrenching his sword free and getting his shield on to his arm. If that blow had missed, he had a poor hope indeed, being now armed as he was. If the Count had taken a wound, it seemed that he gave it no heed. He turned in haste, thinking to strike before his foe could get his sword clear. He came on for three strides, but as he turned he felt his leg fail.

He stood still at that, hoping his weakness had not been seen, and as Sir Lanval stood back they faced each other for a time, very silent and still. The Count was more in anger than fear, that he could not chase his foe as he did before; but he felt that he could stand well enough, if he stepped with care. He threw all the weight he could on his sound foot, thinking that there might be relief in time to the numbness and pain if he did that.

He saw that Sir Lanval would not advance within the sweep of the axe, and he threw it down, and drew his sword out. He thought that he would tempt Sir Lanval to advance, seeing that they were now armed in the same way, as, at last, he did.

There was a time that was loud with the din of blades, and of smitten shields, and then Sir Lanval stood clear again.

He had a piece shorn from his shield, and the mail was shredded from his side at one place by a great stroke, where the blood spread. But he had no care for that, for he knew that his life was won.

He saw that the Count's shield hung low at his neck, for he had a wound from which his left arm had lost its power, and he knew that he was so lame that he could not turn. He breathed hard as he stood.

"Count Raymont, will you now yield?"

"I yield never. You can come on again, if you so dare."

"Count," he said, "I have no lust for your death, and still less that I should bring you to any shame. But you must see this. If you can stand long as you are, which you must let me doubt, yet you are so hurt that you cannot turn in a quick way. Will you guard your back if I move round with the greatest speed that I can? You would be no better than dead. Would you rather that than make terms of accord?"

"Will you tell me," the Count asked, "what your terms are?"

"I will tell you in few words. You have but to swear that you will yield this castle of Faucon-haut, with the town and lands that Count Gismond held, to the Lady Doette, to be held by her in her own right, and I will ask naught beyond that."

There was a pause while the Count did not reply. None could tell what he would say, nor what he thought, not seeing his face, which the helmet hid. But they knew that Sir Lanval had offered him life and honour in a way which few would have done, having him thus in their power. For he might have claimed that he should become servant to him, with all the lands and wealth that he had, being the hard price at which a knight must often buy his life in those days, if he were worsted thus.

What else could he do but swear? He might be bitter and loth, but there could be but one end. Life is dear to all.

There is no more to be said of him. He could mount a horse on the next day, and he went back to Lucia, who would nurse him well.

But Sir Lanval was in better hands than hers, being nursed by Doette, in the castle which he had won for her at a hazard of life which made him of higher fame in the Latin lands even than he had been before that. For men could no longer speak of him as a trouvère who was less certain of sword than song.

And when the next day dawned, and the road that fell through the hills was bright with a new coming of spears and the blue pennons of Poitou, Doette could send them back to her mother's court with a tale that was good to tell.

Nor did they go back in an idle way, for she would have them ride as escort for her friends through the troubled lands of Périgord and Toulouse, for Halt would go back in haste to his own land, having resolved that it was there he would wed.

But, before he did this, he placed in the army of which he had become lord in so strange a way in Bernardi's charge, giving him larger power than he had had before, as was due to one who had shown that he could be trusted well at a great need. And he made Raoul second only to him, as he well deserved, not only for what he had done before, but because he had quelled those who would have taken the treasure which was in his charge, and gone their ways, leaving their captain to his own fate. And after that, having first slain with his own hands the leader of those who rebelled in that way, he had found a road through the hills by which he could join Bernardi between Avignon and Nîmes, and had led him back by that way, to the good end we have seen.

How Yvonne came to the English land, and of the great name that was hers, and of what happened thereafter, is a good tale, but it is one that cannot be told at this time; nor can that of how Sir Lanval went on the next crusade, and proved his valour anew against the turbaned infidels who denied Christ while holding His holy tomb, nor of the song which he made for Doette before that, in the spring days, as he had promised that he would do.

# ABOUT THE AUTHOR

**SYDNEY FOWLER WRIGHT** (1874-1965) penned over seventy volumes of science fiction, fantasy, classic mysteries, historical novels, poetry, and non-fiction, many of them being published by the Borgo Press Imprint of Wildside Press.